LA ON LSD

A Short Story Collection

by Sean Aeon

Haley,

Thank you so much for interest your energy and your time. Great luck on tour. However you don't need. You have everything you need. You have more than you need, and when you feel like you don't, remember feelings come and go. Thank You,

Sean

ISBN 978-1-959810-00-1

LCCN 2022920075

Editor, Cover Artist, and Photographer:

Sean Aeon

www.aeonaes.com

This book is dedicated to all.

I would not be who I am without all else.

Thank you

• PREFACE •

Los Angeles is a matrix of eclectic and profound experiences, providing the inspiration for this collection.

LA on LSD is a maximalist portrait by a minimalist.
It is a portrait of a city as well as a community.
It is a portrait of expressed inherent interconnection.

LA on LSD is also a psychedelic, magic-carpet ride, flown next to angels wearing glowing halos between battered horns.
It is a celebration of self-solidification.

Through the exploration of dichotomy, oneness is apparent.

LA isn't for everyone. Nothing is.

You see where this is going. Or would you like to?

You're welcome to come along for the trip.

As always.

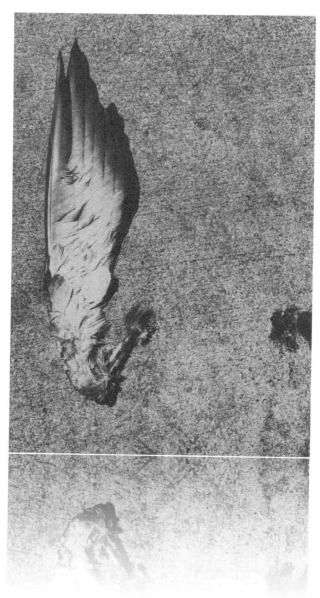

THE GRIM REAPED

FOR LANDSLIDE

A few mornings a week I walked almost twenty minutes to the nearest diner to get work done. My place was too relaxing at times, a characteristic I didn't really want changed. An uncharacteristically large amount of rain poured over the last few days, sidelining my usual trip like it received a red card. The overcast skies and persistent showers reminded me of how dreary it was when I went last, although the weather was objectively better. The orange rooibos tea and blueberry brioche I ordered were near perfection every time, but a thing required my attention before that. This was the story of that thing.

***

A text message informed me a friend of mine died. Well, a question was asked first, then came the real news. I was just about to pull out a chair and sit under an umbrella on the patio, but I stopped and walked across the street instead. The text gave me the chills, and it was already sixty-five degrees when I left the house. I needed to be in the sun, and I spotted what looked like a carpentry error creating a bulge on the side of a building perfect for sitting. The faint, whistling breeze gave tenderness to the sunshine, complimenting the warmth from my hoodie. I sat down and read the text again.

"You heard what happened?"

That question was explicitly reserved for situations no one wanted to hear about. It was right up there with "I'm not racist, but..." and "With all due respect." It could be argued it was worse than both, since whatever happened always happened to someone close.

"Nah. What happened?"

"Landslide's dead."

"What?"

It was April first, and everyone I knew played around like kids more than their kids did. Most of them couldn't see their kids or didn't. The people we needed were only there when we needed them. Parents were people too. A response was sent to me.

"I'm serious."

"I'm sorry. Really. I don't know what to say."

It was Landslide's girl, Ashlyn, who was texting me. Everyone called her Ash; I called her Ashlyn because that was her name. She told me she didn't know how she could forgive herself, but I didn't know what to say to that either. Forgiveness was earned no differently than respect. Forgiveness and respect were granted to self before granted to others. Without self-forgiveness and self-respect, weren't our interactions rooted in anxiety and fear? I didn't know how she could earn her own forgiveness, and I didn't know her well enough to guess. I always thought it interesting how so many believed only God could judge them, yet when they stopped judging themselves they believed God had done the same.

Landslide and Ashlyn weren't together long but she was cool, but they weren't together long. I didn't know Landslide long either —almost two years maybe—but that was the homie. He was just a good dude. He went up and down like everyone else, but mostly up, and up was the plan. Not for all, but some. Some didn't want to get clean, or get educated, or open their mind, or find purpose, or raise their vibration, they just wanted to get by doing the least they could. How was that path different than any other? Would it not lead to either sorrow or satisfaction? Was the answer to the necessary question not provided? Our problem with the personal decisions of other adults was our problem exclusively. There was an event or series of events making us believe what we believed. Most of what we considered true was only true some of the time. Balance was a solid example. Only asking for balance signified not knowing what we asked for. Balance only broke even. Did we try losing as much money as we made, or hating as much as we loved? Did we ask for the same quantity of what we wanted as what we didn't? I doubted Ashlyn wanted to feel fifty percent better and fifty percent the same. Aside from it being pointless, we usually didn't wish for half of someone back either.

If all of something wasn't for us, none of it was.

I think Landslide wanted all of Ashlyn. He spoke fondly of her often and they were essentially inseparable. She said he shot himself in the head. If Landslide killed himself he was just another suicide. He was the third dude I knew for a fact who took their lives in Venice Beach; second in a year. That was just from who I knew and I didn't know too many. I didn't believe what people told me. People lied about things I was surprised they took the time to invent a lie about.

Ashlyn wasn't lying. Landslide was gone.

Rumors swirled within days like soft-serve. More than one person said Landslide was shot twice; his weed starting popping up for sale everywhere. Nothing felt right. Ashlyn was gone the next day, off to San Fran, Seattle, or Oregon, depending on the information's source. It reminded me of playing Broken Telephone in school as a kid, no further along than third grade. How would we have known what a rumor was before then? How would we have learned how exhilarating it was to control a narrative? Peculiar lessons were chosen to teach to children. The parents pushing their kids in the stroller who were old enough to do jumping-jacks were no different. The parents who physically fought others in front of their children were worse.

Adults taught children how to be adults. What about that was confusing? It took me awhile to realize how the parent-child dynamic silently confessed. Kids were students.

Disorderly children were reflections of parental disorders. God didn't make us, our parents did.

I put my phone faced-down on the ground beside me and leaned my head against the wall. The sun didn't feel warm anymore, it was just hot. I closed my eyes and thought about the last time Landslide and I spoke. It was two days ago at the beach on Westminster Avenue. Venice Beach boardwalk. Sunny, breezy, loud. I think he started it.

"Yo, you still write?"

"Always. What's up?"

"Bro, you gotta write my life story."

As an indie writer, people checking-in to see if you were still writing out of casual interest didn't happen often. Writers were not rockstars yet. The recognition of celebrity potential often associated with artistic notoriety and incoming wealth was historically exclusive. I was changing that. Why did we decide to reward acts of physical prowess so far above those of the conceptual? A Nobel Prize winning scientist was awarded roughly a million American dollars, for a discovery that could save millions of lives or alter the way we understood the contents of the universe. Why weren't intellectuals and concept creators endorsed the same as athletes? Steve Jobs revolutionized cell phones and computers, but how did he not have a line of turtle necks? Fashion and functionality had more love to make. Sex would sell forever, so it made sense to utilize it. Sexy was the old sexy. A renaissance was raising its face to the sun and I was lifting its chin encouragingly. Inquisitiveness was the new aphrodisiac. Philosophers fell in love with models once they tired of their mind dehydrating their body. However, some found joy in drought. Models fell in love with philosophers once they tired of meat being the only entree on the menu. However, some hated vegetarians. What resulted from challenging our conventional and conditioned attractions? An industrial revolution was blindly pursued when a philosophical one would've sharpened our sight. We were dangerously overdue. Every other path was trampled. The idea-pushers all deserved lazy millions collecting

dust in diligently active accounts. Inquisitive minds maneuvered the miracles moving us forward.

Inquisitive minds made the money that mattered.

However, as was evidence of Landslide's purely personal interest, there was still written material required for release to properly portray the paradigm shifting like manual transmission. His sincerity was appreciated regardless. *Not* asking me to write his life story was also an option. I was flattered.

> "Uhh, you want *me* to do that? When?"
>
> "Matter fact, you're free next Thursday?"
>
> "Next Thursday? What's today?"

Mario was behind me standing with his bike, and chimed in to solve the mystery.

> "It's Wednesday, fool."
>
> "Next Thursday, bro. I'm getting some other writers together, just figuring out where."

Sounded good to me, but I knew how things usually went—they didn't.

"Okay, cool. Yeah, keep me posted and I'll see if I can make it."

"That's what's up. I don't know if it's gonna be a movie, a show, a book—all of'em—I don't know. But, Ivan, you already know, my life is too crazy."

I actually didn't know, but I didn't have to. If pictures were worth a thousand words, how many words filled a feeling?

We were all standing next to Charlie's. Me, Cello, Mario, Landslide, and I think Zill was there too. Landslide went on to summarize how wild the last six months were, how much money was coming in, and how him and Ashlyn recently moved into a place. He was excited about being here, and it was obvious even before he made it known.

"Like bro, my life's already a movie. I just can't write for shit."

We both laughed. He was right. The stories were everywhere in LA, they were just waiting to be recorded. Mario passed me the blunt and I took a hit before replying.

"Nah, I get it. Just let me know what's up once you get the details. Who's next on this? That way?"

Cello pointed to Zill—he was definitely there that day—and he pinched the blunt from between my thumb and index finger. Landslide dapped me up.

"I'm fucking trippin' balls right now. Goddamn. I'ma bounce."

"Safe travels, sir."

He said peace to everyone, hit the blunt once, then rode his skateboard uphill and past the hotel on Westminster towards Pacific Ave.

That was it.

I didn't get a bad feeling, nothing strange was in the air, nothing was out of the ordinary. Everything being as it should didn't change when a friend died. I didn't like that part, but it was the quintessential example of what so much of life entailed. I didn't like when the things I didn't like were needed.

What surpassed our understanding was out of our control.

Necessity and utility were found and accepted, or we accepted a life of animosity. Many chose the latter. The reality of the fragile floor we walked on was enough to make some not want to move at all. Immobility was often a symptom of ignorance, but was just as fair an option as any. Nothing happened without everything.[1]

The cohesion of all matter was blatantly expressed. Catastrophe called us to find ways to keep our clarity close. Few motivators more powerful than the reminder of our mortality. It was death moving my mind to contemplate life deeper. Loss specialized in making us feel like there was more and less in the world left to love.

Capitalism wasn't required to fuel our hunger when there was plenty. The subtracted made room for additions. My life was added to from a life removed lived enthusiastically.

Enthusiasm was my favorite infection.

I spoke more of Landslide in memory than I did in his presence. I wished that was different, but I knew it couldn't have been for reasons beyond my scope. Landslide inspired me. A short, chubby dude with short locs and glasses perpetually broken and taped together, could have the same effect as Jesus of Nazareth. The New Testament wasn't a memoir, Jesus surrounded himself with note-takers to capture his life also. The symbolism was clear. What wasn't physically recorded was easily forgotten, mistaken, or misrepresented. The game of Broken Telephone was an ancient one. I hoped Landslide kept a journal.

***

The loud exhaust of a bus approaching its stop made my eyes open and head ease forward from the wall. Was a ride what I needed? Aimlessly traveling to the end of the line to see what happened or didn't? I was in the state of mind to do anything since there were those robbed of that option forever.

---

[1] Compasis (from the Greek *com-passus* which meant "a step together,") stated that all possible was necessary, and none happened without all. Each step taken in time being taken by everything in existence at once (see page 263).

Death was the truest slavery. I watched as the bus stopped to my left and let off an old lady pushing a black, two-wheeled cart. Each of her steps were carefully executed, one foot definitively placed in front of the other as the bus pulled away. She was probably in her mid-eighties, still alive, still living. We lived a story which could end after eight pages or eighty-eight.

Landslide's book closed at twenty-four.

The bus stopped at the next light and I didn't regret remaining seated. Did we only experience regret when we made misaligned choices? I was sweating. The moisture congregated on my forehead like Sunday Service recently adjourned. Shade would have been nice but I didn't want to move, and the last time I was on the bus it was more than I wanted to deal with. This was the story of that bus ride.

***

Sitting in the back of the bus was a man yelling about something. At first I assumed he was having a screaming match with himself—which happened pretty regularly on public transportation—but I judged incorrectly. I was scrolling some endless social media timeline and didn't feel like interrupting my momentum. Although curious regarding what the loud man looked like, I didn't want to risk making unwanted eye-contact. He was going nonstop, but I could barely hear the details over the sound of the bus's motor. I was sitting in one of the blue handicap seats near the front. My attention was held once the man yelled the next sentence with additional passion and poise.

> "I have a message for all of you!"

A Mexican accent was easily detectable once his voice was projected.

> "I have a message, and you better be listening. You need to pray to *God!* You need to pray to *Jesus!*"

I stopped listening. People got on buses and trains and did that all the time. Public transportation was the new soapbox. How was the soapbox method really supposed to work anyway? Was the plan to yell our personal perspective into the ears of strangers, berating them into thinking in a way we resonated with? Very strange. The bus stopped and let two people on who sat across from me in the adjacent handicap seats. The bus was at a stoplight and the man in the back took advantage of the added silence.

> "Yeah, I'm an addict and an alcoholic, and I gotta gun charge. But you know what, I walk with God! I escaped prison when they locked me up! He was *with me.*"

Some of us understood villains. Why did we get locked in a cage and consequently find a connection to a higher power? Two reasons. Humanity was on an eternal quest for freedom. Some required the removal of physical freedom in order to free their minds. The removal of one freedom only motivated us to find another.

The second reason. The light was not understood before the darkness. Light was brought into existence. Every version and level of wisdom captured and shared the same view sensibly. We were all at home in the darkness. We are all at peace in the light. The light and dark were options with differing outcomes for ourselves and those we encountered. That man walked through the valley of the shadow of death. Most looked inside, turned around at the entrance, then spoke of their intimate exchange with the shadows. Nothing was gained when afraid of loss.

A snake keeping its skin from shedding only weighed itself down.

That man was alive and I was listening.

> "Everyone who prays needs to journal that! You hear me? If you pray you gotta write that shit down! You write it down and you guard that book with your life! It *is* your life!"

I was nodding my head to every sentence since he hadn't been wrong yet. I looked back to face the orator. Shaved head, leathery-tanned skin, tattoos covering his face, one tooth missing on the top and bottom, and a dirty-blue Detroit Lions jersey. He spoke with the growl of fearlessness I imagined a lion would. Our divine characteristics would rather rot than whisper. I was too far away to hear the bass in his voice, but the passion carried, pregnant with twins.

The light was green but traffic was going nowhere, so the man's audience was at a disadvantage.

> "I hope y'all listening! You hear what I'm saying?! I broke down in from of a

church. My car broke down with no gas."

A car breaking-down and a car running out of gas were hard opposites. I foresaw comedy on the horizon and was excited.

"When I start to walk up to the church, something says, you know, 'Look up! Just look up!' So I do, and I get a vision."

The man stood up from his seat in the far, back right corner, and walked slowly towards the back exit. He was still going with the story.

"I see it, and it's in the sky. It's above the church, you know? And the sun is shining. The rays are coming down on the church and it's beautiful. And the vision—in the vision I see Jesus!"

The man didn't describe what Jesus looked like. What did a "God-turned-man" from present day Israel look like to people when they imagined him? Did they imagine anything, or did they conjure the pale-skinned, blonde-haired, blue-eyed face painted by Warner Sallman in 1940? Wasn't the base of every religion that all was made from one source of creation? Shouldn't every face be the face of God? Some wanted to say those things didn't matter, but we knew they did.

We only took time to alter the powerful.

The man began to paint a picture.

"Jesus is walking down towards the church, but not just him, he has a army. A whole army's behind him kicking up dust, all marching, you know? On horses! And Jesus is holding a child—a baby—in each arm, like, protecting the kids! We gotta protect the kids! We gotta tell'em to write down their prayers! If we don't protect the kids what they gonna be when they grow up, huh?!"

The man looked in my direction and I moved my eyes down quickly, then remembered I was wearing sunglasses. He jumped over the two steps separating the back section of the bus from the front, landing hard on both feet. A woman in pink medical scrubs standing in the area next to the driver was audibly caught by surprise.

"Oh, my god!"

Her neck whipped around like she suspected a sneak attack, and her face twisted at the man. His eyes closed and his head bowed at her humbly. The bus continued inching its way down the street.

"Sorry about that, miss. Sorry, everyone."

He grabbed onto the pole next to the exit and pressed the stop button.

"Everyone, I apologize. I just know this is true. I don't know who to tell this to. I don't know who's supposed to hear it. I don't know who to tell this to, you know? I don't know what I'm supposed to say."

He pressed the stop button two more times but the request was already sent. Still holding onto the pole, he looked down at his shoes and wriggled his nose every few seconds. The woman in the scrubs was still looking at him, but her agitation departed. The reason behind her stare changed, relaxing her shoulders which were stuck in raised anxiety. There was more to feel sad about than there was to feel anxious. The lady turned back

around, stayed facing front, and I knew how she felt. People-watching wasn't about the people we watched. The only reason to watch people was to remind ourselves of ourselves. Our anger at others was often for reasons neither of us understood.

Anger was expressed, at anger expressed, regarding ourselves or what we couldn't control.

We were mad at others for being mad about the same things we were. Not only did we need to let the ego speak, we needed to listen.

The man got off the bus at the next stop silently. I couldn't remember if the rest of the trip was quiet or if I was, as I felt bad and great for him at the same time. It was clear something big suddenly made sense to him, something so big it justified yelling it from a soapbox. He was doing what more of us needed to, he was just doing it in a way making him look mentally unstable. The SoCal frequency was partially responsible. People overflowed and subsequently drowned in a connection they felt but couldn't describe. Raw energy bubbled in Los Angeles; the residents resided in a cauldron. The same energy generating genius incited insanity. Plenty of possibilities became palpable because they could. A friend from Canada asked me why Americans fought so much. After thinking about it I realized it was by design, at least in Cali. The energy making people fight for no reason made them fight for all of them. The gold rush never ended in California since the golden energy never left. LA was another way to spell OZ, as in the one with the wizard and the time-bending red heels. Every road was paved with yellow bricks and we came to taste gold. That appetite took us wherever we allowed it.

Too many more were like the man on the bus, and Landslide, and everyone else I didn't know or who were forgotten too quickly.

Some asked for answers and received obstacles.

Others could only offer us obstacles if we struggled the same. If only we were taught that misdirection was worse than having none.

> ## When standing at the edge of a cliff, it was better to stand still than move forward aimlessly.

I didn't know what happened to Landslide the day he died, but it felt like an aimless step. He did what we all did, it was an expensive mistake, and he paid for it as called for. Reflection before reaction. I think he followed an Emotional Truth[2] as if it were absolute, which was the same as trusting the blind to lead.

Presence in the moment brought progress, enslavement to it brought us nowhere. We could still only serve one master at once.

***

I opened my eyes and was glad I wore sunglasses, the sun was yelling at me. My phone was still on the ground, and I didn't flip it over to check the time as I usually would have, I just stared blankly and listened to the traffic. I still wasn't interested in writing Landslide's life story—or anyone's —but I wished I knew more about it. From him. I would tell

---

2 Emotional Truth Theory: self-inflicted suffering associated with presuming the thoughts and actions attached to emotions are any less inconsistent. The words are genuine when they are said, the actions are genuine when they are performed, and the thoughts are genuine when they are thought of. These truths are to be understood as transient (see page 263).

people all I knew about him; he represented the city to me.

Gold didn't shine in the dark.

My friend wasn't lost, he was misled without understanding. We all visited that place but some became locals. Losing something wasn't the same as having it hidden from us. The weight of California gold weighed many to the bottom of the California coastline.

The city was screaming to have its story retold so the narrative could change, but too much cash was being made to hear anything over the money-counters.

Artist: Kendrick Lamar

Song: The Recipe

Album: good kid, m.A.A.d city

"Got the women, weed, and weather/ Don't it sound clever? Come and play/ W-what more can I say/ W-welcome to L.A."

People were killing themselves for others living like they didn't want to be alive. Then there was

Landslide. He did what he wanted as he wanted and was excited about all of it. Ironically, Landslide also represented how quickly the ground could feel like it was disintegrating beneath our feet. The eyes of many were opened to what entered without their knowledge. Similarly, I was still doing the same—staring at nothing—when a guy on a bike rode passed me and around the corner. The tires squeaked as he peddled, then I could hear the squeaking circling back in my direction. He stopped in front of me and put one foot down to balance the bike as he sat.

"Yo, bro."

"I'm good homie, thank you."

Usually I listened to the pitch, but I just wasn't in the mood to present like I cared. But I tried not to be rude since, well, none of us asked to be here. Or if we think we did we didn't actually know how. That dude didn't leave though, he kept talking.

"Wanna buy some weed though? It's gassy as fuck."

"Nah, bro. Definitely said 'I'm good'."

"Don't even wanna smell it first?"

Tipping point. That was the bad example we all unfortunately assisted in perpetuating. We were used to having an inconsiderate level of persistence produce, what I called, an Annoyance Buy. The Annoyance Buy disproportionately awarded universally annoying actions with the sellers requested currency, causing their actions to appear reasonable, effective, and acceptable. None of which they were. I could stick a fork in my retort, it was ready to be served.

> "See? And now look. If I *spazz* it's a problem, right? I politely say 'I'm good.' *Twice* I say that. But you really can't fucking leave me alone? Blew his brains out, bro. That's what a friend of mine did today. So I'm wrapping my head around a few things right now. Can I *pretty please* have a moment of privacy? Is *that* okay with *you*?"

The squeaking kind of sounded like a song as he rolled away, like the ones played for cartoon characters making their footsteps sound like music. The ego wasn't bad, the ego was our inner-child.

The ego was the simplest part of who we were. Without the ego, we would give away all we possessed and starve to death on the street somewhere thinking we did the world the same service it would do for us. It never did. Not in a neglecting way, just in a it-wasn't-all-about-any-one-of-us kind of way. The ego said fuck that, and told annoying people to get the fuck away just in case being annoyed to death was a real COD. The agitating grew more pleasant once we were distanced from it.

Distance wasn't always a punishment.

Wherever Landslide was I hoped he felt at peace and at home, or distanced from feeling anything else.

Love live Landslide.[3]

---

[3] "Love live" is used instead of "Long live", demonstrating a life loved; a celebration of those moving-on to continue living in their next form.
What good is living long without living with love?

THE UNREVEALED SEEN

THE TRUTH IS MAGIC

I have been lied to a lot. I've been looked in the eye, smiled at, laughed with, and lied to, and it was always a show worth the cover. It was a unique experience to know a factual and provable truth while someone fed you an alternate they invented. Deceit was not unlike murder, but life was mutilated instead of taken. We took what was real and true and turned it into a blindfold. We tied it over the person's eyes, took hold of their hand, and led their unsure, shuffling steps into a cage doused with the sweetest smells of childhood. However, the fragrant aroma was rendered charmless once the flame from the welder's torch ignited to seal the contraption shut. Luckily, for those who fell victim, the blindfold couldn't stay tied on indefinitely. When their sight was restored they were faced with a new, undistorted truth: they were made into a slave. The act of deception locked away their ability to make an informed decision, and when robbed of that element they were robbed of liberty. To lie was to attempt to enslave.

I was a slave once. Inverted truths stained with ill-intent made a believer of me, and I was almost permanently ensnared. I wanted to believe. I wanted to believe those closest to me would never willfully misuse my trust, but I was wrong. Patience and understanding held lies hostage, inspired altruism, or spawned sadism. The roulette ball would tumble onto one of them, and we held our breath and prayed to gods we avoided in anticipation. If not for the unforeseen, it was a lesson I may have never learned although I experienced the solidity of the consequences. How many layers to a lie could I uncover? There was only one way to find out. Within me seethed a masochistic spirit recklessly driven by unrelenting curiosity. I was desperate to know if my eyes could adjust to the abysmal darkness they'd been dipped into. My affinity for plunging shovels into the shallow graves of buried secrets bordered closely on addiction. The initial offense wounded deeply; my ego splintered and was ready for use as kindling. I realized I, of all people, could be taken prisoner by the fraudulent—that was always the worst of it. Four or five years passed since the last time that happened. Four or five years ago I was presented with an item on par with the mythical Icarus returning to Earth with fire.

We were still surrounded by treasures awaiting our inquiry.

***

It was my niece, who was only nine years my junior, that for my thirty-first birthday handed me a gift neatly wrapped in vintage, sepia newspaper. The bow was tied with natural twine. It was nearly a shame to have to disturb it, so I handled the unwrapping process like I was disabling a live explosive device.

> "Uncle, you know you can *rip* the paper, right? That is what it's there for."

> "Shh! My birthday."

Slowly revealing itself like the tips of green grass through melting snow, was a black, hardcover notebook held closed by a flat, black, elastic band. My living room lights highlighted the pebbled-leather finish, smooth, yet textured to the touch. When I turned the notebook so the spine faced away from me, sparkling gold paint lightly dusted onto the edges of the pages sparkled in my eyes. To say it was beautiful was an understatement.

> "I don't know what to say. This is…this is amazing, Xarissa. Seriously, thank you."

My brother, as always, beat her to a response.

> "Aww, you gon' make Ian cry."

> "Man, I'm not crying. You crying!"

I threw in a few fake sniffles, and pretended to wipe heavy tears of joy from under my eyes.

Xarissa and her girlfriend, Carina; my brother Jackson and his wife, Serene; my sister Glory and my other niece Bella; my twin sisters Terra and Paula; my cousins Gerald and Xavier (and his girlfriend, Maria); and my lone nephew Marcus, all laughed. Xarissa could then finally respond.

"Now, you know I give the best gifts, right? Figured you could use something new to scribble in."

"Always."

"Don't forget my birthday's in two months. Just saying."

After a few hours and almost two bottles of tequila, the third and fourth happy birthdays were said, take-home plates of food or dessert were wrapped, and separate ways taken for the evening. The last time my birthday was celebrated at home with family, there were more of us still around to do so. Our loved ones were time sensitive. It was nice just sitting around, eating, catching-up, and cracking jokes. I also didn't have to pretend as much to be happy, I was. I stacked the dirty dishes in the sink and left them there to sleep it off. Cleaning the kitchen could wait until after my favorite morning-after-drinking meal: fresh watermelon. I grabbed my new notebook from the coffee table and sat on the couch. That time I opened it, and was greeted by the soft, crackling sound resembling milk being poured over toasted rice cereal. It was the song of a new notebook. As I picked up the first pen I saw waiting around with nothing better to do, I thought

about writing something. However, unlike the old cliché, I wasn't much of an articulate creative under the influence of alcohol. I honestly didn't know if I was much of an articulate creative outside of the influence either.

Walking with a crutch made it easier, it didn't teach us how.

Since I was about ten years old I was an amateur poet who consistently wrote inconsistently. I didn't consider turning it into a career, it was just a way to flip the cookie jar of my thoughts upside down and shake out the leftover crumbs. I stared at the page a moment longer, tapped it with my pen like a magician with their top hat and wand, but there was no magic. In consolation I decided I could, and should, write my full name on the inside cover to claim the elegant notebook as my own. Ian Mays.

What happened next I could never explain. Below my name, slowly materializing without me touching the page or pen, was line after line of writing. The notebook was writing in itself. I watched as it happened and felt my heart beating in my chest like it was an inch away from finally breaking through my body. The first two lines were from a week ago, March 12, 2021. I knew the conversation.

> "Baby, you're not really still entertaining her, are you?"

> "Mom, why would I lie to you? I only called her to talk about Sonny. That's it. Swear."

It was something I said verbatim. My mom made me promise not to call my wife—ex-wife—Rosa anymore for any reason. I told her I'd only call Rosa if it was about our dog, Sonny, but I lied. To her face. And the notebook knew about it. How the hell was that possible? What the hell was I given?!

Every line was the same: a date, a question or statement, and a lie I told or a truth I'd hidden. The page was turned into a bulging burlap sack of words I wished never escaped my lips. When the notebook kindly concluded its exposition, I counted my twenty-two indiscretions with disgust. Was I dreaming? Maybe I passed out. I didn't remember drinking

that much though, then again, that could be the problem. I felt tired. Watching a notebook write in itself removed my brain through my nose then blended it into a pulpy juice. Apparently it was done now. How was I not dreaming? Falling into a lucid dream I couldn't recall because, tequila, was mildly comforting. Blaming what couldn't defend itself was safe for the moment. Only.

As gently as I could, I closed the notebook and placed it on my coffee table like a newborn baby I was laying into a crib. I didn't want to awaken it again. My unblinking side-eye of suspicion lingered on the item, then I tiptoed away towards the short hallway leading to my bedroom. Maybe going to bed would kick me out of my bizarre dream.

Ironic how sleeping woke us up.

***

It took awhile for the shock of what I possessed to vacate, but life was increasingly more eventful once it did. I never spoke to Rosa again; lying to my mother like a child was over with. I wrote her name down shortly after my own and discovered she'd been cheating on me with her ex. She divulged to him any humiliating story about me she remembered. To my face, Rosa assured me she wanted to fix our relationship and loved me as much as ever. Later I found out she only continued to speak so sweetly with me so I'd go easy on her in the divorce. Her and her ex deserved each other. Throughout their relationship he was mentally and physically abusive; she told me I was her hero. The notebook proved her statement to be fictional. Were heroes made to vilified? The easiest person to lie to was a loved one, they wanted to trust us the most. There were truly malicious and heartless people in the world, and they weren't the ones screaming "I hate you," they were the ones whispering "I love you." Still, I kept that between me and myself.

> We didn't get to cry over the damage we caused and think we were helping ourselves.

Options were presented and I kept choosing the same stupid one. Rosa showed her true self repeatedly, and I repeatedly chose to involve myself with her. Who was I really mad at?

***

The notebook and I crowded half of its capacity with varying degrees of the unrevealed, but my borderline addiction soon turned water to steam in the riverbed of my mind. I was shown my brother, Jackson, regularly hit his wife, Serene, and did so their entire relationship. And he loved it. He married her because she silently took whatever violent act he forced on her. She married him because he wanted to marry her. He was six years my senior, I looked up to him, and yet he was the kind of sadist reminding me of life's passionate complexity. They both did. Only the weakest people alive picked fights with those they knew they could beat. I wrote Serene's name down also and she was used to being treated the way she was. In her mind, getting hit until she cried then hit until she stopped was just part of being in love. The situation she was in made sense to her like the ones preceding. The aggression became so routine, if it didn't find her she went looking for it. Masochism was real, and it was learned. Pieces were coming together I wished would stay single. My mom mentioned talking to her about some "women's health" stuff, but that Serene knew the lifestyle she wanted. We couldn't tell a mermaid they were drowning. Serene was pregnant, due in two months, and they were having a girl. What would that child's life look like? What would they have to endure? Kids didn't have a choice, and that was the most unfair part of life I saw. Perhaps contentment with trauma as part of humanity would come to me when I was older and wiser. Or when I was ready prepared.

> The experiences taking from us left behind incomprehensible magic.

But the anger I wanted to see past wasn't see-through.

Xarissa and Carina were dating for a little over a year and were radiant around each other. It took Xarissa awhile to open up again after the heartbreak of her last— and first—real relationship, so I was happy she was happy. Unfortunately, it wasn't real; Carina was using her. Xarissa wasn't rich but she was doing well for herself. She worked nights at a nonprofit hospital as Lead Pharmacy Technician, and was probably better at saving money than I was. Conversely, Carina loved to shop, eat out, and always wanted to be doing something or going somewhere even though she wasn't working. Xarissa loved Carina and didn't want to lose her, and Carina knew that and used it to her advantage. I tried to tell her

about my "premonition", however it didn't go well.

> "This is about you and Rosa, right?"

> "What? This has nothing to do with—"

> "Like, I know it sucks what she did to you, but that doesn't mean it's happening to me, okay?"

> "Yeah...yeah, maybe you're right. Forget I brought it up."

My cousin Xavier's girlfriend, Maria, slept with my other cousin, Gerald, last weekend like she'd been doing for seven months. The two of them did extremely well at keeping their affair concealed. Xavier was clueless, planning a proposal, and Maria wasn't planning on pleading guilty to her crimes. After how things went with Xarissa, I decided not to share my discovery. As a substitute, I made it a point to audibly make known the psychologically deteriorating effects of infidelity whenever in Maria's presence. If I could spark her guilt to eat her alive she would walk herself out.

Marcus, my nephew, was a twenty-four year old alcoholic— not a secret. He drank to wake up, to put himself to sleep, and as a snack in-between meals. His mother was my late sister in-law Tina, and his father my late older brother, Corvin. Marcus refused to discuss the root of his drinking problem, and like most roots, he let it extend down deep into the soil of his identity to create a hidden home. Both of his parents died in a car accident. Who held the authority to question his coping mechanism of choice? A coping mechanism felt like a cure when its caress was warmth as we lay bare and shivering in darkness. It pulled us close, kissed us gently, and replaced the abrasive sandpaper of clarity with a silk robe of temporarily softened lines and rounded corners. Succumbing to its embrace, our senses were swayed into seeing the darkness as impossible to escape or understand.

> Coping mechanisms convinced us they were our sole means of survival or solace in an unending cycle of anguish.

They functioned flawlessly that way. They lied.

Marcus killed his parents. He killed my brother. He killed Corvin.

Marcus only wanted to kill his mother. His dad wasn't supposed to be there with Tina when it happened, but he was. He loved surprising her, and the only time I really saw her happy was when Corvin was giving her something or taking her somewhere—she was very much a Carina. Marcus studied rigidly to become an auto mechanic, and worked on cars since he was in middle school. He knew what wouldn't be noticed or traced once disabled. Corvin was the smartest of us, but he didn't have the best luck with selecting women—Tina was an especially addictive personality. But wasn't that always the case? Two people coming together to provide balance for one another? No argument altered love being an act of completion. Corvin was the guy you wanted your sister to date; Tina was your sister that you knew needed someone like Corvin. Initially it seemed like she was lovingly addicted to her husband and the father of her only child, but soon prescription pills were her priority. When Corvin was away she disciplined Marcus like an unruly pet, and unfortunately for Marcus, Corvin was away often. My brother was unnecessarily patient, and as it turned out, to a fatal degree. Marcus inherited only half of his dad's empathetic demeanor. No one knew the truth except me, and Marcus, and the notebook. That should have been my definitive reason for seeking to know no more, however the hypnotism of my masochistic mentorship made me greedy. My mother finally stopped me. Coworkers, acquaintances, and friends were exposed as intricate tribal masks: they looked human, yet were hollow. My mother's secret was an anvil she carried like a tin lunchbox from the 1970s. I remember exactly where I was when it fell on me.

I was sitting on my balcony in my favorite gray sweatpants and a black v-neck with my feet up on a short, black, leather topped stool. It was definitely a Sunday evening if I heard Mr. Jenkins practicing his clarinet next door, and as always, my ears were happy to be alive. He was also the one who told me hippies invented v-necks as almost a ceremonial garment. According to him, the shirts allowed crystal pendants to be in direct contact with the Sun and their owner simultaneously. While said hippies could have a shirt on already when they went into stores to buy rolling papers. Mr. Jenkins was the old guy next door I wouldn't mind being, but in a penthouse somewhere overlooking the ocean. Anyway, my notebook was to my left on a round, wooden side table only a

few inches taller than the stool. I was thinking about something my mother said before we got off the phone that sounded...off. She was turning fifty-nine in two months and we were never closer, so I knew when something was wrong. I was a bartender sampling a cocktail through two skinny, black coffee straws knowing there was an ingredient missing from the recipe.

Knowing who someone was meant knowing when they were being someone else.

"Wait, what'd you just say, Mom?"

"That I don't know where your crazy came from. You been crazy since you got here. I got good genes, baby."

"Uhh, well it's either you or Dad, obviously."

"Ha! Boy, who knows."

Who knows? Who knows what? Where else would the sections of my personality materialize from? My mom incubated a sense of humor worth coveting, and was constantly cracking jokes, but, "Who knows?" was unusual. I couldn't recall her ever saying anything like that before, not even in jest. Reluctantly, I wrote her name into my notebook and I immediately wished I didn't.

That woman wasn't my mother, she was just some woman. My siblings weren't related to me. My dad wasn't lost on a fishing boat deep in the Pacific Ocean. I was kidnapped.

Kidnapped.

Years ago my mother showed me a documentary about a string of unsolved kidnappings in the first hospital she worked. It was only a year or two after she graduated nursing school, and in the documentary she was a person of interest later ruled out of the investigation. She joked how having her name associated with some criminal's activities was the closest she would probably get to fifteen minutes of fame. However, she was the one. Five children disappeared from that hospital and I was one of them. She stole me. Thirty-one years of deception, and she made it look as effortless as an enchanted ballerina en pointe moving across stage. Loretta Ames was called Mom, Mommy, and Momma, when she should've been called Monster.

I was a motherless child.

The truth could set us freer than we wanted, free like a leaf lost in the wind. The situation reminded me of my last attempt at impressing people.
I told a joke: we were currently experiencing the sixth Ice Age. We lived in it and were living in it. People were so cold the world froze without feeling a thing. The sixth Ice Age froze hearts and minds instead of earth and water.

I didn't think the joke was properly appreciated at the time. The laughter played hide-and-seek with my ears, and I gave up looking before I looked foolish.
I didn't find the joke funny anymore either.

Artist: The Beatles

Song: I, Me, Mine

Album: Let It Be

" [song intro] Ohhhhhh, silver day. / I, me, mine/ I, me, mine/ I, me, mine/ Eeeeeeven those tears. / I, me, mine/ I, me, mine/ I, me, mine."

***

I trusted no one. Trust was a lazy concept, a waste of effort, a waste of consideration. Yet, the baking drought within me ignited a blaze I could never have imagined. I wrote feverishly. Locked away from humanity and their festering fallacies, endlessly entangling themselves like jungle vines between the twisted strands of their DNA, I wrote. Each fabrication I spun into verse, and ballad, and sonnet, and haiku, clothed me against a world furnished with people as cold as the lies glaciating my heart. The Ice Age.

For over two years I wrote in solitude. I sold my condo, took the money, moved to Mexico, and wrote. Everything. My eyes were opened during that time.

Loneliness was not a low point, it was a launch point.

Whenever backs were turned and no one looked back, it was safe to assume you were about to blow up. It was just like the movies. A dark, deep, and cathartic collection gazed back at me once my fingers were peeled from my laptop. Thousands of poems, transcribed from my experience with the gold-dusted pages of my notebook, made flesh and bone of all I was haunted by. I was an emptied vessel. The ghosts of the graveyard I trudged through for almost three years cleared my vision like morning dew wiped clean from a window pane. It was

Falsehood Theory come to life. The lies and truths were no different than one another since they were both stories we believed or denied. I wasn't the only one needing that reminder.

Following seventy-two rejection letters I finally found a literary agent who understood the material. Within three months my book of poetry, The Obscured Observed, was picked up by the third largest publisher in the country a week before my birthday. By that time, my on and offline following was substantial due wholly to my agent who knew, what I considered, real life sorcerers in Marketing and PR. He was your favorite puppet-master's favorite puppet-master. Although the money from my condo went a long way in Mexico, most of it was spent on tequila, marijuana, LSD, and the freshest seafood ever prepared for me. It also paid for every streaming subscription available. I didn't go completely broke, but the money tree was in the midst of Autumn with only a few leaves left desperately clinging to the branches. I regarded each expense as necessary; I needed tools to properly tighten or loosen the bolts of my mind. The marijuana kept me gleefully present and forgetful (and hungry); the tequila elevated my passion, desire, and sociability;

the LSD encouraged internal and external perceptual exploration and enhanced my emotions; the streaming subscriptions kept me distracted, and at times, inspired. The seafood kept me alive and appreciative. All the while, my puppet-master of an agent was proficiently pulling strings like he was crocheting a sweater. When I made the trip back to the US for the contract signing, a $20,000 advance awaited winking as welcome. I didn't know what to expect when I arrived, but I wasn't expecting that, and I think that was exactly the way I wanted it.

> Expectations were the assassin's bullet striking joy once in the head and twice in the heart.

I was physically overcome by the offer. The tears of joy I shed on that day were nameless, but even with a name to write, the pages of my notebook would rest easy in tranquil silence.

Chapter Three

MERMAID DROWNING

A FABLE OF WOE

It was my first time in California. I landed at LAX, walked outside to wait for my ride, and I noticed the palm trees first. At 5'10 I was taller than most girls, yet my head and neck still titled back like a recliner to see the top of the nearest one. It didn't look right. I saw palm trees in-person before, but none of them looked like the ones in Los Angeles. Florida palm trees were thick with relatively short trunks, and long palm leaves often shaded the wild green coconuts growing beneath. They were easily only half the height of the LA variety. While watching a documentary about the birth of Hollywood, I discovered the notoriously iconic trees were imported. They were brought to the city to consciously create and sell a fairytale. Dangled like shimmering lures in the sun, the trees dazzled early America into taking a bite of Southern California. I'm sure the hope was one bite would have them would

be hooked forever. Some things never changed.

The iconic symbol of one of the world's most recognizable destinations towered above me with its spaghetti-shaped trunk. On its head was a visor of green and tan leaves varying in stages of youth, and the whole thing swayed defiantly in the wind. I could imagine one strong gust blowing it over until it bent into a perfect arch, but of course that never happened. To me it just looked out of place, like, I don't know…a soccer mom in a strip club. Her drink firmly holding onto its virginity while sipped nervously, paired with a pinky finger protruding like she was using it to flick someone off— which she would never. Then, like the soccer mom, these trees were stuck. Would they have enthusiastically volunteered to be Angelenos if given a choice? Would they have opted to be part of the fantasy, like the tidal wave of starry-eyed artists rushing to flood the cities studios and stages? I would bet they wouldn't. Out of place and stuck here: maybe these trees were indeed the archetypal LA resident. Why my mother felt she belonged made sense.

My dad told me she was out there somewhere, comatose on the street with the rest of the dreamers. The City of Angels was more like the city of Atlantis: underwater, shark infested, lost. My dad's words. My mother bled ambition and didn't realize the consequences. The predators knew she was prey and she knew less than she needed. My dad told me that. He said he was her life-jacket and tried to save her, but his rescue attempts felt more like kidnapping attempts.

We couldn't convince a mermaid they were drowning.

The danger was real only once they realized for themselves, their sparkling aquamarine scales ensnared in desperation's jaws. By then they were too far from the surface and too weak to fight their way back. One by one the bubbles no longer floated upwards, and the water held its breath like an impassioned lover. Somewhere, submerged at a depth where sunlight was ancient myth, my mother was there, and hopefully still alive.

***

Seventeen years passed while no one in the family heard from her, and after year seven no one was listening. When Ms. Lynette Arthur grandly proclaimed her plan to leave The Jungle without my dad and me, it didn't go over

well with the relatives. Not everyone with a child was a parent. Stars didn't belong on Earth, and Los Angeles was the closest thing to outer space. I was ten years old when she shared her inflated views of Hollywood before handing me a signed copy of her headshot. I burned that stupid picture on my eighteenth birthday and I was eight years late to lighting the match. It meant too much for too long. King Arthur didn't pull the fabled sword-from-the-stone, finding me worthy enough to bestow it to me as my birthright. At eighteen I realized that picture was a cursed relic given to me by a woman who probably didn't understand the magnitude of its power. I found it sad how family could treat each other. We thought love was this elastic band woven from spider's silk, so those closest were pushed and pulled the hardest. I saw no evidence supporting love held such strength. I wanted to hate Lynette but I didn't. I loved her for who she was to me, yet couldn't believe she felt the same although she told me daily. That was also a long time ago. Ironically, my mother is who signed me up for gymnastics, ballet, singing lessons, and dance lessons, and was front row at every recital and practice I could recall. Joyous memories became Judas to the Jesus of my better judgment. She connected with me enough to try making me just like her, but left before sampling the flavors her recipe created. Although my mother started it, fortune seemed to favor her over me for reasons unknown. The unforgettably bittersweet taste was one lodged between my tongue and cheek like a sarcastic remark.

Lynette dreamt of broadway, performing live in musicals where she could witness the audiences reaction, but she couldn't handle the east coast after Autumn. Remembering her without her voice was impossible. My Girl by The Temptations let the sun shine on my slumber, and No Woman, No Cry by Bob Marley fluffed my pillow and tucked me in. I heard her in the mornings from my bed, warming up at the end of the hall for the matinee show. Her voice was soft, raspy, and each note felt like it told a little story of its own. Adopted, she was never on good terms with her parents but didn't tell me why. The little tales told by the notes she sang never went away. Her voice was an image echoing off the walls in my head, like the last gentle chime from a maturing music box. There was always a glaze of heartbreak even when the song was a happy one.

> Pain was hard to sing through, but when it was, tangible beauty reached out reluctantly. It's hand was outstretched for empathy, not synthesis.

The sentimentally protective sensation inseparable from her song was the most motherly thing I recalled about her.

***

The antiquated idea stating one day every man or woman should have children was deadly. My mother was never mother material. Six different doctors told her she would never have kids, and I was the miracle baby God sent to the wrong set of praying hands. Freedom flirted with us like a private dancer possessing Satan's tongue. A spell was written all over Lynette's body, "Reclaim who they took from you". The novelty of having a little version of herself couldn't survive the savage terrain of an artist's mind left for starvation. Conversely, my dad remained overjoyed; his father never wanted to be one. Every opportunity to beat the hell into my father was accepted ardently by his. The abuse was activated like explosives were, turning his childhood home into a minefield made for soldiers where civilians slept. Any reason would suffice to wage war on the weaker, and when none could be found war was waged all the same. My dad couldn't wait to be the dad he always wanted, he just didn't know he would be doing it alone. He did the best he could. He learned to braid my hair, taught me to respect my mind and my body, showed me what love meant in every way he could express, and taught me the value of currency.

> Having money without discipline would leave even the richest penniless.

I was taught incomparable life-lessons, but a girl still needed her mom. Our relationship inspired my pursuit of Behavioral Psychology. Blood filled my veins and moved through my heart with the same electrified urgency moving my mind to research without rest. I felt compelled to understand how and why our thoughts and actions were how they were. People—my mother especially; myself included—made no sense to me. Humans were strange and perplexing animals as extraterrestrial as any alien in Science-Fiction. What did being human mean? What did acting human look like? Was our

personality not just a set of traditions, habits, and standards? I spent my academic and professional career holding a gold, tiny-linked, tangled necklace of questions twisting more violently as I picked and pulled at it for answers. I tried fitting-in but nothing fit. My parents thought it was a phase, however it was one I grew further into instead of out. Nothing grew inexplicably, growth's direction was chosen or forced. I was a prime sample of Stabilizing Assimilation Law. I followed what was generally accepted by society for the sake of my survival and mental stability, however I was disconnected from all of it. I was playing the role of a character, playing the role of a character, who knew they were in a movie and didn't think it was written that well. My mother left more of her residue on me than I cared to admit. I too was an actress.

***

I would catch my dad sitting alone drinking in silence next to a flickering tea candle. The light knew where to illuminate his face, a prosecuting attorney presenting his pain to the court as evidence. How well did we know those unwilling to show us how they hurt? Although he only drank after put me to bed, I knew he wouldn't check on me until after watching sports news. Our house was old enough to have raised my great-grandparents, so I would sneak from my bedroom to his and peer at him through the skeleton keyhole on his door. He would stare at the fire as if they were conversing, blinking so slowly I thought he would fall asleep—he never did. We considered slowing down to be the same as stopping to our detriment. Dad always sat there until he finished his drinks, placing a shot glass overtop the candle to quietly extinguish the flame. Watching him in that room he was a necromancer, but the ghost he was attempting to contact was himself. I suppose, like most addicts, each drink was another shovel full of dirt thrown over memories he hoped to entomb. He didn't know that was useless. We couldn't drown or bury our sorrows when air didn't fill their lungs, regret did.

Memories didn't die, they waited.

A simmering brand was left on our minds, ever-tender to the touch, carved in the shape of hurt endured. As the smoke cleared, what remained was a scar reminding us of how we never wanted to be hurt the same way again, yet we were scarred nevertheless. Our hands were stained with our own blood as long as the difference between the blade and the hilt was forgotten. No matter how he tried to anchor his emotions at the dismal depths of another bottle, he couldn't weigh down the force of his love for her. My mother was his siren. I believed in some mysterious, unscientific way, it was their love bringing her song to his ears once again. Love letters were still rolled into corked, glass bottles carried to the shore by foam-kissed seas. About nine months ago he said he was on his lunch break at the post office, when two of the new guys were watching something on their phone.

"And of course they have no headphones on. I don't understand why these young guys can't just listen to the phone with headphones, or know having the volume all the way up ain't acceptable. So now I have be the big bad manager. Put my fork down, walk over, and inform these gentlemen as to how one should be considerate of others. But that's when I heard it, Leese, I'd know her voice even if my head was underwater. And now I know I should've told you sooner, but after everything that happened I didn't even know if I should. But it was her. I knew it before I even saw her. You remember how her voice would crack when she sang too high, but still stay in key? Yeah. Yeah, it still does."

Some of us loved in a way others never wanted to love anyone. It was like his lips were happier just to say her name. Was I ready to be loved that way? Someone had taken a video of my mother singing on the corner of some street—somewhere on Skid Row —and it was making its rounds on the internet.

"Leesie, baby, she didn't look good. That's another reason I wasn't in a rush to tell you. Her voice? Her voice still spoke to you like it was...like it was answering questions you didn't ask yet. But she wasn't herself. She wasn't your mom."

"My—okay, Dad. When was she ever my mom? Really? For how long? Four years? If that?"

"She went through a lot, and—"

"And that's, what, an excuse?! Because it's not an excuse and you know it isn't."

He sighed one of those old man sighs. The type of sigh saying "I'm too old for correction...even when I'm wrong," but he knew he was. He knew what I knew.

Using our trauma as an excuse to cause trauma to others was inexcusable.

He said it didn't look like there was much life left in her, so if I wanted to try seeing her again I was already running late. I bought a ticket, flew to LA, and booked a hotel with my homegirl's discount—thank you Gianna for sticking it out in that job you hate. My mission to Skid Row started the day after I landed, with night one dedicated to some mild sightseeing. I needed a drink, somewhere near the hotel keeping the odds of me staggering into my bed or someone else's near fifty-fifty.

***

Los Angeles was a city of idolized demons and fallen angels. Souls rose and fell daily, and demigods made domiciles from dust. Broken people came from all over and lined its streets like broken glass and shattered expectations. The homeless weren't the only ones braving the elements. Men thought the only thing worth offering women was money, and women thought the only thing worth offering men was sex. We hurried to volunteer what our miseducators taught was most desired. How could personality alone ever suffice? Who cared what we thought or believed when dealerships, designers, and destinations didn't except self-awareness as legal tender? The droughts in SoCal weren't only due to the forest fires. A different kind of thirst dug through Angelenos one drop at a time. In a city where someone became the only thing everyone talked about every fifteen minutes, love and attention were pronounced almost identically. Hoses and lips were the tools used to extract sex, money, and adoration, passing it from one anxious enthusiast to another. The elemental mixture created more hunger, staining the teeth a dark red-orange.

Many of us chose to starve ourselves with what we ingested.

Although I was unfamiliar with the traditional ups and downs of the mountainous California landscape, the summation shared with me after a morning,

late afternoon, and evening, felt fair and transparent. Exceptions to the rules were sure to exist, but they would be just that, exceptional. We loved what was special and wished all could be, but if all were special then none were.

The conversations I came across were what made me into wet clay ready to be molded. Los Angeles spoke with an accent from all over, all under, and everywhere in between. Some exchanges I shamelessly eavesdropped into, others were so loud I couldn't help but overhear, and a few were started with me directly. Apparently I stood out like an erection and that made people chatty; I was easy to talk to once I got going.

***

Last night I ended up wandering around Hollywood for longer than I planned, and the more I surveilled the city the more I realized everyone was addicted to something. Meth, cocaine, pills, alcohol, money, fame, attention, intimacy, stability, instability. The list was bold, brash, and infinite. Meth was very popular. I saw eight separate people smoking it, in plain view, over the course of maybe five hours. I felt like I was the only one who showed up to work on casual Friday wearing heels and a business suit. Regardless, money was still the most addictive and most dangerous, and there was way too much of it here.

Cash was the conductor of the Crazy Train. Passengers tenderly held hands while riding alongside self-destructive behaviors in exchange for fast money.

Before the night closed, I found myself conversing alongside a petite escort with dyed blonde streaks in black hair. She was between customers and needed a lighter for her joint while I smoked a cigarette outside. Thin, gray clouds were sketched across the overcast night sky in small groups. The moon was full and bright, shining like the last wishing-lantern released upwards to grant its requests. We ended up discussing money after she handed me my lighter. Ten-thousand dollars was the most she made in a month, and a month later it was gone—she wasn't bragging about the second part. Doing it again was possible, but she said it was tiring as hell and she wanted to be done with coke. The lines kept her awake so she could pull it off. Her name was Natalia. She hated escorting, said it made her feel like she was selling her soul

—whatever that meant—but she couldn't go back to working a regular job like a slave when she could make three-hundred dollars in thirty minutes. Did she think a regular job was slavery, or was she manipulated into thinking so? Too many used "slavery" to describe any challenging circumstance ranging from mild to medium. If we believed that, what did we think freedom was? Natalia used to be a dancer, hated the hours and having to split her money with the club, then started escorting freelance. Aside from making her feel like hell, it was easy money; she smoked or drank the shitty feelings away anyway.

"Life only sucks when you think about it."

Her words. Natalia's booker was a guy she met while dancing, and he set up the "dates" where she would see men or women. A booker was an extremely politically-tame term for a pimp; I gleaned that from context. Natalia was twenty-three. I was thirty-two with a masters and a few relevant certifications, and I never made the kind of money she made as fast as she made it. The security of my soul also wasn't one I worried about being jeopardized either. She offered me a hit of her joint—which smelled amazing—but I stopped myself in the middle of grabbing it from her and itched my shoulder.

> "You know what, I probably shouldn't. I always think I'll be good but then I end up paranoid in a corner somewhere."

The tail-end of her right eyebrow stood to ask a question, thought about it, then decided to sit back down. I'm sure my awkward smile was basically one of those "Hi, my name is…" stickers, but mine said "Hi, I am one hundred percent, definitely a tourist…" Natalia scoffed, looking to her left and nodding to herself in return. We both knew why I wouldn't smoke after her, and she was more offended than shown.

Our eyes were connected to our brains. How we viewed experiences were how we thought about them.

I felt bad. She was doing what she felt she needed to in order to survive, but I stood by my decision. Her throat cleared but the air between us did not.

> "Right, wouldn't want you paranoid. Anyway, my booker's probably blowing

my phone up, and I left it in the room on purpose. Nice meeting you…sorry, I suck with names."

"Ileese."

"Ileese. Right."

Natalia held the cherry of her joint against the wall behind us, and the loose ashes disappeared before landing. She removed a small, aluminum can from her black, leather purse, picking out two mints and placing them in her mouth. The rest of the joint was laid on top of the paper covering the mints, the lid closed, and she pushed the can back in her bag.

> "I would've offered you one, but, you know, your paranoia."

The wink she flashed at me felt like it pulled my pants down in the middle of a middle school hallway. Natalia clicked away in black ankle boots towards the hotel entrance, delivering one last message in front the open automatic doors.

> "Be safe, Ileese."

"Thanks, you too."

"Don't die out here on your last day."

***

I saw video footage of refugee camps on news reports but never personally. Skid Row was a homemade refugee camp. Both sides of the street were paneled with camping tents and wooden shacks, made from assorted pieces of graffitied and less-graffitied plywood. The sidewalk was clearly a front porch for the residents, so I walked on the street and watched for traffic. Nearly every structure was covered with the same blue tarps used for disaster relief, yet I saw no relief present. Portable outhouses with attached handwashing stations were positioned near the larger clusters of tents, but the entire block smelled like one. I walked with my head and eyes down as if they were weighted, and moved my feet to an imaginary treadmill spinning beneath them. Bass-heavy music played from a couple of the makeshift homes; laughter echoed off the asphalt. A barefooted man, wearing only a black garbage bag as short-shorts, hobbled passed me in the opposite direction on muddied feet darker than his attire. A woman sat on a rusty paint-bucket next to the curb, pouring water over her head from a shallow, plastic container to rinse soap from her hair into the gutter.

Was creativity accelerated by the death of comfort?

With me were the essentials: a fanny-pack with my wallet, phone, room key, lighter, a joint, and a travel sized shot of tequila —just in case. Calling attention to myself wasn't the goal. I was already on 5th street, and according to my phone, once I crossed over San Pedro street I was there. I was absolutely there.

The YouTube video was recorded near 6th street & S. Central Ave, so a few blocks still lay ahead. I turned right at the intersection and there were two, short, gray-haired men with dark skin sitting and talking on the curb across the street. I asked if they could help me, introduced myself, and showed them the video of my mother. One of them said yeah, he knew her, and his name was James. He spoke with an accent from somewhere between the westside of New Orleans and the eastside of Atlanta.

> "A lot of people move out here and they give up, you know? They chase the dream until things get too hard, and when they...and

when they get too hard they look for the easy way out as soon as they can. Miss, they just scared to try. Scared to work. Some think failure exists, which is why we fear it. Those people live and die and they are forgotten. Nothing against them, you know? I'm in the same boat they are. Then there's other people like your mother, miss. They came here and this is where they belonged. They tried, and they tried, and they never gave up, even when it, well, even when it was too hard. Even when it became impossible. Some never make the decision to quit, they just never make it. Now *those* people are what LA is all about, they're about the dream.

Being alive is about doing what we are meant to do— what we are called to do— even when no one is looking. Even if no one ever looks."

He grinned, and his cheeks looked like they could take an elevator to his forehead. He let them ride back down to the first floor, then his story went skipping along, arms swinging forth and back.

"It's been decades since they brought new palm trees into LA, and we all know these trees don't grow here naturally. So where do the new ones come from? Whenever one of the dreamers chase the dream until their last breath, if they end up out here, well, when they die they get put in the ground. When they get put in the ground they get buried, and when they get buried they fertilize this soil and they grow into one of these palm trees. It's the palm trees that let you know you're in LA as soon as you get here. They represent the spirit of this city. The spirit of this city is the dreamer who chases the dream until it is finally time for it to rest. They are this city, and you're looking at them everywhere you go. They are here now, forever, just like they wanted to be."

"My mother's dead?"

"I'm...oh, I'm sorry. But yes. Been gone awhile, now.

That's an old video you showed me there."

And there it was: a baseball bat to the face. An old video, of course. The internet was eternal. Since my dad saw it not too long ago I just...I just didn't check. That was it, "Been gone for awhile, now." I didn't ask what that meant, since I didn't see how any possible answer could possibly make me feel better.

"And you say she's a tree now?"

"I'll take you to her."

"To my mother? Who's a tree?"

"Did you *want* to go, or did you not?"

It wasn't a challenge, it was more like he just wanted to know which direction to head towards. I thought I would live my entire life without someone asking me if I wanted to see my mother who was now a tree.

Everything could happen in LA.

I changed the locks and left my emotional responses outside. Keeping me company was the jaded and the detached. My mother was dead. What could top that? When in Rome.

"Sure, fine."

"Okay. Charlie? Char-lie! I'll be right back, yeah?"

Charlie nodded without breaking his fixed stare at the ground where he scratched streaks into the pavement with a pebble. I was curious.

"Is it far?"

"Far? No. The Moon is far. We can walk where we're going."

The limp he carried made his left foot drag a few inches behind him. I followed the likely-to-be-delusional man back down S. Central Avenue towards 5th Street.

"Hey, we're just walking back to where I came from."

"Then you passed her."

I wasn't keeping track of the side streets we passed as closely as I should have, but maybe three or four were behind me when James stopped abruptly. It didn't feel like we arrived anywhere, but like we were in a car with a dead battery. I was trying not to be rude.

"Uhh, is everything okay?"

"It is."

"So, where is this tr—where's my mother?"

"I forget."

"Excuse me?"

"She's close. I just don't remember which street she's on. She's not *my* mother."

I needed out of the asylum, lunacy reigned supreme. I just followed a crazy homeless dude to nowhere; I might be crazier than he was. And where were the palm trees? When I looked around I didn't see any nearby. Abandoned warehouses with busted windows and spray painted tattoos lined one side of the street. A park was across from them, filled with camping tents playing a residency like Legacy artists. Then there was the community center and some other older office-type building, but no palm trees. One more time and then I was giving up.

"So we've been walking for like twenty minutes and you don't even know—"

"Shh! I'm trying to listen. If you would stop talking for a one second."

"Listen? To what? Traffic?"

"Shh!"

"Goddamn, this is insane."

I said the last part to myself. I would never consider it wise to call someone crazy and homeless the "I" word, not with no one around to witness my possible homicide. James listened with closed eyes and the bottom of his chin facing straight out in front of him. He swayed his head from left to right as if it were too heavy to hold straight. For maybe a minute he did that before his cheeks rose and his lips strolled into a smile.

"Ah, I can hear her, now. She's just over this way. See? I knew we were close."

"You can hear what? I don't hear…I don't hear anything."

"It's impossible to hear when you're not listening.

Come on."

I was honestly over it. He said my mother was dead, which I was prepared for anyway, so the next step was going home and breaking the news to Dad. Judging by the way he didn't want to tell me about her in the first place, I assumed he was ready for that also. For now I would entertain the homeless dude, look at a tree, then call a ride back to my hotel and order takeout. Get a pizza and a beer, and be fat and happy. Gianna was going to fall on the floor laughing when I called her. James turned around and walked passed me back in the opposite direction.

"Uhh, where are you going?"

"Just up this way."

Down another street for about five minutes, then a right on Stanford Ave around a green porto potty and a gray, single-person tent. The tent was horizontally wrapped in either clear packing tape or plastic wrap, but I wasn't getting close enough to confirm. Mr. James leading me here and there would have made me nervous if it wasn't the middle of the day, and I wasn't at least five inches taller than him. I didn't think about how much higher my weight-class was.

Ahead of us was a diamond-pattered, wired gate, with green nylon strips covering it from top to bottom. James turned to me, nodded confidently, then put both hands behind his back before holding his left inside his right. A few more buoyant steps

were taken forward, stopped, then he turned to face me. That time he grinned wide enough to bare his teeth, clearly proud to present the two rows resembling browned corn occupying his mouth. Tint aside, all were present and accounted for.

Beauty was a chameleon with peacock feathers.

He stretched out his hand towards the nearest palm tree.

"This is her. Singing Lynn."

My feet took three deliberate steps towards the tree, as pebbles and other small pieces of street trash crackled under each step. I examined where it was rooted to the ground. It was the only palm tree in the area, and it was in the corner of a small, gated parking lot—not exactly the picturesque palm tree palace. The feeling of James staring into the flesh and bone of my back was unpleasant, and when I glared at him he bowed his head and stepped back like a butler dismissed from dinner service. My attention returned to the tree, and I tilted back my head and neck like a recliner to see the top. Like every other spaghetti-trunked tree in LA, it didn't look right. It was...out of place, but different. Why did it seem out of place yet differently?

Apparently the homeless man was also a mind-reader.

> "You hear it don't you?"

> "No, sir, I don't."

> "Then get closer."

> "For what? It's a tree."

> "One thing doesn't only have to be one thing. Get closer. You can touch her. She is *your* mom."

> "*You* obviously didn't know her."

> "Or maybe *you* didn't."

I held my tongue. It felt like it would slip free from my grip at any second, but I held it. With my whole body I held it.

How did we formulate opinions on what we knew nothing about?

I would walk up to the tree, touch it, then get the hell out of there. If I reacted out of character I would morph into another character happy to spaz on Homeless James. As I made my way to meet a tree face-to-face, an uninvited overgrowth of optimism spread its weeds within me. I didn't want to feel hopeful. What was there to feel hopeful about? I wasn't the naive ten year old girl anymore. Nothing about her made me want anything to do with her, but the feeling wouldn't leave. I stood an inch or two in front of the palm, and although James was staring again, I didn't acknowledge him. Radiating anticipation lifted my arm mechanically, levitating it towards the tree's trunk. I didn't know what to expect when we touched, but it was...nothing. I rested my hand on the trunk of the tree and felt nothing. I kept it there and stared up at the palm leaves, looking for sign or something resembling one. Anything. But there wasn't. I studied the spot where my hand was, then slowly removed it and put it back in my pocket.

We chose hope or preparation.

> "You're a liar. It's just a tree. Just like I said it was. You're crazy if you think people turn into trees. But what does it matter? You live out here. You can think whatever you want."

I put my hand on my forehead and laughed at myself. James was confused.

> "Did you listen for her?"

> "There's nothing to listen for! It's a GODDAMN—

never mind. Thank you for wasting my time."

I walked passed him so I could get anywhere else, but I didn't get five steps away before I could hear him quietly singing. I began yelling before I could even finish spinning back around to face him.

"Are you really serious?! You think that's fun—"

He was not singing, he was aggressively digging something out of his molar with his index finger. There was no one else anywhere near us. I didn't get it.

"What was that about?"

"Huh?"

"The singing? Just now. How'd you do that?"

He stared at me, blinked once, didn't blink again, then smiled his curled-lip smile making him look as happy as I would be once pizza and beer bounce-housed off my tongue. Otherwise he was silent.

When I got nervous or anxious I bit the inside corner of my bottom lip repeatedly with my canine teeth. The tender nibble steadily increased in pressure until consciously stopping myself was required. The habit followed

me since I could remember, and I went at it as James smirked coyly. I glanced at the tree, then back at him, then back at the tree, and after taking one step away, I heard it again. A warm, raspy voice rose up and moved all around me like the smoke born from the death of a fire. I held my breath and tried to quiet my thumping heart, it distracted me, and nothing mattered more in that moment than what I couldn't believe I heard. I could distinguish that voice even if it were smeared into a choir of a thousand choirs. My mother was singing to me—only me—and using the words of Bob Marley to tell me not to cry, and that "Everything is gonna be alright." Did she know how long ago the well of my tears went dry? Still, I felt I could raise my arms straight out on each side, close my eyes and fall backwards, and the sound I was surrounded and saturated by would cradle my body against the inevitability of gravity. I was blissfully weightless. My eyelids were buttery quilts in mid-melt, growing heavier and more comforting, tucking me in and putting my sight to rest.

When mesmerized we mingled with the magical.

A sobering breeze blew through me and gave me the chills. The face of the earth was turning away from the sun and I would need to leave soon. My mother sang continuously once she started, seamlessly transitioning from the end of the song back to the beginning. I gradually made my way closer to the tree she inhabited and sat with my back leaned against it. I thought about how the years without her clawed their way from the pages of my calendar. The vibration of her voice moved within me like the affectionate purring of a feline held close. A cool gust of wind raced by me, handing out free goosebumps which turned my legs into Braille faster than I could read.

"Mommy, I have a to go."

I didn't know the last time I said the word mommy, but it fell from my lips as naturally as ripened fruit. My mother's voice gradually faded to complete silence, my eyes opened, and my entire body relaxed. James was gone as I hoped. I pushed myself off the ground with both hands, stood, and faced the tree. I spoke calmly.

"Thank you for singing to me again. I missed that. But you know what? Your pretty voice can't fix you abandoning me and Dad."

I whispered.

"Pretty doesn't fix ugly."

Her song sprung forth from her again as if she was given a cue she almost missed. Not every apology was saying sorry, and most of them changed nothing. I took out the small bottle of tequila from my bag, poured the contents around the tree, and took out my lighter. Even the dead were predictable.

We were quick to forget we didn't forget quickly.

I personally believed in the universe balancing power of retribution. I held the lighter to a spot visibly stained with alcohol, then watched the consummation of fire and earth in their union. James telling me when or how my mother passed away wouldn't have made me feel better, but that did.

Artist: The Temptations

Song: My Girl

Album: The Temptations Sing Smokey

"I...guess...you'd...say/ What can make me feel this way/ My girl...my girl, my girl./ Talking 'bout myyy girrrlll—my girl!

The fire was a rock climber, scaling the tree's trunk inch by inch until the whole thing was an oversized candle wick. It burned melodically with crackling oranges and yellows in the late city evening. The heat leaned against my skin as I stepped back from the blaze, closing my eyes to better focus on its pulsating weight. The sound of sirens awakened in the distance like rolling thunder before rain. My departure time was signaled. A small, distinctive snapping sound crackled from the tree; the large wick wouldn't be standing for much longer. Everything fell. I walked into the night with my mother's song still following me, her raspy voice like firm fingers through my hair. Nevertheless I ignored it, kept walking, and didn't look back since I would never travel there again.

Was there a reason to convince those who turned their backs on us to do otherwise? Didn't they leave us so we could find us? And if we should ever find them again, they should know we didn't find them to befriend them.

People didn't change unless given a reason, not even those who changed into something completely unrecognizable.

Goodbye, Mother.
I hope it was worth it.

BEVERLY HILLS

YOU GO WHEN YOU HAVE TO

Why Marko decided to make me wait at that boldly bourgeoisie establishment was pretty funny. Granted I made him wait nearly every time we met, my menu was known for that appetizer, Marko's wasn't. He was doing it on purpose and I knew it, and the girl he was with outside was the reason. Once Marko was around a girl, getting him to focus his focus was far-fetched; I didn't stop to think if I was much different. The wave of momentum I was surfing was a tube with space for two, and I knew it was no business of mine when it would end. I was holding on tightly. Seated at bars, perfecting million dollar projects while half-drunk-high-ish, was not something I planned to have work for me. Sometimes serendipity was on our side. I knew many requiring offices, desks, cubicles, and distilled glass-bottled water to complete any work of value. I was happy for them. Even working after sunset was a stretch for me, something felt right about finishing my day with the Sun. However, I almost always ended up working when I was bored.

The bar stools were designated by their leather-padded backs and armrests married to suede. The cushioned seats contained an unmistakable memory-foam interior; I was very comfortable. The width between armrests was an obtuse sociological statement regarding the size of those welcome to sit. I made the cut by only a few inches and almost felt proud. I also almost throw-up in my mouth at the moment of pride felt for being "included," but it happened to the best of us. The Rodeo Drive-adjacent bar-restaurant scene was...fine, objectively, although I usually chose elsewhere to enjoy recess. Where I waited wasn't presented differently than any other, but it was authentic. There was nothing to disagree with when it came to what was presented authentically, there was only the choice to engage or not to. The authentic wasn't for everyone and wasn't supposed to be. It pissed people off. The authentic did what it said it did. The authentic didn't have to be different, only honest. Daily we decided to demonstrate the existence of insincerity, authentic sincerity, or Beverly Hills. Each meant something different depending on whom was asked.

Regarding the authentically insincere, I hoped they fell asleep and I woke up at their funeral. The story ended in my favor if justice was served by a waitress dressed in a miracle. The story always ended favorably as long as I was alive at the end, but that wasn't how I saw miracles made. Miracles took the most work. Too many didn't want work, only what work awarded. Regression was available in an array of makes and models. The mirror world was one of the more tangible delusions, it stared back at us the same way silence did. Was that why there were tales of vampires with no reflection? Did we need to invent creatures unable to see themselves backwards?

How did we find self without first experiencing its loss?

What were we mad about? Vampires were interesting. They lived forever, never experiencing the loss of life, and consequently fed on life like Neapolitan ice cream sandwiches. Vampires represented those who hurt others instead of finding a way to heal themselves. How could they see themselves as the source of harm without a reflection? The

thought-process producing their actions came from those utilizing the same. Vampires created vampires. Backwards was how I witnessed the majority of lives, a confident observation made from recognizing my own previously backwards inclinations. People saw me and wanted to know how I was so lucid, but when I told them about the work their demeanor changed. I didn't avoid the work, it was all I felt was mine. We drowned in variables. I liked sailing with the wind at my back, and people were crosswinds. The majority of my interactions began feeling like unnecessary murder trials. My guilt could be yelled from the top of my lungs, yet I sat silently through the proceedings instead. I didn't care and didn't care who did. Death sentences were the only ones of true consequence. Static exchanges occupied more of my experience than I found reasonable. Time was spent recklessly from meager earnings moaning about what would never get done or wasn't known enough about. I would say it was a joke, but it wasn't funny, not even ironically. Still, I laughed out-loud, quietly, but out-loud nonetheless. I was so far into my head I forgot Athens was sitting next me; she was my ride.

"What's so funny?"

I was still smiling from the laugh.

    "What?"

    "You just laughed."

    "Okay?"

    "Christ. Whatever."

She got up and stood with her cousin Laurren, who was with her guy friend at the other end of the bar giving me the Evil Eye. I didn't know the guy friend or his name. I was friendless because I was a dick without provocation. I put my glass to my face and tipped it nearly all the way upside down, holding two of the ice cubes in my mouth that fell in along with the alcohol. They shattered between my molars like they'd been stepped on by a giant, and the cold chill from their demise ran through my jaw and down my neck. I was ready to go home but it was early and I was bored. Life was so fucking boring sometimes, or I don't know, maybe it was just me. There was always a possibility it was just you, and you didn't reach some advanced level of self-awareness—or any other kind of awareness—you were just being a dick.

It was easy to be a dick, all it took was balls.

***

The music was momentous. It was this jazz-dance mix, and it set the mood in a way where the concept of time felt like an odd one to measure. Relief also sat with me, as I was finally as floaty-high as I needed and wanted. Marijuana allowed me to mingle with manors. It was halfway through the second joint that always elevated me to the height I liked. I didn't get stoned anymore, I elevated. No one wanted to be stoned, everyone wanted to elevate. Mostly everyone. We could be stoned to death; did we ascend to life? Were verbal descriptions of interactions dictator of our psychological perception of them? How about the description of interactions we received? Did we reach for those descriptions when ours were unsure and second opinions were absent? Was communication mangled by connotation? Were we saying what wasn't meant as frequently as what wasn't understood?

The lighting in the bar was perfect. Warm, soft orbs glowed shyly against the walls they were fixed to; shadows of geometric shapes decorated the burgundy backdrop's monochrome. It was almost eight in the evening but it felt more like eleven. The winter solstice was poking its chest out and I was over it. The Sun was gone by the time I finished washing my hands if I took too long in the bathroom after lunch. In a way it was always like that. Excessively directing our time towards mundanity made us the same. Time was the energizer not the enemy. I loved the nightlife but hated having it pushed on me, and I hated the cold. It was coldest at night, and the layer-worthy temperature crept silently into the sky behind the daylight like a second thought. Los Angeles was much colder than advertised, and that meant a few things.

The words hammered into our tombstones never spoke to us. For that reason the only people I dealt with were business owners or artists, as I couldn't make time for anyone else. I paid for sex when I wanted it because it made the most sense. The vision of me being some unsuspecting girl's horrifying boyfriend could be made into a halloween movie, or at least a Hallmark one. And effortlessly finding a way to be an even worse spouse sounded, well, effortless. There were men arrested for paying adult escorts for voluntarily selling their bodies which...said seller was the owner of, correct? Struggling with understanding fundamentally flawed methods was a tendency I kissed tenderly on the forehead

daily. The inconsequential was worried about lavishly, and the stress attached physically debilitated. Prostitution clearly came with real consequences, they just weren't ones warranting any new thought since they were anything but new. Prostitution wasn't slavery—those who were literally sex-trafficked being an exception, for every obvious reason. Those deciding which civil rights issues warranted what level of social acceptance laughably surpassed a sphere of influence most lived and died without imagining. For as smart as we were we shouldn't be as dumb, but we existed in a system far larger than we understood collectively.

Could ignorance fulfill a necessary role in existence?

I was justifiably exhausted, but the housewives who spent all day at the gym—and were stepping out after their evening power-nap—were entering two-by-two and three-by-three. I needed another drink. The music was loud enough to mute a normal speaking volume, which needed to be doubled for the person next to you to hear what you said. The colors of the paint grew richer as the evening matured, and the soundtrack more sensual as the night candidly shared more about itself. Each bartender wore a black bow tie and suspenders, with skin tattooed like members of an undisturbed Amazonian tribe. Every heavily tattooed person I knew—with twenty or more pieces—was similar; perhaps there was something in the ink. The skin I wanted next to my meals and beverages was intentionally scarred to solidify the owner's dedication to what inspired them. Those with an ocean of tattoos understood a specific pain, which was why they also understood a specific art. Was that why so many people wanted to be artists? Did we know there was something otherworldly they reached out to commune with that may have reached back? However, the Michaelangelos in our world didn't buy their own paint. If everyone was an artist there would be far less art. I didn't know why we weren't taught that religiously. Being an artist wasn't for everyone, and it especially wasn't for people wanting to be. Passion wasn't about want, it was about hunger. A *calling* was what we heard even when not listening. Those wanting to work the comfortable job with the benefits and the schedule, but also wanted to saturate the pool of public creative material with work from leisurely sessions, were actually

patrons, right? Patrons meant everything. An artist was still an artist without an audience and art was still art, but the power of art was its power to communicate. Creation without communication was distraction. Art without the pursuit of an audience was...a hobby—or therapy—which for many was sensible. If I didn't care what people thought of my work I wouldn't share it, I would marvel at it privately. Creatives sacrificed comfort for their creations like tribal offerings to demanding deities. Experiences begged on bended knee for interpretations from the observer. The risk attached to sharing our interpretations was having them translated by the language of subjectivity. Artists volunteered themselves to be judged. The walk to the courtroom was on red carpet, and it wasn't red before they got there. Others didn't choose to be artists, they only chose to be themselves. Artists used the broken pieces of themselves to build bridges. Others did other things. Art did not exist outside of meaning.

Art was how artists were able to breathe.

I ordered coffee along with a gin and lime. I didn't want to miss anything and I was high enough to see the skyline—figuratively. With the countless rooftop bars operating in LA, that distinction called for clarification.

I loved the effect of marijuana. Me and my thoughts were usually more than enough company for the room, but it was a big-ass bar in a big-ass room. My espresso arrived in a tiny white tea cup in the middle of a matching saucer. Both were placed in front of me by the bartender, reminded me of the dinner scene from Beauty and the Beast. Ordering an espresso at a bar at night was a first for me, and the second one I ordered with honey. I wanted to leave, but the coffee was required if I wanted to be awake for longer than an hour. If only Magic Marko would hurry up and get his ass in here.

A glass broke on the other side of the restaurant; a balding man at two o'clock spoke with his hands to a woman with surgically enhanced lips which looked hard to move; a pair of women in party dresses laughed from their stomachs over twin, gold-toned colored cocktails. One wore a mint-green dress, the other was in peach. The handle on Ms. Mint-Green's purse was shaped like a cheetah in mid stride, and was a surprisingly original statement piece. Eighty-five percent of everything in Beverly Hills looked sloppily overpriced,

but the cheetah purse looked like someone took pride in their talent. Art was always art to the creator whether it was art to anyone else. Artists put their soul into their work and then sold it to support themselves like everyone else. Artists knew what selling a soul felt like. The purse owner sat the bag upright in front of her on the bar—it was rectangular. I hoped she knew the pride she took in her item was beyond justified. Only the people who cared told us when to be proud of ourselves. I did whatever I could to make Me my favorite person. It wasn't selfish to love ourselves. No one was looking out for anyone, and if they were, the person they were looking out for was likely looking in the opposite direction. Love was labor, and sincerity was an endangered species. The last time I was sincere it nearly killed me. Twice. Some would sit you in front of a mirror, buckle you to a chair, and make you watch as they ripped your heart out of your chest, then accuse you of being heartless. My heart was wherever it needed to be. My mind stood confidently, working like a pair of batteries pulled freshly from the package. Our minds made sense of the senseless.

Our unconscious mind repeated the lies loving us most, and the truths unable to see us seduced.

I wasn't bitter, I was mindful. I was aware, and due to said awareness I was bothered by subtleties many didn't know were taking place. The music switched along with the vibe, which I did earnestly mean in a real way. The evidence supporting the theory stating all physical matter was literally vibrating at a subatomic level was overwhelming, correct? A "vibe" was experimentally examined and relatively simply explained science. I believe it stopped being considered New Age, spiritual dogma, around the same time people starting posting useful information on web 2.0. The frequency of the enveloping sound effected the frequency of the room and everyone in it. Humans were still seventy percent water. Music represented the collaboration of perception-altering, ancient magic, and hyper-sophisticated technology. The magical and technological shared more similarities than most were at ease with admitting. Marko walked back in with the girl I didn't know and stood next to me.

"What'd I miss?"

"Ms. Athens is mad at me."

"Again?"

I shrugged; he shook his head.

"You have that effect on people, don't you?"

"Well, I wouldn't say all—"

"Carmen—my apologies. Irshaad, don't forget what you were saying. But this is —ah, you know what? I'm actually trying to let people introduce themselves. Please."

He extended both hands in front of himself, and in one motion crossed and uncrossed them over the other. He looked back and forth at me and, whom I could assume was Carmen, to complete the essential hand-eye signal for "introduce yourselves." She was intently watching a commercial on the nearest TV, and her hair was in a loose bun on top of her head. Not my type but she was cute-ish, with naturally long eye-lashes fanning with each blink. The commercial was for dog food, and she slowly turned her head towards me like she couldn't take her eyes off the screen.

"As Marko mentioned, I'm Carmen. How are you?"

"I'm good—Irshaad—nice to meet you."

I peeled my hand from my glass so I could shake hers, but realized it was covered in drink-sweat. I wiped it off on my thigh and presented her with the dried version. Carmen's handshake only applied enough pressure to let me know I was holding one. I did my best to match her delicate touch, but a shot of tension touched me also.

"Sorry about that."

"No, not your fault. One of my rings."

She lifted her hand and waved the three silver-ringed fingers. Maybe it was her fault, but I kept that to myself.

"Gotcha. You, uh, big into dog food?"

I motioned with my chin at the TV. Her head pivoted and leaned slightly with such precision, she would've duplicated a robotic malfunction if a second faster. She detected the sprinkle of sarcasm like it was a sprinkle of hot sauce. Her lips pressed together.

"Do you hate dogs?"

The question was asked too loudly, and Marko looked up at the ceiling and smiled to himself from behind Carmen. Marko was the homie, but he dated out of pure boredom and his selections seemed to display that plainly. We all knew hating dogs was not a wise Southern California stance to assume.

"I *do not* hate dogs, I love them."

I responded too loudly in return, looking to my left and right, confirming no drinks were aimed at my head for the accusation. I turned back to Ms. Carmen to complete my thought.

"But I'm more into doggy-style and less into canines."

My attitude regarding how I treated people I didn't know or didn't need was growing easier to execute by the month. Disengage with disharmony.

If someone or something wasn't directly linked to the maintenance of my food, shelter, clothing, or means of acquiring such, they were not a necessity.

I was now okay with paying the price for being whoever I was, it felt refreshingly like being given free money. There were like, eight billion people in the world, how many friends did I really need? How many people did we need to like us if we loved us? I was proud of myself until I realized she didn't flinch. What's-her-name, Carla? Carmen—pulled the left side of her face into a grin saying she'd outwitted me mentally before saying a word. She chuckled.

> "You know the funny thing about doggy-style is that—"

Marko cut her off.

> "I think that's enough meet and greet, yeah?"

His cape was still invisibly waving in the air. I shrugged.

> "Athen's is my ride if you two wanna joi—"

> "No—no, thank you, Irshaad. Carmen, you're ready, right?"

She was still goddamn grinning at me. Marko laughed nervously; I laughed amused. That girl didn't know who I was which was cool, although thankfully I was doing well enough most people I didn't know already knew me. I didn't hate being marginally famous and a little more than marginally prosperous. I knew people who wouldn't live in America for less than a million

dollars a year, and others who wouldn't know how to live outside of America even with a million. I was in the former category now and going no where. It felt like centuries passed me by, but my season finally arrived—about a year ago. But yeah, that girl couldn't care less if it was what she wanted to do most, and it wasn't. I didn't know where Marko found them or how they found him. Surprisingly, she kept going.

> "Where are my manners? Irshaad, would you like to learn something?"

> "Wait. You're teaching me something about doggy-style?"

Carmen deliberately blinked once, then stared. If she was a foot closer I think I could have felt the breeze from her lashes.

> "I'll take that as a yes. 'Dogs' are guys. All dogs. That's what the word means: male canine. Unless you're into guy on guy which is none of my business."

> "Okay, you can—"

> "But then I wouldn't understand why you haven't stopped gawking at my

boobs since I got here. Flattered by the way, thank you."

My eyes shifted to Marko's less than a second before his did the same to mine. I assumed he was angry with me now just like Athens was. Although awkwardly neither of us looked away, I didn't know what he was thinking. Did that really happen? I couldn't relate to stories of looking into someone's eyes and knowing what they thought. I never experienced that and knew no one who did in any way striking me as tangible.

I spoke to what I witnessed. I didn't pretend to know anymore than my experience.

I'm pretty sure that attitude got me kicked out of Catholic school, and Sabbath school, and Sunday school, and...I was forgetting one.

Marko pretended to be on his phone—he did it all the time. Carmen cleared her throat softly.

"I'm curious. What's your superpower?"

Marko's eyes rolled up from his screen like a convertible top opening. The conversation almost felt staged, but it was LA. I didn't even know what to—

"My what?"

"Superpower. Your gift. The thing you do that feels like it happens so naturally it's like...your blood flowing through your veins. It's everything keeping you alive that you don't have to think about."

"Have we...do I know you from somewhere or..."

She smiled and folded her hands below her waist in front of her.

"We all know each other once we know ourselves."

I didn't know what that meant and felt like I wasn't meant to. Maybe her second job was a fortune teller. She persisted without pestering.

"Will you be answering?"

"I, um—"

Goddamn it, Marko, was your cape caught in the telephone booth? I said nothing audibly, but his timing was the bullseye I needed.

"Carmen, we can go."

"We can. Irshaad, can I know your superpower? Pretty-please?"

Oh, and she could be funny now too? Marko shrugged in defeat and returned to the rouse of busy-on-the-cell-phone-guy. I picked up my gin, swirling the ice around so it circled the glass like models of planetary orbits. My index finger rose towards Carmen as I continued spinning the cubes. She nodded once.

"Please, take your time."

Marko wasn't happy, but this time it wasn't my fault.

"Take your—? Yeah. Okay, sure. "

Not *all* my fault, anyway. A bartender with "FREE" tattooed across four fingers scooped up two unfinished drinks to my right, and something about the angle of their bow tie made everything feel backwards. Marko raised his hand, drawing their attention.

"Excuse me. Just tequila and ginger. Well is fine."

It was familiar. The whole scenario was familiar, so I was in a leup[4].

My stomach muscles spasmed in slow waves too well-trained for one deep breath after another to pacify. Moving through it was my only option. Presence. What was my superpower?

"So, would you like to tell me?"

"Depends. Are you reading my mind?"

"Do you think that's possible?"

I didn't know how to answer that logically. I supported a healthy amount of proclamations with no defense other than…other than, I don't know, some shit made sense and other shit didn't. And if I did say so myself, I was pretty goddamn good at pointing it… wow.

"I know my superpower."

"You do?"

Only Marko's eyes moved as he glanced up from his phone and

---

[4] A leup (pronounced 'loop') is life-cycle set in motion by conscious or unconscious decisions continually leading us back to the same people, places, and possessions. The individual choices creating a leup are often viewed as unrelated. Leups vary in intensity, often signaled by repeated deja vu or the recognition of a repeated experience. For instance, a leup can be a cycle of making money, it can also be a cycle of choosing unfit romantic partners.

promptly looked back down. I answered her question.

> "Yeah. Pretty sure."

> "Okay."

She waved her hand in front of her, gesturing for a display that wouldn't take much from me.

> "I show people who they really are."

> "That's Interesting."

> "Is it?"

> "Depends what you do with it, I suppose, which may be worth considering."

Marko threw another look. I wasn't staring at Carmen's tits anymore, maybe I was waiting for the next weird thing she wanted to say. She kept going.

> "I heard there's a name for that."

> "For what?"

> "Those who saw the truth in people and places."

> "Hm. A strangely specific bit of information to come by?"

> "Depends."

> "On?"

> "Where you get your information."

One short laugh, that was more a thud from chest, answered her quick reply respectfully. I kept my mouth closed and continued listening.

> "A Clarif—from what I've heard."

> "I have not heard."

> "Maybe you should try hearing."

I smiled as humbly as I could manage, patiently. If she was going to start knocking on the window, I was going to cut the conversation short.

We always opened the door to let people in. We could always leave them outside.

I chose courtesy.

> "Are 'clarifs' some kind of common knowledge I missed?"

She thought about that, pushing her lips to the corner of her mouth.

> "I don't think so. Is *common* knowledge the kind that interests you?"

"Uhh, I guess sometimes?"

She leaned her back against the edge of the bar and her elbows sat on top of it.

"I knew another like you—"

"Ooh, let me—can I guess? Talented."

Carmen licked her lips casually, then angled her face to the ceiling as she searched for the word.

"Almost. Troubled."

She smiled her same little smile again before looking at Marko doing whatever on his phone with his cocktail. My aunt called it a Shepard's Smile. I was informed from too early of an age it was like Mona Lisa's, yet smarter and less slutty. Her words, not mine. I could Shepard's Smile too.

"Oh, didn't know there was a difference."

"I only found out recently. I've seen how knowing we aren't alone in an experience makes some feel better."

I raised my glass. Maybe there was some sort of conference that these girls frequented, Marko knew about it, and he just camped out and hit on all of them—as he should. She cleared her throat again and I decided to be a gentleman.

"Did you need a drink?"

"No, thank you, it's just the weather."

"The worst, right?"

"Maybe not that bad. But I was wondering, do you know who I really am?"

I pretended to think about it; I wasn't going to start that conversation. I knew when a trap was being set.

"Dog lover, right?"

Carmen smiled and moved off the bar.

"Nice meeting you…"

"Really?"

"I am truly that bad with names, yes."

"Irshaad."

"I was kidding, Irshaad. I know who you are. I'm excited you're finding yourself. Long road from here."

The single, friendly touch she gave my arm was light enough to leave the cotton on my jacket undisturbed. She turned to Marko.

> "Don't let that thing eat your patience."

> "Huh?"

She flicked the side of his phone with her middle finger.

> "Let's go."

> "Oh, you're ready now?

I interjected.

> "Uh, Mark, if you wouldn't mind?"

I waved him over and then addressed his guest.

> "A moment with my friend, Carmen. I'll give him right back."

Her eyes rolled playfully, and she turned to hide what I guessed was a smile. Marko arrived while my inquiries battled their anxiety.

> "Sir, you're friend? What the fuck?"

> "What?"

He shrugged as nonchalantly as he did innocently.

> "Bruh, that girl is *very* weird. And if she rubbed off on me at all, you're paying to remove the contamination."

> "How about I get *her* to rub-off on *me*, then I let you know if it's fatal."

He winked. That was the wittiest thing I recalled Marko ever saying.

> "That was goddamn hilarious. Holy shit."

He chuckled and shook his head.

> "Call me in morning, bro. Before noon."

> "Yo, she called me a Clarif? You heard that part, right?"

> "Yeah."

> "Do *you* know what that is? I don't."

He hesitated, wondering if it was something dangerous enough to turn lack of knowledge into lack of life.

> "Uhh…man, I don't know!"

> "Yeah, me either. The fuck is that about?"

He hid his teeth behind a grin growing so large it became a short laugh.

"What's funny?"

"You. I'm off to see how weird my new friend is. *Before* noon."

" '*Before noon.*' You know it's always sunrise somewhere, right? In which case I'm always up before noon. Not that I need to be."

"You wanna know something?"

The question came with the asterisk of him knowing I didn't know what he did. My right eyebrow looked up slowly with intrigue.

"Are you about to tell me something your little friend let you in on?"

Marko put his right hand on my shoulder, and squeezed like he was my dad cheering me up after striking out in my first little league game. He smirked and leaned closer.

"You ready?

The sun doesn't rise, we do."

"Are you drunk?"

"Perfectly."

He about-faced in one spin, got to Carmen and put his arm around her, then held up the peace sign at me with his free hand. I lifted my gin and took another sip before I put it down. The anxiety returned noticeably louder, its volume raised without an invite like the volume of TV commercials. The bartender returned also.

"Hey, man. Last call for food if you want anything."

I shook my head and tried to move my lips into a happy shape, however I didn't get very far. The bartender tapped the bar top, nodded, and picked up a white towel they tucked into their back pocket. If I was right, as he walked away he tripped and...

"Oh, shit!"

...then the girl bartender turned around...

"Whoa!"

...and then caught him in a hug. She was shorter than him, and his momentum caused his arms to naturally fall over her shoulders.

Neither of them moved, and then they did. It was just how I remembered, although they didn't. The girl apologized first.

"Sorry, I—"

"No, I guess I'm still learning to walk, or something."

They both smiled.

Deja vu was unsettling, but knowing what happened next then seeing it happen in front of you was terrifying. It was one of the more obvious signals. The terror cane from not knowing how best to react. Should I do anything? It wasn't like I could see the future, I could just finish the deja vu. Nevertheless, it was never what you wanted when you were somewhere in life you drastically wanted to change. I was stuck in a leup and didn't know how I got there, but something of consequence needed to be done differently.

The cycles we were lost in were the same we created.

Imagine being lost in an unwanted, undetected leup for your entire life. Similar people producing similar relationships followed you. Same places, same problems, the whole time not knowing why or how. Were you crazy? How could you tell? You didn't realize you were doing the same thing over and over because you didn't have to, that was the point. All of life, all of the universe, all that ever was or ever would be was following the same pattern as what came before it. Once I realized what I wasn't seeing and then kept seeing it, a lot changed. Recognizing every part of life was cyclical made what was difficult to ignore impossible to. Why would the seasons be the only Earthly condition to occur in consistently reoccurring seasons? Women menstruated and gave birth rhythmically; we could forecast when crops would grow; all lived for a time and all times came to an end—as it did before. Divine creations creating divinely created consistence. The cyclical nature was the only one. I didn't see anything otherwise, nor did anyone else, we only used different names.

Athens was still sitting to my far right, and I realized we should have slept together and then left each other alone. She was my type though, the whole look, but she was an easy type to like. The eyes, the lips, the tits, and the small frame were always on display, and the "Let's just have fun and forget about our problems," personality was the plus-one. It was a good time in doses. We both desperately needed to grow, and I figured that was why we couldn't leave each other alone. That, and the sex.

Narcissists didn't grow out of their narcissism, they grew deeper into it.

She looked up as I was staring and I turned too quickly and left to get some air.

I walked passed the wine bar next door peppered with every style and color of bodycon and wrap dress. On the stocky wooden tables and wood grain floors were the fancy shopping bags with thick, braided-cotton string handles. Those were the bags retail stores didn't suggest. The bag was opened and stood on the counter, the purchased item was placed inside along with the receipt, and lastly, the bag was picked up by the customer service team member and handed to the customer. Each one of those pleasantries was included in the price of the overpriced novelty obtained. The bags were still meant to be discarded; decadence was part of the capitalist consumerism extravaganza. Although the disposable income of said variety was at my disposal, I chose to feed Poppa Capitalism in more

creative and mutually beneficial ways.

I stopped on the other side of the wine spot and looked up, greeted unexpectedly by a glowing white marble in the sky. I was absolutely a moongazer. A teacher I unwisely didn't listen to wore a bracelet with a quartz on it resembling a full moon. Wearing a full moon was a reminder it was always full; phases were a matter of perspective. She said the full moons held a special energy, and I believed her—I listened to that part. Staring at the full moon was the closest we could get to staring at the Sun. My eyes focused and I could make out the shadows of the craters, but I also saw something else. An intimate relationship was shared with the moon, and the eye contact it held with us maintained the romance. Prolonged eye contact scientifically made us feel closer to other life forms. That one fact was monumental.

The magic in everything was seen easily once we chose patience over presumption.

Presumption put a knife in our neck. Ancient cultures, and some current ones, could confidently arrange marriages knowing they would work if both partners chose to look into one another. Seeing the magic took time, we chose whether to take it or not. Choosing the magic was easy for me because it was the first thing I remember searching for. Our inherent belief in magic was a connection severed. The adults were amputees, the kids were fine. The adults thought they knew everything, an arrogance passing blindness to their offspring. Then the kids were cut from their connection as well. A kid threw a temper tantrum because they wanted candy. The kid was more than likely suffering from sugar addiction due to dietary direction from their guardians. The parents physically disciplined their kids for the behavior they caused, then were nice to them. The physical aggression came again, nice to them again. Kids weren't dumb, they new. Children conditioned to associate attention with love realized anger was a strong form of attention. Aggression was gravitated towards because it was easy, and anger, attention, and love were already made psychologically inseparable. Then when they're in abusive relationships we acted baffled as to why that lifestyle appeared reasonable. The aggression often struck without understanding of its origin or outcome. Some actions were committed with purpose, others as part of it. How much of what we did was done so for reasons beyond our field of perception? Conditioned responses then turned into the curriculum we used to manifest the cyclical once more. The "big picture" was comprised of brush strokes smearing millennia across the canvas with each movement. Ignorance was the only enemy.

We were taught we all changed like shapeshifters, yet many remained who they always were. It was the twenty-first century, and passengers on planes or trains still acted shocked when assigned a neighbor. Humans of all ages were still getting bullied because they enjoyed reading. That was still a thing. Were we surprised basic prejudices still plagued our perspectives? We were still mentally attacking each other for wanting to get smarter. Wasn't that a large part of the the problem? And we said nothing, no one did, we just kept finding ways to be entertained enough to gouge out our eyes but keep them at the same time. That was hardly an excuse.

When we surrounded ourselves with distractions, everything was.

We were what we allowed. What we allowed represented us directly.
As always.

Artist: Nick Drake

Song: Pink Moon

Album: Pink Moon

"Saw it written and I saw it say/ Pink Mooooon is on it'sss way./ And none of youuuuu stand sooo tall/ Pink Mooooon gonna get yeeeeee all."

***

My eyes were still on the moon when I heard Laurren.

"Hey! Athens is looking for you."

"Okay."

"Okay?"

"Yes?"

"What's your problem?"

I sighed.

"Bruh, I don't have—"

"Like you're talking to a whole bitch in front of us, Irshaad. Who was that?"

"Did you know the word 'dog' referred to male canines, like 'bitch' referred to the female ones?"

A laugh starting as air escaping Laurren's nose, moved down her face into a smile, then crackled along into her sentence.

"What are you fucking talking about?"

"Nothing. That girl came with Marko. Weren't ya'll here last…whenever? Pretty sure you *saw* when he picked her up."

"We *saw* her all in your face."

I continued moongazing.

"Hello?"

"You said Athens was looking for me. I'm here. You can let her know."

"Whatever, asshole. She cares about you."

"She needs help."

"What?"

"Nothing."

"Did you just say 'she needs help?'"

"No. I said 'nothing'."

"What does she need help from? Giving a fuck about you?"

"No. She needs help from all the shit she's addicted to."

"You're serious? You're drinking in the same fucking place we are. God, you're such a…such fucking millennial."

Although I didn't consider her insult to be a skilled one, I knew I was being insulted. I stopped moongazing although I shouldn't have.

We dishonored ourselves and opposed our divinity when choices were made based directly on emotional reactions to external stimuli.

I wanted to moongaze, not have the conversational equivalent of telling a Knock-Knock joke to an empty room. However, I engaged against my better judgement.

"You see how you keep shifting the focus off of your own family member and back to me? How does that help her? Who gets help when they have people around them convincing them they don't have a problem?"

"You're legit putting words in my mouth."

"Am I, Laurren? Because I don't think you know how this—actually…"

I stopped myself and my hands from talking, and slid each of them into their respective holsters to relax. An urge was in me to keep wasting my breath that was harder to kill than Beatrix Kiddo. My stop button was broken.

"You know what? You're right. If she doesn't think she has a problem then she doesn't. Part of life is being okay with people being adults and making choices, right? So I'm actually glad you brought that up. We all rescue ourselves by choosing to search until the answer is found. What could the answer do for us alone? Detectives found clues because they were trained how to see, and they put those skills into action. Most of us—most of us ain't even looking. Athen's ain't, right? Because she's fine; she's chillin'. And you're right.

Those who aren't looking for help aren't at the point where they need it yet. It's everyone else who's acting out of fear instead understanding.

Personally, I'm done acting like I don't see what the fuck is going on."

"Whatever. You're mean as fuck and dramatic about everything anyway."

She walked away. We were often categorized as assholes, or mean, or dramatic when we protected our energy and our boundaries. Sometimes we were legitimately just being dicks, however that was relative. Being nice without being honest only misrepresented ourselves. We would soon be called to defend the misrepresentation, and nothing went well after. I would be mean, I would be an asshole, I would be dramatic, whatever it took to keep my intangible space invasion-free. The derogatory

terms grew more endearing every time they were used incorrectly.

I turned my attention back to the moon and remembered the significant: my cup overflowed. I couldn't keep track of all deserving gratitude. In a past life that was close enough to remember, there was always some compounded worry. Too deeply I appreciated shedding the burden of how much money was in my bank account or when it would arrive. While traveling as a second-class citizen, I was blatantly informed how those who spent more on a ticket would be given greater access to accommodations. I literally couldn't buy the better food, even though I wanted to, unless I paid the additional money in advance. It was called coach now; coach was synonymous with steerage. The Titanic sank but it's philosophy didn't. Class was never meant to separate, only designate. We messed that one up too. What sank was our understanding of honesty and why it was important, but that was true of a lot. The majority of the world was still in survival mode, a setting with more minor comforts now than previously, depending on demographic and locale. Honest observation led to the greatest gifts. We knew what we wanted when we wanted it, and either decided to reach for it or watch it walk away. Passengers stumbled past me in planes where they needed that first-class seat close to the entrance more than I did. The voice of god spoke to everyone about everything from what to wear, to the appropriate number of wipes prior to flushing. Hearing the voice of god was unrelated to religion, yet kin to creation. That voice, that vibration, only knew progression, and I knew that spoke to a level of existence exceeding my understanding. A single voice led me to a city where the people who were from there said everyone was fake. Everyone. That same voice was guidance to an angelic alter allowing me to live at an angelic height. I loved LA.

There wasn't a perfect moment to wait for, they all were. Intense gratitude was owed for our time here, and we saw it everywhere once our eyes were opened. Some deeper insights were difficult to identify when roaches were roaming my bedroom wall, but they were no less critical. Ignorant instruction led to assumptions of, "If I couldn't see it, no one could." Personal success was not the only one of consequence to us personally. Envy existed out of ignorance.

The success of one was one example of the success available to all. Reminders were mistaken for reprimands.

I was grateful our moon spoke to us. I was also grateful for the way the drinks and the edibles simultaneously induced their effect. The spirits and the plant medicine worked well with me.

A plane passed overhead low enough to read the airline name in the moonlight. To my left I heard the approaching heels of boots I purchased digging into the sidewalk like I didn't.

"Uh, *hello*? You're leaving?"

I sighed.

"B, where does it look like I'm going?"

"You call me 'B' now?"

"Should I not?"

"It's fine."

"Okay."

"Okay, what's with you in that girl's face?"

I tucked my lips under my teeth, bit down, and took a breath. Then I spoke.

"There's no way Laurren didn't run back in there and tell you."

"So? Why were you in her face?"

I thought about it; Athens was impatient and drunk.

"Uh, hel—"

"Don't say anything else, please. At least give me a second to answer. *You* asked *me* something."

"And it takes you *this* long?"

"I don't—"

I stopped myself again and smiled. My dad was a pot head and my mom loathed it. He got high and turned into The Joker, finding any and everything unbearably hilarious. Vivid memories of him laughing in my mother's face was a bandage covering self-inflicted wounds I was taught how to execute. The desperate attempts she made to communicate her feelings moved her to tears, the situation called for her to stop.

The first to find comedy found victory.

Victory was layered. Laughing at a clown was easy. My parents separated, then my mom filed for divorce and raised me herself. I'm not sure who should claim the prize there. Did The Joker cut a smile into his face because he realized nothing warranted a frown? We hated a joke we would love if we saw we weren't the punchline because there wasn't one. Life was one of those "whose-on-first" jokes. It went in an unending circle growing in hilarity as long as there was no attempt to dissect it. My dad was who he was because of his parents, as was my mom, as was I, as was Athens.

Growth was often written in eraser.

Athens didn't get it and I doubted she wanted to, she just wanted to feel anything. She also didn't want to let anything go, which she proved with each question.

"What were you going to say?"

"Really…it *really* doesn't matter."

"Oh, my god. God, I *hate* when you do that."

"What do you *like*?"

"What?"

"What do you like?"

She scoffed and shook her head. It was only an insulting question when answering the opposite was less work. The smirk landing on Athen's lips warned me her response may not impress.

"Money."

"What did—did you say 'money'?"

"I'm joking."

She wasn't.

"No, you're not."

"Jesus. Whatever, Irshaad. What's funny is Josh used to act all serious and shit just like this too."

"You know what I love more than anything? You bringing up your goddamn ex who I saved you from. *Please* keep going with that shit."

Her eyes rolled. How was I supposed to take her seriously? She wasn't completely facing me, but her back was turned enough she didn't see the woman walking up behind her.

"Yo, watch your back."

"Huh?"

"Behind you—watch out."

As she turned I stepped back, held onto both of her arms near her shoulders, and moved her out of the woman's way with me.

"Can you stop?!"

"*Relax.*"

The woman slowly limped closer. She was homeless and walked like both of her legs were too short but in different places. Staring at the ground, she mumbled to herself loud enough to be heard if you weren't already in conversation.

"I'm tired. I'm tired of tearing my life apart. This is not what I—I did *not* imagine this. I'm tired. I'm tired of tearing my life apart. This is not what I—I did *not* imagine this."

She repeated the same thing and kept walking. Six or seven dirty-white shopping bags hung from both arms and shoulders, and her short, frosty hair was matted to her head. The back of her right calf and ankle was stained with a line of blood.

"I'm tired of tearing my life apart. This is not what I—I did *not* imagine this."

She was stuck deep in an unbroken leup. I remembered being where she was—not homeless—but stuck deep and not knowing how to get out. The longer we were stuck, the further we drifted from the coastline of conscious existence. The return trip, from endlessly repeating a single sentence while limping through Beverly Hills on a Sunday, was a series of layovers and connecting flights. Our energy shifted like Earth did. We did everything Earth did. We did what was done, we just did it in different environments. The homeless woman was a mirror, as we all were.

Honoring our conditioning over our calling was the quickest way to lose ourselves.

We listened without pursuing understanding when nothing was understood without listening. Moving forward in ignorance was moving no where. I didn't listen too well, I knew that, thankfully some couldn't be ignore. I forgot I was still holding Athens until she said something.

"That was old blood on that lady's leg, right?"

"Hopefully."

I let her go purposefully but she didn't seem to notice.

"I'm going to check on Laurren."

"Yeah, okay."

She faced me.

"You're not coming?"

"Smoking first."

The hesitation she flashed was just, but her intuition was visibly dismissed, a decision seldom working in our favor. Athens was the type to pass by a mirror in public and stare at herself genuinely impressed. Then again, so was I. We understood the parts of each other we needed to change, but they were the same parts where we allowed laziness to preside.

Her steps clicked back to the entrance like a metronome, and it reminded of that song about the boots made for walking from the seventies. Was it possible for our purpose to be walking away? Could our life-cycle be one of seeing the choice changing our direction, but acting comfortably instead of courageously when deciding? What if we did that until we died? Winter was cold every year and we weren't ever surprised. What if Athens was Winter for me and everyone she met? What if that was who she was? I wondered if she knew we would never see each other again. Some knowledge made us do things differently, most just made us say we would. The latter was much easier for those raised by parents consistently attaching professions of love to the tail of broken promises. When I thought about it, I didn't know if I knew Athens or the version of her she was made into. I didn't think about how I would be able to recognize the difference; I didn't think about whether or not there was one.

It was hard avoiding someone in the city if being out mixing for clients was necessary. Thankfully, I recently graduated. The right people were fans of my work and the wrong people understood it. My good fortune enabled me to stay home and really only interact eye-to-eye with those I wanted to, when I wanted to. It would be easy never seeing Athens again, assuming there was anywhere left in the city to stay where people liked her. Perhaps what her and I shared was...complimentary. Some just didn't know how to take a compliment. What I lacked in

connections I made up for with passion and persistence. LA was my city in the way that everyone I met understood I represented its soul selflessly. Traits like integrity still mattered to masters.

We chose to walk away or in circles.

I chose to walk a few blocks before ordering a ride. I didn't want any uninvited exchanges with friends, foes, family, or other.

One cycle was broken by the next.

THOUGHTS DESCENDING

THE ONLY FALL IS FORWARD

I loved everything about planes and loved nothing about driving. Generations of Homo Sapiens sadly lived and died without flight. Traveling through the atmosphere at extraordinary velocities was an exclusive privilege for us inhabiting the future. For example, my cruising speed on the 405 averaged eighty miles per hour, while a Boeing 747 cruised at about five-hundred and sixty. However, it was in a car where I felt like I was flying the way everything flew by me. Whether it was time, people, or places, they all looked and felt blurry, which didn't change even after the car was parked. Everything I saw was melted candle wax to my eyes; I felt distortion and panic. The anxiety swam excitedly beneath a delicate surface like fish in a frozen lake. Too fast, it all moved too fast, and even at my maximum speed I couldn't find a way to keep up. Everything I did felt useless. My heartbeat played at a tempo somewhere near the speed of light, a reaction to my inner dread whispering, "If you can't save yourself, were you ever worth saving?"

How much control did I really have? Was I in control at all? I was supposed to be but it didn't feel like it. Was that all there was to the winding road of life? Living one wrong turn away from ending it all? Is that what made it worth living? Life was saturated with instability by design. It was a game. It was a game we were all forced to play—we were forced to. I'm glad I was invited to the party, but I also didn't have the choice to decline. We were stuck playing the game so long our bodies broke, or, we were randomly thrown off the game-board entirely. Our next move could always be our last, erasing the entire game as we knew it. The rules were all made up and the points didn't matter—it was just like that improv show Whose Line Is It Now? I loved that show. Not only were the rules made up, there were countless versions of the rules, and they were all right and all wrong simultaneously. In life, not Whose Line, but it still kind of applied to both.

There were no rewards for sincerity, or honor, or integrity, or honesty, or compassion. That was part of the game too. It wasn't always like that, but it was currently. What was valuable and what wasn't was collectively decided. No one was ever actually rewarded for anything because no one kept the rewards. We couldn't keep anything. Ever. It seemed like there was so much time to keep things or do things, but our longest lifespan wasn't even long enough to be measured by anyone but us. I thought about that and it was endlessly hilarious. There were dead people more celebrated than live ones, and live people no one cared about until they died. There were too many of those. None of it meant anything, yet everyone wanted it. We wanted all of the Its—possessions, attention, admiration, control. It was vile and insatiable gluttony. I often hated the same things I loved about life, and tried finding something to love in what I hated. The latter seldom benefited me much, but it felt good. It was easy to forget feeling good about something was the reward.

Artist: Nina Simone

Song: Feeling Good

Album: I Put a Spell on You

"It's a new dawwwn, it's a new a dayyy, it's a new li-iii-fe/ Fo-ooo-r meee!/ And I'm feeling goooood."

I saw myself sitting in a car flying off a cliff, and everyday I got a little closer to the ground. That was my reality. Sitting in a two year old, blood-red, Aston Martin Vantage with seashell interior, that was seconds away from breaking into more pieces than my fragmented thoughts. It didn't matter what model car you were sitting in once it flew off a cliff. The plummeting vehicle was a purchase I made because I thought it would make me feel better. That was what we killed ourselves to make more, and more money for, right? So we could finally feel better than we did before, or at least better than someone else. I didn't feel any better, I felt worse.

Retail Therapy was real and one of my favorites. The things we owned didn't leave until we lost them.

Then I realized it was no different with people. People weren't genuine they were human, and I was no exception. When the opinions of others was a source of joy, we started living to maintain approval. We only lost what we were going to lose, including ourselves. Fortunately, we only found what we were going to find, and that went for the good and bad alike. Good and bad were both words I wanted out of my vocabulary. Good and bad were lazy ways to describe rewards and lessons. What we considered words to represent defined much of our perspective.

Words defined our lives, yet we used them like we hated them.

Those words were either defined by ourselves or others, and those definitions informed and gave direction to our decisions. The same happened earlier that evening. Passing by The Virgil I thought of Virgil Abloh, knowing because of Virgil we knew there was a Virgil in all of us. The name Virgil was popularized by a Roman poet, but a poet of another medium redefined it. New definitions, new direction.

***

The car was getting closer to the ground.

***

Everything started last night after the bar. Me, Lonzo, and AJ ended up back at Lonzo's Zen-inspired condo in North Hollywood. Bamboo trees were in every corner of each room, and at least one Buddha statue sat serenely in meditation on each table or countertop. In the center of his round coffee table was a bronze singing bowl with a bronze Buddha on either side. The table was cut from a block of brown jasper, predominantly tan, with cinnamon, dark burgundy, and black tones swirling throughout. It was too nice of a table for the three, powdery, parallel white lines Lonzo separated onto its surface. He was a self-proclaimed *vibrarian*, a descriptor of his own invention most accurately capturing his essence and the essence of those like him. Of course, that was how he described it.

Vibrarians "vibrated" at their highest and most authentically.

He would do a line side-by-side with Buddha and equally respect both teacher and tool as their contributions were without contradiction. It was a joke he thought of that never stopped. Him and AJ would more than likely be producing an official vibrarian anthem within a year if they could create interest. After tapping the center of his nose twice and inhaling some leftovers, Lonzo made a statement.

> "Everyone does blow in LA, homie. You'll finally be one of us."

I was sure I didn't want to be one of them, not in that way. Neither myself nor my two counterparts were notoriously tender, but we stayed up for hours doing coke and talking about everything we ran from. It felt like stopping, turning around, and finally facing off with the serial killer chasing you through the forest—walking, as usual— waving a machete. The most sobering conversations often happened when we were the opposite.

Some used drugs to silence the pain, others used them to feel the pain they silenced.

All three of us broke down emotionally, confessing our sins to one another like the good Catholics we never were. After more than twenty-four hours without sleep, the aftermath of our revelations were the barely remembered stragglers and I was starving. Lonzo and AJ wanted to keep running lines like they were rehearsing for a movie scene, but

I was done and needed to go home.

Lonzo walked over to his dining room table, poured three shots of what I correctly assumed was tequila into plastic cups, and brought them back to me and AJ.

> "Bro, you might as well just crash here."

AJ picked up his shot and motioned for me and Lonzo to do the same.

> "You ain't got nothing to do in the morning anyway."

I chuckled then tried to get things moving.

> "Are we toasting these shots or what?"

AJ responded first followed promptly by Lonzo.

> "Let's go. A toast to a bigger bag?"

> "Because the bag brings us any kind of everything."

I raised my cup higher before making an addition.

> "To the bag, and only moving forward with it."

"That part."

Once the shots were gone I stated the obvious.

> "Nevertheless, gentlemen, I
> do have work in the
> morning."

The two musketeers were ruptured by laughter.

> "I hope you know how
> much I truly can't stand
> y'all."

That only made them laugh harder, which was why I said it, because that's what friends were for. Lonzo and AJ were easily the two people closest to me in LA, but neither of them would ever have work in the morning. They both shared accounts of enjoying handcuffs, but it wasn't sexy when Routine was dangling them. Their seventh year in Hollywood recently came and went while I slowly approached my third. The music industry treated them well and valued their talent as songwriters/ producers, so they possessed considerably more leisure time than I did. The business and creative side of executive producing and public speaking worked well for me, but I wouldn't have been able to afford an Aston Martin if I didn't buy it used from Lonzo. There

were projects to complete before I was alongside my companions in their comfortable tax bracket. But I wasn't complaining, or at least was trying not to.

What we loved doing should be loved while doing it, as it was never done the same way again.

Nevertheless my frustration remained buoyant, knowing a millionaire's mind was behind my forehead. The wealthiest business owners either built frameworks, knew unimaginable ways of using them, or employed the people who did. My mind knew what to do with a well built framework. I could revolutionize books right now. The metaverse was looking like the next iteration of the internet as we understood it. There was an idea I played with for how users would experience reading in a digital world: "meta-books." An immersive visual and auditory experience where the book was virtually moved through rather than pages being turned. The scenes unfolded visually and audibly as the narrative was read. Words scrolled through the environment at the users desired speed and style, and could be stopped at anytime for use of dictionary, etymology, and pronunciation functions. It was the evolution of reading without having to employ another's voice. A resurgence in wonder for the written word made sense because we were digging again. The monetization of fabricated information awoke a sleeping sleuth in many who slept for a lifetime. Fact-checking was a fact of life. The energy the audience was asked to expel when receiving creative material was compounded and returned to them. Higher-level experiences required our participation. I saw users still utilizing the part of their brain traditionally activated by reading, but doing so in the environment they were reading about while experiencing it in real time. An audio-track would be made available as an option instead a focus, with the captions unable to be removed. The reading experience was about the reader telling themselves the story just as much as the author. Was innovation's goal making life easier while removing the work revealing the lessons lending wisdom? There were never enough opportunities to practice listening to ourselves. Users selected their vantage point for the story from the available characters, moving through the narrative as they did. Finer details illustrating the world and characters, such as the way they chewed or the texture of an item, would project as an enlarged

semi-solid image to be viewed. One "page" could be the interior of a rum-soaked pirate ship, and the next a sun-soaked beach with white sand on a forgotten island anchored by treasure. I knew it was at least a million dollar idea too many would try to buy me out of before my name was even attached. I wanted to take it a step further, including gender and race neutral characters readers made look however they envisioned, but one step at a time. It would be an AeMersive Meta Book—an AEM file. It was a PDF on acid. An investor was coming soon—figuratively—I just needed my patience to hold my hand. I received remarks meant to discourage me, reminders that any and everyone had ideas, as if that diminished my skillset.

Those who minimized the power and importance of concept creators forgot how every version of society was formulated.

Without the concept there was nothing to create. Elon Musk, Bill Gates, Steve Jobs, Walt Disney, Philip K. Dick, Arthur C. Clarke, Plato, Leonardo DaVinci, every notable theoretical physicist. Some built with their minds in specified ways giving purpose to those who built with their hands. Those who built by hand gave purpose to those who built with the mind. When what we brought to the table was valued, the table was more bountiful for all. Anyone could do anything, yet most did nothing.

Lonzo did another line and then pinched his nose like he was going underwater.

> "Isaiah. You're not really leaving though, right?"

I was really leaving but I shouldn't have been. I should've just called out of work and slept it off in the condo. How much we did begrudgingly reflected how much further we could grow.

No obligations existed while options operated, and a life of bondage awaited without that understanding.

AJ arranged a line for himself while Lonzo refilled each of our shot cups.

> "And don't say you can't chill because you don't feel good, yada, yada."

> "Yeah, none of that 'I'ma kill myself' shit from earlier, bro."

I looked over my shoulder and then back towards Lonzo.

> "Who said all that?"

Lonzo and AJ glanced at each other before mutually crumbling to the floor in laughter. I was confused but connecting the dots, while Lonzo's eyes watered from the wave of comedy.

> "Stop playin', bro!"

> "I mean…that vaguely, I guess, kind of sounds familiar."

AJ sat up on the floor with his back against the couch.

> "No, it doesn't."

I confessed.

> "You're right. I don't know what y'all talking about. At all."

> "Bruh. That's crazy."

Lonzo wiped the last trickling tears away.

> "And if I can be extremely Capricorn for two minutes —"

> "Sirs, gentlemen—"

> "In the middle of my sentence, though?"

I bowed my head humbly.

> "Where are my manners. Please, continue."

> "If I can be especially Capricorn for just a minute, we live in North-goddamn-America in the 21st century. Is suicide *really* ever the most fun answer?"

> "Is that rhetorical?"

He thought about it, pressing his lips together and up towards his mustache.

> "Yes. I'm being funny but like...when you think it through, you know? Like there are people who *didn't* kill themselves during the fucking holocaust."

I looked at AJ and I imagined my face looked the same. I couldn't tell if Lonzo's observation was profound, or if the drugs made me appreciate everything more, including thoughts of minor consequence or coherence. That was the first time I could recollect my mind going blank as a response. AJ was literally slack-jawed, his lips begging for more water and less tequila. Lonzo was still hot.

> "Like why, you know? I've absolutely thought one-hundred percent yes to suicide before, but the holocaust? The fuck? Yeah, I would've pulled the trigger on that one in a snap."

He chuckled to himself.

> "I got lucky on that pun, by the way. Not planned. It'd be in poor taste to accept artistic credit."

Lonzo's remark was deserving of the moment of silence it received, like after a national anthem was performed—or at funeral. Then we laughed, and the perfectly chill downstairs neighbor confirmed how insane we sounded. Three knocks came from under the floor in the kitchen, followed by a woman's voice, seasoned with a fading Jamaican accent still rich with flavor.

> "Bredren, can't send me nuh invite!"

We laughed too hard again, sounding like skeletons inside of carnival haunted houses. Once that subsided, I miraculously remembered something useful.

> "Lonzo, do not 'all-aboard' regular people onto that

train of thought, brody. People will probably *not* get your…suicide sense of humor."

He over-acted, sticking his nose up as high as his neck could reach.

> "I happen to find me hilarious."

> "You kids have fun. I'm out of here."

AJ stood up while patting his pockets.

> "Bro, you're too high for that shit. No, you know what I mean, you're coming down and you might as well chill. You're too all over the place. And somebody call my phone."

No one was "too anything" to do what they wanted, which was usually the problem.

I didn't believe in good or bad choices, or good or bad outcomes. Choices were made, and the events following either went the way we wanted them to or they didn't. Something not happening how we wanted didn't negate its benefit. I gleaned that from The Catalytic Principle, the only philosophy I could almost remember. The real reason I wanted to leave so badly was because I was trying to feel better—whatever that meant—and coke didn't make me feel better, it just made me feel awake. I was tired. I was tired of doing the same things with the same people and thinking somehow I'd be able to create a different outcome. Not Lonzo and AJ though, they were cool. I knew the famous Einstein definition of insanity, yet I was acting it out anyway. Each of us were the sum of our actions, even if we did the math wrong.

***

I could see the cracks and indentations on the boulders that lay no more than arms reach away from my bumper.

***

The first time doing a stimulant, and coming down on an incline that was almost vertical, was as fun as it sounded. I remember being in the car for what felt like five minutes before the impact slapped me back into reality. I fell asleep at the wheel and didn't know how long I was out for. There was no way I could survive, and no time to think of a way to shift the odds in my favor. What if there wasn't just coke in whatever we did? It didn't feel real. What did I really know about reality? If one part of life didn't feel real then maybe none of it was. Merrily, merrily, merrily, life was but a...contradiction. We hated our jobs and loved our hobbies. We fell in love then pushed it away once it caught us. We hoarded money and wasted time. We met the right people and said the wrong things. We loved what we wanted and hated what we needed. We got what we asked for only to look for something new. We chased what was running away from us and ran away from what we were given. It was exhausting and I was exhausted, which was why I shouldn't have gotten in my car. The initial crash jolted me awake —was I in another dream? Did I wake up into a nightmare? My life wasn't flashing before my eyes; I wasn't dying the way I was told I supposed to. We watched movies based on real life then expected real life to unfold like a movie. It was like sniffing an origami rose and feeling betrayed by discovering the scent was notebook paper. What struck me as stylized was how the

closer I was to dying the slower everything went. I finally made a wrong turn I couldn't correct; I had time to think.

Slowing down was how we remembered what we never wanted to forget.

Nothing worried me. I possessed nothing aside from the next few moments, realizing no other day was any different.[5] Dying taught me a lot about living. I closed my eyes, took my last, deep breath, and prepared to sleep peacefully.

*** ***

The collision erased my car and body like a typo. The odds were always in favor of the "chance" in second chances. Accepting responsibility wasn't fun and wasn't meant to be. My last mistake was a cross I would've carried while dancing in the streets, if only another chance was spared. The immaturity was easily seen. Did we need protection from any choice not taking our lives? The highest possible capacity of conceptual

---

[5] General Ownership Phenomenon: We are born into a world grounded in the illusionary ideal of possession. From the items we purchase, create, and collect, to the people we befriend, give birth to, and love, none are exempt. The illusion of ownership is then revealed to be the most feeble and ultimately destructive device used to validate humanity's existence. The promise and expectation of permanence is either introduced through deception, ignorance, or irrationality. We own nothing, we keep nothing, therefore we lose nothing. We are free. Everything is borrowed (see page 263).

absorption mattered in assuring our decisions were our own. The body only moved how the mind allowed.

The connections between the intersections of life required comprehension, or we would cut our umbilical cord while still in the womb.

The line between innovation and indolence suffered from the occasional Purple Haze. The price of ignorance wasn't bliss, it was death. Dying taught me a lot about living. Clichés existed because they replayed a recording of a repeated truth. The journey on the way to any destination was revered as paramount since the destination was always the same. Arriving where we planned to be only inspired the next adventure. Destinations didn't exist the way they were taught to us, they were only rest stops we visited while we traveled. Our planet, solar system, and universe were continuously in motion, and by extension, so were we. Like the moon, all we experienced occurred in phases from our perspective. It was adorable considering ourselves exempt from universal law. We were celestial bodies born on, and relegated to, a celestial body ourselves.

To live was to grow, to die was to transform, to stop was to alter direction. There was nothing more. With each new piece of information we perceived, and each unit of time we passed through, we were shaped into a new creation. Logically, the afterlife was conceptually no different than the present. Without training the difference was invisible; I remembered now. Aside from time, I considered memories to be our most prized possession. Our memories made us. They held our past lives, were the footprints to where we stood, and the colorist shading our potential selves. Through the knowledge and practice of IMM, I regained my memory of forgotten lives and events. It was like seeing the videos your friends recorded of you during a blackout night of drinking, and suddenly having every detail of your debauchery reignited. It was also like feeling the touch of beauty for the first time. IMM is. IMM described the immortal nature of consciousness, and the accessibility of eternal navigation. *Imminism* could be described as the study and use of the energies and pathways connecting one instance of existence to the next. Through the knowledge of IMM and the meditative practice of Reflection,

I was able to see part of my first *Ocurrents*—the events leading to the car crash—where I lived and died. An Ocurrents was what Hinduism called an incarnation, what others called a "past life", and I was now on my third. Our completed lifetimes created energy that was not destroyed, however we needed the knowledge of how to look, not only where. It took time for my appreciation of meditation to develop when not understanding its base functionality. I was told witnessing my thoughts was important but not why. Part of meditation was the practice of objective observation. While alone, we did so silently and internally as preparation to do so expressively and externally. Separating ourselves from a thought or emotion was like separating ourselves from people, places, or perspectives. When we meditated we could listen to our unconscious. As we sat, if a thought arose we didn't consciously or willfully bring forward, we knew it was an unconscious one. Simple.

The conscious and unconscious mind were Yin and Yang, no different than our present and previous lives.

The parts of our minds we overlooked or avoided were on display. If we could see our unconscious thoughts and emotions swirling in front of us mentally, and how they didn't effect who we were presently, we saw how we chose to be altered by the stimuli we made contact with through our voluntary or involuntary ignorance. If our first death was from unawareness, our second should be from understanding. The process of intelligent life was the same from the least to the largest. Reflecting into a past Ocurrents utilized the same principals as observing the unconscious mind and the conscious reality. Fractality and Dichotomy. I believed in both heaven and hell because I experienced them. We saw either or both before our physical burial. We Ocurred, or reincarnated, many times between physical birth and death. The ancient explorations of IMM, of Hinduism, of Buddhism, of Abraham, all spoke of life and death and lives lived physically, as well as spiritually. Did we live the same life at thirty-three that we lived at ninety-three? Did we not look back on our journey and say, "I don't even recognize the person I was at that time in my life"? That was because that person was no longer who we were, that person was dead. Our lifetimes, incarnations, and Ocurrentses were as material as they were metaphysical.

During my second Ocurrents I was guided back to IMM by another. My name was Trémar during that life, and I stumbled upon a man named Tommy discussing sharp-edged concepts snipping at the stitching of what I thought it meant to exist. It started how it always started: observation and inquiry. Tommy's first insight he shared with me was, "Those who ask the questions will find the answers to questions they never asked." Many of us fiercely defended involuntary conditioning. None returned to alignment without choosing to look deeper, so many never did. The deeper we went the darker it was, so the

light necessary came from within or we went blind. Tommy also never wanted to be thought of or called a teacher, he was a student. Students didn't become teachers, no one did. Technically, a teacher was someone teaching something to someone else in a given environment, not a permanent state of being.

There was a time to teach, yet no time when we didn't learn.

The last insight he shared was, "People give you their word then act shocked when you expect them to honor it." It wasn't about IMM, or past lives, or death, or Shadows[6], or Relims[7], it was simply about the experience of interacting with another Existant[8]. He shared a piece of his journey. IMM was all. IMM is. All were created with the knowledge of IMM within them, so none were taught, they were reintroduced. My weaknesses told me I was human, my strengths told me I was more.

---

[6] Shadows: memories of past Ocurrents presenting themselves as visual, auditory, or physical hallucinations at varying intensities.

[7] Relims: those who use their knowledge of Ocurrents, Reflection, Fragments, and IMM, to maneuver their soul from one lifetime to another.

[8] Existant: one with the following characteristics: consciousness (the awareness of internal and external existence), self-awareness (the recognition of consciousness and the capacity for introspection), sentience (the ability to feel pain and pleasure), sapience (the ability to think and act utilizing wisdom and insight). A combination of the words *existing* + *internally* (creating the term *Existant*), since the essence of who one is lives within; not characteristics exclusive to Homo Sapiens.

For that I expressed gratitude, and there was more than could be described.

I always hated driving and never owned a car. I was never in a car accident in my present Ocurrents, but every time I saw one on the side of the road or on the news, my head turned away before the thought entered my mind. The reason was revealed. The unnamed and impassioned parts of myself were traceable. All was from another. I was always who I was presently, the same way an infant was an adult who only required the time to develop. Each life we lived affected the next whether we knew it or not. None existed irrationally. None existed irrationally unless all did. Now I saw how humble my beginnings truly were. I was grateful. All taking place while pursuing our passions was necessary. Humble beginnings weren't humble for long. Life was good.
As always.

II THOUGHTS

THE ONLY THING BETTER THAN THINKING ONCE

Identifying what we were was difficult. A deeper and more dynamic connection was formed with those we traveled with consistently. There used to be four of us, but we lost one and I missed them. I was glad we met and were able to spend time, share space, and go places. Wherever their energy went it was being utilized as it should be, although how I felt didn't change. I was okay with that. The sadness of loss was accompanied by immense appreciation. Tears cleared our eyes allowing unobstructed entry to life's luminescent light. I sipped on my surroundings a little slower, earnestly hoping to pocket every penny of the moment before it changed. No one wanted their hand held forever, and joy was no exception. Nevertheless, we were high on shrooms and weed and wax, and time was our master no more. The skyline was in front of us like the future, shining brightly without bias for everyone. Anything could happen in the future and I liked that. I would never again fall in love with potential, but I didn't mind flirting for inspiration. The new moon made the city lights smile with tears in their eyes. Reds and oranges, yellows, greens, and blues, with the drops of neon violet. Downtown glowed with every frequency the legs of our naked eye spread for, and we penetrated the entire spectrum on our journey. It made sense the city pulsated with energy. A concrete jungle was erected with antennae stretching into the heavens and veins branching beneath the soil. Gods left footprints on the surface of an immortal being. The magic knocked on the window to our souls like it knew we were home, patiently waiting while we made preparations. The magic spoke to us all, few chose to continue the conversation. I wanted to talk about everything until night turned into morning.

I loved how difficult it was to get lost in the city; no turn was a wrong turn. As long as we knew where we wanted to go and kept trying to find it, we found where we wanted or somewhere better. Perfect example: our ride-share driver from a few months ago.

He was a Christian hip-hop artist with over ten thousand followers, and he was arguably more humble than Andre Benjamin. He performed two full songs for us in the car—while driving. I could confidently say he didn't know who I was and didn't care. No attempt to hit on me, and only glanced at my chest once; he was a class-act as far as the evidence. The names he mentioned as collaborators suggested his industry standing was legitimate, yet he wasn't bragging about his connections. A bold invite to his first major album release party was extended. What if one of us was on the sex offenders list? How would he know? Sexual misconduct wasn't gender exclusive. Preferential treatment produced parasites. Lemma heard later he grew to be almost as influential as I was, and "almost" was closer than most made sense of. Wasn't that life also? "Almost" was the end or the ignition. Most performances presented nothing more than novice transparency, yet unlike most performing in LA, his was believable. A recent flyer I saw pictured him covered from hat, to backpack, to shoe, in multi-colored, Italian-designed apparel. He transformed into everyone else. Wearing that much of one brand symbolized how much we still struggled to define ourselves. Something was missing for him. Knowing where we excelled quieted our concern of where others did. We walked on water in our own divinity, or crawled through contradiction to fit into someone else's. The over-display of status symbols was a symptom of generally having unhealthy attachments. The unhealthy attachments came from inner-misalignment. That wasn't really my crowd, but that was what that goddamn, majestic, piece-of-shit, ever-golden, Atlantean In magnitude of a city was about: believing. When believing beasts to be beautiful was beneficial, we witnessed the confirmation of the anomalous. Miracles still came hard like women who were listened to, but I thanked every god they came at all. The miracles could decide they were needed elsewhere, in which case I was excited for whomever shared their company.

Time passed but certain aspects existed outside of it.

Los Angeles was a permanent residence of transcendence.

The rats were still the size of adult squirrels, and ruder than cashiers with no ambition. I've watched them audaciously almost run humans over. People be dancing and shuffling to get around those wild bastards—it was insanity.

Tons of tattoos, piercings, and random bruises, meant more than likely she was either an active exotic dancer or one on sabbatical. I could definitely always tell by her boobs if nothing else. How many twenty-whatever year old girls had boobs that sagged unless they kept them out professionally? Unless they were, like, a hippie-hippie? Nevertheless, the effects of the professional mindset produced forecastable results easily overlooked. If she could sell her body in one way, she could sell it in any of them. Arynn used to dance and she stopped counting her tattoos after the twentieth. There were exceptions to the rule also, same as all of them. I danced for a year and half before I got my first tattoo. I couldn't go under the knife though. The BBLs and boob jobs were all investments with returns Wall Street stock brokers would approve of. The prices for services rendered went up post-op; it was hardly ever about a relationship or self-esteem. She could get a man or woman without the cosmetic surgery, the surgery was to get one who bought her everything. It was a lifestyle like any other paying better than most. A lot of us asked to be saved, but we were just saying what we were told we should. No one was saving me. No one was saving anyone.

The younger pimps dressed like rappers with one hit and shitty management; the older pimps dressed like shitty managers. If an advantageous circumstance arose, they doubled as rappers and managers, respectively. They possessed no creative vision but presumed they did. Selling one's body and managing the sale of another's body were both trauma responses. Trauma responses lived in the unhealed who were products of their caretaker's egomania. "Toxic" was the more common descriptor for the affected. Those labeled as toxic fulfilled societal roles we created and collectively participated in. If that were not the case then strip clubs, brothels, drug dealers, pimps, politicians, assassins, and serial killers wouldn't exist. The sons of unhealed mothers were romanticized, and daughters of unhealed fathers, sexualized. Those taught to smile as they bled knew where to cut so others did the same.

Traumatized adults fed the black hole within us we ignored with star-spangled eyes.

The Existant[9] experience was dichotomous. Cops and Robbers wasn't a childhood game it was kindergarten conditioning. Who would law enforcement enslave without the traumatized? They still rode on horseback through downtown like they were back on the plantation. The theatrics truly respected no boundary. Not to suggest we all didn't have a level of trauma to navigate, however the spectrum contained highs and lows lifetimes apart.

The undercover cops still dressed like SoCal residents imitating tourists. Tourists wore whatever they considered to be different, consequently leading them to all dress identically. *Different* quickly became a category due to many consciously attempting to do the same thing. We couldn't be "different" and be ourselves at the same time.

The security guards dressed like cops, walked like hitmen, but were neither. What baffled me was the unbridled arrogance. The cool ones realized how ridiculous their job was and visibly didn't take it seriously. The others were usually very large physically, convinced they were the opposite intellectually, and consequently lived with testosterone-driven Napoleon Complexes. Oddly, the bus drivers weren't much different. Some realized they chose to serve the public by driving a bus, that the public sucked most of the time, and they didn't take it any more seriously than needed. The less-aware drivers would sit at a fresh green light, until it turned a sour red, because someone wanted a ride with only a dollar and didn't have the seventy-five cents. Could the combination of no ambition and no appreciation be classified as an infectious disease? I wasn't sure how it was spread, but once it set-in it seemed terminal more often than not.

The homeless still yelled in the streets as loud as they could, cursing unseen adversaries unaware of their anguish. During the heatwaves there was an exodus indoors to any coffee shop with cold air conditioning and open seats. If aliens took over Earth, downtown would be the Lion's Country Safari, and they wouldn't need anything but a gate to seal it off. LA at its highest and LA at its most genuine were contrasting views. Did everything move faster here?

---

[9] Existant: (see page 95)

Did time move faster? Cars move faster? Money? Relationships? Friendships? Women? Men? Ideas? Recognition? Love? How could we have time to hold on to what mattered, let alone figure out what did? We could all apologize to each other more. We lived in a vortex beyond the boundaries of our most brilliant minds. We were all holding on for dear life; we could be a little nicer.

"Bitch, where we going?"

Lemma and Arynn laughed. I barely liked being around either of them, and I was talking to either of them.

"Anybody? I'm about to turn around."

"You're not though."

Fuck Arynn—especially. I kept walking and thought about why I hung out with them—the traveling thing. I needed new friends, but it wasn't easy to find people who were fucked up the same way you were. They weren't even friends, more like fellow patients. L.A. stood for La Asylum if anyone asked me, but no one ever did. You met people, you lived a fairytale for a while, and then it was over. And if you were serious about why you moved to LA or chose to stay, you got over it because the next showtime was in fifteen. I joked about ending up in a straitjacket if I stopped the psychedelics and the smoking, but I didn't joke about my conviction to continuing my preventative treatment. And I only hung out with these bitches because I was bored and lonely. All of us were supposed to be so aligned, but I didn't know if they were and they could think the same of me. They still talked about good versus evil and spreading positivity like the depths of what we'd been introduced to were still holding their eyelids shut. They weren't the only ones thinking that way, but that didn't make it better. Perhaps I wasn't gracious enough.

> Once freed from the imaginary constructs of morality and polarity, we only saw functionality and utility.

There were no confines only cohesion. Too often the hands holding us back were our own. Satan stood closer than the person behind us in line. We weren't as connected as we thought we were if we still saw evil in the world. We acted on each other's behalf so organically and interchangeably it was comical not to see the obvious. Much less made me angry once I understood our interconnectivity. Compasis.[10] We were told everything happened for a reason as if that alone was substantial. *This* happened because of *that* because causes produced effects, and if the effect was observable it was considered purposeful. Through IMM we saw each Ocurrents shared universal qualities. At first the memories were like scratches on an old photograph, but soon the blemishes formed images of their own. Whatever was possible was necessary.

Admitting ignorance initiated illumination.

It bothered me the way we could have the knowledge of more than we put into practice. I was trying to practice more.

> "Ladies, help me out: where are we going?"

> "You can tell her, I don't care."

> "You said you wanted to tell her."

> "Yeah, but I *said that* because I thought—"

I cleared my throat.

> "I'm not high enough for whatever this is, and I really don't want to be mad—I really don't."

Lemma stopped walking, and Arynn and I stopped after realizing she wasn't a step behind us, she was like ten. An approaching police car with sirens screaming between horn flares distracted all three of us. I snickered because the cop's horn sounded like Morse code, and the result was not what I think they expected. No one got out of the way for cops with their sirens on if there was traffic downtown, no one except for the pigeons. The cops were left figuring it out just like anybody else would: on their own. They got two wheels onto the median and rolled cautiously past the civilians, still honking their horn, just not as much. Having to struggle as others did bothered misplaced privilege. I looked back at Lemma.

> "Destination?"

> "First, allow me to commend you for coming on this adventure with

---

10 Compasis: (see page 16).

minimal information to begin with."

"What do you mean? Both of y'all told me—"

"Oh, we lied about most of that."

Arynn put her hand on my shoulder, which I didn't like, just to tell me something I didn't want to hear.

"Basically all of it."

"Okay, so…"

"We're going to Book Club."

"How?"

I looked back and forth at them both.

"Arynn was invited like uh… like she was…hmm. Do you like Cinder-Arynn, or uhh… Arynnella, better?"

I was so excited I didn't feel Arynn's hand on my shoulder anymore, until she moved it to place a crown on her own head only she could see.

"Either pleases Her Majesty."

Lemma laughed while I shook my head.

"Okay, so we have tickets?"

"They don't do tickets. Our name's on the list."

"You're serious?"

Arynn winked at me then looked back at Lemma to correct her previous statement.

"I take it back, I'm fucking with Arynnella."

She kept walking then stopped so abruptly I felt compelled to check if she tripped.

"Gee-zus! You okay?"

Arynn reached across her body and waved her left index finger towards her right, indicating our next turn. She took a step to her right, stopped, turned back to her left, opened her left hand and waved it in the air, then pointed straight ahead (now on her original left) as she walked across the intersection. She thought we were going right, but clearly not. Arynn was mostly hell to be around, but at least she was funny sometimes. Another perk was her shameless use of every physical feature she could sexualize, getting us free drinks, drugs, food, whatever. I think she was on her fifth or sixth Ocurrents—second as a woman of color—and she was jaded in ways that could be worse, but weren't great. Neither me nor Lemma were anywhere near as smart as her, so I appreciated she was only a dick about it sometimes.

Intelligence was odd that way: some were taught it was important, others it was a waste of time.

Intellect aside, she was getting reckless. When we first met she would say things like she was in love with love, however that perspective was as temporary as everything else, and not enough cared to prove it rational. Arynn wouldn't be winning any awards for rationality herself, but she hated looking dumb. I didn't think she would know what to do with love if she did attract it, we were twins in that way and no other. Getting random guys to spend money on her was easy, and I was fine going along for the ride until I thought of a better idea. I didn't have one yet, so for now I followed the leader.

> "It's this way for real, for real. And one of y'all need to take this bag from me before I eat the whole thing."

> "Yo, don't even play!"

Lemma's mom made the most insane brownie edibles. Her oven tray was broken in a way where the THC from each batch would settle in the crust around the edge of the pan. Six figures swam laps in her bank account for the last two years, courtesy of her cutting the crust into strips and calling them Stoner Stiiix. After the last kitchen she worked at closed down, she started baking and packaging her own stuff. Her last job was at a small, all day breakfast diner making any kind of breakfast sandwich imaginable out of either French Toast or French Toast Donuts. It sounded ridiculous, but the food was decadent and the sauces were licked off fingers knowing anything else was disrespectful to the craftsmanship. I missed *Frenchie McFrench*. Her mother didn't touch the oven once while she was there, she was on the grill. The owner was anal about the settings and worked more than necessary to keep their secret vaulted. Lemma's Mom, Sandra, bounced from one cooking gig to the next until her springs broke, and the only choice was trying something for herself. She taught herself how to bake and how to bake well.

> Life didn't test us, it gave us opportunities. We were always gaining. We didn't fail, we found out what didn't work.

Arynn had a question.

> "Y'all want beer, right? The store is right here!"

Me and Lemma skip-jogged across the street to catch up with her, but she ducked into the store giggling before we could. She was already passed twisted. When I looked into the liquor store entrance, Arynn a giraffe-necked beer bottle dangling between the bent knuckles of her index and middle finger. Her hand waved at me goofier than the cartoon character named after the adjective describing her shenanigans. Her cartoonery was inspired by a plant still being outlawed in parts of the world.

> Marijuana made difficult people funny and awesome people irresistible.

I assumed those refusing to partake, or judging others for doing so, weren't as properly informed as they could be. Before I started smoking daily I wasn't either. Cannabis now carried me above conditioned views, and I looked down to see hilarity where others saw hatred. Plant medicine's true value shined in those moments. Marijuana made me forget what I was about to say, but I also forgot what I was forced to. The anxiety some felt was their unanchored mind looking for a thought or task the new energy could be applied to. Eating to slow the untethered ascent helped also. I hoped Arynn didn't kill all the damn Stoner Stiiix. I walked to the far side of the sidewalk closest to the curb and stood with Lemma. She was on her phone silently playing a game making little beep noises three at a time; I leaned against the parking meter to rest my legs. The Sun went down about forty minutes before, but it was still warm. The grill of a taco stand crackled to my left like it did every time we came there. We all took the bus, and that liquor store was right around the corner from the 33. I was trying to eat less meat, but fresh carne asada and el pastor in the air would always smell like a love song. The beef was flipped and chopped sharply on the grill, while the metal of the spatula rang off the cook surface with each hit. The technique reminded me of the cooks in Philly preparing cheesesteaks for lines going outside and around the corner. Years passed since I was in Philly, and the summers there were—

"Hi, excuse—"

"Holy shit!"

Lemma looked up and added.

"Bro!"

The random homeless man, standing too close to me, replied.

"Sorry, sorry. Excuse me."

Why dudes thought they should introduce themselves a foot away from my face while I wasn't looking was wild to me. It happened more times than I could count and more times than reasonable. I was trying not to be rude though but his breath smelled like dead mouse. Not the DJ. I tried to start the interaction again from scratch.

"Hello, sir—personal space, if you could take a step back. But what's up?"

"Can I borrow a light?"

A half-smoked cigarette was held up as proof of urgency. I nodded. There was a time when I never, under any circumstance, loaned out lighters. I was working on my rudeness. I reached into my bag

and Lemma's jaw dropped like Edvard Munch's, The Scream.

The shock displayed at our personal improvement was amusing by design.

Nothing worse than not getting a joke. Or motivation. I didn't stop looking, I just answered her look.

"Don't say nothing. Just let me find my stuff."

The man thought I was talking to him.

"Huh? I—"

"Not you, sir. Speaking to my friend. One second."

"Oh. Yeah, okay."

He looked quickly towards the security guard—sitting on a stool just inside the liquor store entrance by the ATM—and then back at me.

"You know where to get any meth?"

"C'mon, man!"

Lemma stuck her phone into her bra; she liked to fight. I liked to observe. I let my bag fall to my side and zipped the top closed.

"Yeah, can't let you borrow anything now."

"What? Why?!"

"I don't need that energy, bro. Nothing personal."

Lemma clarified.

"*And* that does *not* need to be explained to you, homie."

The man was unimpressed.

"Oh, what the fuck! Who cares?!"

Lemma was unimpressed as well.

"That's your time, bruh."

"Well, do ya' know where I can get some meth or not? You didn't eve—"

"My man, *right now.* Outta here—what are you doing?!"

He was reaching for Lemma's pendant or looked like he was reaching for it. I didn't know which one it was, but his hand found itself near her pendent hanging close enough to her cleavage for clear "hands-off." Lemma shoved him. Four frantic backpedaling steps then the guy hit the ground. The backpack he wore protruded outwards about thirty inches, making balancing himself impossible against any major collision. Good cushioning though.

"Goddamn, bitch! What the fuck is wrong with you?!"

"Who the fuck you talking to, pussy?!"

The security guard appeared on the sidewalk, sliding from inside the liquor store.

"Not again—let's go!"

"*She* pushed *me!*"

The man was using the wall to prop himself up, but security grabbed his backpack by the top loop and yanked up.

"Oh, c'mon! Ayyy!"

"Keep it moving, G. Get going!"

The meth inquisitor wisely listened while adjusting their shoulder straps on the move. Lemma watched him walk away with disgust.

"No—but for real—what about either of us says we know where to get meth, or that reaching for anything near my chest is cool?"

"I think that's a fair ques—."

"Yeah, me too."

Arynn bounced out of the liquor store with a black plastic bag in hand. Her arrival finally broke the laser-beam stare Lemma was still giving the man who was almost down to the next light.

> "Yo, it sounded *crazy* in there! Who did the security guard throw out?"

Arynn laughed at herself and kept going.

> "Lemmy-Lem, did you punch somebody?
>
> "Are you drunk already?"
>
> "Nope! Oh, here you go."

Arynn held up and shook what was previously a freezer bag full of Stoner Stiiix. There were at least nine in there and we all ate one as we got on the bus. I grabbed the bag only containing three left.

> "You're gonna pass out."
>
> "Nuh-uh."
>
> "Okay. Want one?"

I offered the bag to Lemma and she took it and opened it. She shook her head and closed her eyes like she couldn't already see the disappointment inside of the translucent bag.

> "You a wild girl."
>
> "Yeah, yeah, let's gooo."

And the adventure was back on. We walked down 7th for awhile, and I wasn't really paying attention how far. I was thirsty as hell.

> "We need water, right?"
>
> "Shit—yeah."

Arynn slurred something.

> "That izza goodidea."
>
> "Okay, yeah, nobody was talking to..."
>
> "Any free water on the way?"
>
> "Uhh, there should be some if we go...damn, that is a good question."
>
> "By the—izza bythebodega, no?"

Arynn tossed her arm around Lemma's neck. I shifted my eyes towards her and she was already looking at me. Arynn was right, but the look me and Lemma exchanged confirmed it was wiser not to let Arynn think she could be correct right now. I kept the momentum going.

> "You're good to walk for a little bit, Arynn?"

> "Mannn, yeahgirl, I'm chillin'."

> "Okay, you keep chillin', princess."

I shrugged at Lemma and she squeezed her lips together to trap a laugh before it made a run for it. My hand flashed to my mouth to do the same, since her having to laugh was ruining my ice cold demeanor. Neither of us were simultaneously present to see Arynn that high before, and the experience was pure gold. Overall she was still well in the range of being way too much for no reason, but you know, just not right that second.

Did playing with the elements make us easier to play with?

We got to the coffee shop, bought waters, and sat for the first time in what felt like forever but was likely closer to twenty minutes. Arynn put her head down on her folded arms almost before her ass hit the seat. We were outside, and a large moving-truck drove by bringing a breeze blowing like it wanted the best for me. The cars driving by sounded a little like the ocean, which probably meant I needed to go sit with the real thing. Lemma also bought a water bottle because she was bougie, and didn't want to hold the sweaty plastic cup. It was a nice bottle though. The textured design was faux black marble recreated to almost feel like thin stone. The empty bottle was heavy by itself. There was still room in there even with all of her water, so I offered to fill the rest with mine in exchange for using it. She laughed so loud it scared a nearby group of pigeons into flying away.

> "You don't have to *bribe me* to use my canteen, crazy. It's cool—Jesus. You sound like a water-crackhead."

We both cracked up—pun intended.

I held her royal water receptacle and poured the water in, but as it filled my eyes played a trick. The water already in the bottle was so still, it looked like the water I was pouring into it went to the bottom but wouldn't fill it. I kept pouring and didn't know if I should stop. I was mesmerized. Pouring water into a container seeming to never fill felt more familiar than I wanted it to. Silent nails on a gritty chalkboard snuck beneath my skin. I stopped pouring and gave Lemma back her bottle with the cap tightly screwed on.

"Thank you, thank you."

"Yup."

I looked up at the trees and the palm branches were suspiciously swirling into each other. I had a question.

"Hey, Lemma?"

"Hm?"

"Did your mom put shrooms in the brownies again?"

She laughed once through her nose then rubbed her forehead.

"Girl, I thought it was just me. I'm over here like, 'Is Imarra really not feeling this shit?' Wa-vy."

"Cool. That's cool. Okay. Good talk…"

An eye was to be kept on Sandra. Lemma's mom was notorious for spiking any and everything with mushrooms or marijuana. She was definitely a hippie, and passionate about the spelling—and propagation of the

spelling—being h-i-p-p-y instead of the alternative. Hippy was happy with an i. The trees looked pretty cool, moving like belly dancers in seductive slow motion. I preferred to set intentions and state what I wanted to gain before taking anything with a psychoactive effect. Doing so spoke to our unconscious, partnering with it to activate areas of our minds and the associated energy centers our conditioning blocked. I used to party on psychedelics, now I prioritized and parasailed through unknown spaces of untold benefit. It was actually no different than saying grace before eating or making a toast before drinking. We were telling our bodies and minds what to do and how to feel about the elements we were communing with.

Our experiences were easier directed when focusing on the desired outcome and the reason behind it.

The reason fueled our capacity to create, and was excessively overlooked to our detriment. Directing our experiences was also how we learned the most. I was terrified of psyches until I kept hearing them attributed to people loving deeper and fearing less. I assumed one especially good or bad trip shattering my perception of reality was reason to stay away. A splintered window was more obstructive than an absent one. Sometimes we needed things to break.

Was our perception of reality any safer without psychedelics? Wasn't more openness needed? Did our minds not need more clarity now more than ever from daily societal bombardment? Did we fear the same processes that freed us?

Lemma tapped my arm and started giggling before she could say anything. I shook my head at her.

"You're a mess."

"Look before you miss it!"

Arynn successfully drooled enough on her arm for one line to crawl down her skin and make a puddle on the table. Lemma was as thoroughly amused as she should have been. It was plant medicine inspiring us to interpret the world with four year old minds once again.

We truly lived on a planet begging to give us everything we needed, while we manufactured another synthetic biohazard to cure the symptom of the last.

Arynn's drool also kind of looked like a synthetic biohazard, readying itself to erode the table like acid. The burn your skin, instantly dangerous kind, not the trippy kind pushing us to learn something different—LSD. This girl was one step away from needing a stroller, which felt like cause for worry.

"She's good, right?"

"Yeah."

"When did she start eating whole edibles to herself?"

We both chuckled. Lemma remembered something.

"I think after her last Reflection."

"Oh."

"Yeah."

Silence, then I asked the obvious and the intrusive.

"What'd she see?"

"Didn't tell me."

"She told someone though, right?"

Lemma shrugged.

Experiencing a past life wasn't much different than experiencing the current one. What ate at us ate through us when not expressed. Humanity started as many civil wars internally as they did externally. We battled against what we were conditioned to believe held importance. What we didn't talk about was usually what needed to be. I guess I still looked concerned, because Lemma tilted her head so her face covered my view of Arynn's, and smiled reassuringly.

"Yo, she's fine. She's not dead."

"Isn't that what everyone says though?"

"That they're dead?"

"The other thing."

"Oh...yeah, I guess."

Lemma wore a small, pink fanny pack clipped around her waist she dug through searching for something. A blue, disposable nicotine vape was rescued from her pouch and brought to her lips. Pausing, she shared a thought before inhaling.

"You know how it is when you see something connecting the dots you didn't know were there."

"Did she say *anything* about —wait, where was I at?"

"That's the session you skipped when she went to Dominic."

"God. Why didn't she just Reflect herself?"

Lemma shrugged.

"Guess she didn't feel like it."

"That codependency isn't helping her."

Lemma hit the vape finally, and the resulting smoke cloud resembled the kind rain fell from, then it was gone. She sipped twice from her bottle before responding.

"Then she'll have to dig her way out until she learns."

The vape was offered to me and I hit it twice. She was right.

Some wanted to be free, others wanted to be taken care of.

The consequences joining each decision were unique. Not good, not bad, just unique. When others did too much for us from too young an age, learning to do the same for ourselves was daunting. Those born into imbalanced homes were given a different ditch to dig their way out of, just like Arynn. Just like all of us. One flower grew in a meadow, another on the corner of Pine Avenue and Market Street next to a streetlight. Nothing I saw, heard, or felt provided an explanation I understood. I wasn't at the point in my journey where I mastered placing myself in specific socio-economic demographics upon Ocurring. Perhaps I should ask the Ayierrah[11] nicer next time before my Transformation. For now I was happy with being able to confidently exit one life and enter another on command. The undertaking of Ayiuma[12] wasn't to be taken lightly. One life always placed theirs at risk of ending for another to begin.

Lemma tapped the back of her slide against the ground and it popped off her left foot, then she rested it on top of her right one.

We never made it to the event.

Arynn had the address in her dead, locked phone, and we had to call a ride for her to get home. She couldn't walk or keep her eyes open; there was a lot she was running from. The problem was she was trying to run away from the treadmill she was running on. Knowledge was power but wisdom...was wisdom the cross? Was wisdom the cross carried by the wise? The gift that cursed? The eraser of ignorant bliss?

---

[11] An IMM legend. The Ayierrah (i-ee-era) are a personification of a process during Transformation (the energy of one Existant moving on to be utilized in a different form). They are viewed similar to the Grim Reaper in the respect they are said to chaperone Consciousness Energy (the energy maintaining a frequency high enough to produce Existant life) back to the source. Energy returned to the source will rejoin the Life Cycle without the knowledge of their past Ocurrentses. For those within IMM this is unfortunate, but it represents the process most Existant life experience. The Ayierrah legend is they dress in all white (the white light) and can be bargained with to redirect their actions.

[12] Ayiuma (i-yu-mah) The preparatory process completed before attempting to Reflect (looking into a past life) or Ocurr (ending a current life to begin another). A ritual including optional steps, with each additional step completed creating a smoother experience. A spell (mantra/prayer/affirmation) is recited called the Umaiy which brings the Relim's frequency into the correct vibration to explore their experience.

The power of wisdom was the ability to realize our desired experience at will.

With wisdom we desired harmony; shared interactions were of the highest. It was through wisdom we could perform the alchemy of a life turned golden. We knew more and with more to navigate, but an easier time doing so. Eradicating fear through understanding brought a level of ease. All was either a lesson or reminder. Arynn reminded me of what I forgot too often and remembered too late.

Found people got lost too.

It didn't matter what else happened, I understood why I was where I was and with who I was with. When one's utility was understood, all of it was. The totality of true understanding didn't come all at once, even if much came in waves. Only one page was read at a time. The propagation of partial wisdom created the "false prophet". Sure, some people realized they could make a dollar selling the key to life, but that wasn't the majority. Most false prophets were those thinking they were connected but weren't, or who didn't thoroughly explore what they were shown and shared too soon. The choice between patience and production needed to be made, along with realizing the time for each.[13] I understood part of what Arynn symbolized and that showed me the way the mundane hid magic. We were so busy getting places we never saw the places we got to.

Artist: Black Star

Song: Respiration

Album: Mos Def & Talib Kweli Are Black Star

"So much on my mind that I can't recline/ Blastin' holes in the night 'til she bled sunshine./ Breathe in, inhale vapors from bright stars that shine./ Breathe out, weed smoke retrace the skyline."

I usually took the bus home at the end of the night for one of the following reasons: no money for a ride, too tired or too far to walk, or not walking weather. I liked walking, and loved avoiding the unnecessarily treacherous hunt for parking characteristic of every large city's downtown. Walking was our most ancient and most personal mode of

---

13 Authorist Futurism—production vs. Surrenderist Futurism—patience (see page 263).

transportation, and all of us weren't able to do so.

The gift received by fortunate children was a time to stroll the surface of their mothers.

We did well to pay additional honor to the gifts we received without request. Walking taught us patience, preparation, and how the points we approached on our journey could potentially alter why we sojourned. We weren't blocking blessings, we were rolling passed them. I asked myself what I loved about being alive. If I was just here on Earth by myself, what would make me smile in my head and heart? Compasses weren't my forté, but that sounded like a pretty good one.

A sexy friend of mine was only thirty minutes away, but for all that I could just go home and enjoy the rest of the trippiness. Riding the bus won and I was happy it did. I was still practicing choosing calm over chaos.

On the bus it was quiet and I found myself thinking of my last Reflection. I was shown a life where I was a casually dressed, bald-headed Asian monk, sitting one table away from another man and his dog. We were in the corner of a Burger Crown, busy with customers going in and out regularly. I informed the man I would like to be near him and his canine if it wasn't a problem. I started right away with reciting full, audible, meditative chants, in what I could imagine were in multiples of one hundred and eight. The chants were printed on a messy stack of laminated papers stuffed in a worn, canvas messenger bag. I started reading and chanting and just kept going. After one was done, I flipped the paper and continued singing in a deep pitch I felt in my knees, then reached in my bag to grab another. And the poor man I was next to was just minding his business, sitting with his dog, scrolling on his phone. He kept sighing, but I wasn't getting the hint or was too deep into the chants I couldn't hear him. Or maybe I just didn't care —that time it was hard to tell. I knew I was preparing to sing like thirty chants in succession yet chose to randomly sit one table away from someone. But it was like that.

Inconsideration was a default in our mental infancy due to insufficient growth.

The ignorance in that example was me leading in a low-vibrational manor in a situation calling for a lighter approach. It was ego, it was narcissism, it was lower chakra, it was hyper-mechanical thinking. It was knowing how to read the room and choosing to expel the energy to do so or not.

Found people got lost too.

The light of one idea was sent through a prism so those from every color saw themselves in the reflection. We did not learn the same, we did not love the same, we did not lose the same, but each happened in each life lived. We listened deliberately or frivolously, and none gained from the latter. Ignorance only allowed the capacity to be happy for others if what happened for them was what we wanted for ourselves. I was a monk. If I thought singing chants was a blessing, then of course a man and his dog would love it also. No. That never worked that way nor would it ever. Why treat others how we wanted to be treated when we could find out how they wanted to be? Wasn't that more sensible?

The man sighed again, shifting his weight in his seat to lean his left side against the wall. Ten minutes almost elapsed. God, I wish I could stop myself and put him out of his misery, but I was

involuntarily enjoying it. I wouldn't be singing the chants if I didn't—the dichotomy of all. But who was more at fault? The man for not honoring himself and asking me to chill with the annoyance? Or was it me for being a monk with zero consideration for another adult peacefully sitting alone with their fur-covered companion? There was nothing harder to protect or more worthy of protection than peace.

The Reflection shifted from fast food burgers to fast food tacos.

I was sitting outside on the ground with my legs folded watching a girl sitting in the outdoor dining area. A cross on a silver ball chain was in her hands as she said Hail Mary after Hail Mary. She couldn't have been more than twenty-three, if that. She was still in her work uniform. Black, skinny, denim with a hole ripped in the left knee and thigh, and a black t-shirt with a yellow cartoon chicken head on it. The jeans were too cute for work. She didn't work at the taco place, they wore light gray button-ups. On break from her fast-food day job, she was sitting at another one and using her few available minutes to chant Hail Marys. And the Lord's Prayer. I didn't know if those were all supposed to be said together or not, I just heard her say them both. What could possess a teenager to spend their fifteen minute break chanting Hail Marys? How was she conditioned to view her thoughts, her actions, her life? I saw the kids eyes though her thick-framed, rectangular glasses. Whatever she was begging forgiveness for was stealing minutes of youth she didn't know she would kill to have back later. The sign of the cross was made with her right hand starting at her forehead. Did she know what the cross symbolized?

Our crucifixion was both the final opportunity to choose a different path, and the necessary death killing the old to make space for the new.

Without understanding the purpose of the crucifixion there was only chaos, and confusion, and death. The growth came afterwards. The growth followed understanding the only way to live was to die. Her entire break was used repeating a prayer she was instructed to say by people who hopefully didn't understand why they instructed her to say it. We locked ourselves into lives we chose willfully in unawareness, convinced that what felt right couldn't be.

The cycles were generational, created and inherited perpetually in varying ways and degrees, then compounded with each Ocurrents if we didn't know what to look for. New bandages were placed on top of the old, hoping to heal when they could only incubate infection. It was no different than the seasons.

The seasons of our lives repeated like the seasons of the planet if we did nothing to change them.

No one was surprised when every year Spring came after Winter. Yet, we were surprised when generation after generation experienced the same wars, prejudices, accomplishments, and dreams, just on different scales. Cycles weren't broken, new cycles were created. Life and death were cycles also, but I wasn't sure what that implied. Many still thought of death as one event, although more than one took place. How many civilizations exhausted resources attempting to break the cycle of death instead of creating a new one? But what would that be? Did we know what we were asking for? Obviously, I didn't know or I would've already been immortal a while ago. Then again, I accomplished a version

of that in a unique way, in a way
we all could.
Not good, not bad, just unique.

SAN FRAN

WE EITHER GROW, OR OPPOSE GROWTH

Me, Cello, and Mario sat in Jefferson Square around two in the afternoon, and the day was clear, quiet, and sunny. I think it was a Monday. The end of September creeped closer, and according to Cello and a few locals, we were witnessing a meteorological miracle. There were trees and bushes growing all along a paved, winding path, cutting through larger grassy sections. The three of us were located at the top-right of a short set of five, concrete steps. Shade was abundant, the temperature was just right for a hoodie or light jacket, and there was no breeze. We were either sitting in a park, or in an open living room with a view and a skylight. It wasn't too good to be true, it was as good as it was supposed to be. People were jogging, walking their dogs, and sitting on the green, wooden benches also lining the path. My friends and I were traveling together with two large hiking backpacks with us—one of us planned to head home early. The sky was the same bright blue found in crystallized labradorite, and there were hummingbirds flying in and out of each tree. My eyes could barely follow the hovering and buzzing birds flying around and passed one another, and it was better than TV. Did we really watch more television than life? Interpreting the world around us, deeply enough to appreciate its beauty, was close companion to the audacious assumption our inventions echoed its likeness. We actually took time out of our lives to try out-creating the Earth we were born from. Our antics were cute, assuming mischief was still considered to be. Hummingbirds shrugging at gravity like a five year old with an attitude was an unparalleled entertainment experience. Smoke trails in the sunlight, twisting circles through and around themselves in midair, was a close second. Finding something better than watching that, well, I would want to see that too, but nothing in that park was more magical than those birds.

While speaking with Mario I decided hummingbirds harbored some genus of insect in their DNA. I didn't verify my suspicion with any research, it just seemed to make sense. As far as I knew, birds rode the air currents when they flew and used their wings for direction and altitude. So, if there was absolutely no wind, could the average bird still fly? Hummingbirds flew around like honeybees looking for their next flower to pollinate. They hovered —what other bird did that? Their wings moved so fast the movements eluded the naked eye. Were they literal expressions of a high-vibrational beings? Two of them did the hover-thing above a tree at about two o'clock from where we were. Earth's subtle wonders still impressed me beyond description, and for that I was immensely thankful. I was thankful for the gift of appreciating what wasn't often noticed. I was thankful my inner child still enjoyed magic shows. As I watched the small animals fly in an organized frenzy, it was quickly becoming my favorite, albeit puzzling. If hummingbirds moved fast to us, did we move slow to them? Their speed, as they experienced it, would feel as natural as ours did to us, right? Did their speed make twenty-four hours feel like twelve? What if flying wasn't the only action their speed was applied to? Did their minds move as fast as their wings? Relative to us, were they time travelers?

More beauty than our brains could organize surrounded us constantly, which I suspected was a source of collective agitation. Firmly misplaced anger was expressed we couldn't locate a reason for, an emotion fostering frustration more than anything. Was our frustration developed from the countless available ways to enjoy our lives, and our limited capacity to undertake each captivating option?

Beauty also came in forms we turned and looked away from.

The woman who walked over to us was frustrated as well.

> "Hey—hi—you wouldn't happen to have any papers, would you? I left mine at my friend's place and he smoked them all."

The nervous laughter was in a hurry to be heard, making her statement sound accidental. That word, "friend", was encrusted with an unending number of nuances. Some friends went out of their way to help us, others helped when it was convenient. Friends chose to be family and family chose to be friends. It already sounded like that lady needed new ones. Perhaps of both. I answered her.

"Yeah, I got some."

"Oh, my god, I love you, thanks."

I heard it wise to be weary of those who said they loved you before they knew you.

Those who loved in haste often hated in the same fashion.

A few loose locks of hair were tucked behind her ear, and she stood up straighter so her chest was more prominent. I couldn't tell if she was messing with me, thanking me, or genuinely flirting. Her short, petite frame was topped by curly, black hair and fairer skin, with face makeup noticeable in places she couldn't have wanted it to be. Eye contact was only held for a few seconds at a time, a gesture representing creativity or insecurity. Both came from a dark place I recognized. It was easy seeing ourselves in a mirror when our eyes were opened.

I reached into my jacket pocket, found my papers, and handed her two of them before sitting down. She thanked me, folded the papers neatly, then stood awkwardly while looking at the pavement by her feet. She was sitting by herself on one of the green benches before walking over, yet no movements were made suggesting her return. My other friend, Cello—who was preoccupied with his dog—looked at me and then at Mario. Mario shrugged while balancing a toothy grin on his face; Cello shook his head in disapproval.

"C 'mon, Aqua, let's go."

Aqua was Cello's dog's name; Cello owned a Chihuahua. They both walked away and I turned my attention back to our fun guest. Her right hand was hard at work switching through the sections of her purse while she supervised. She asked the question she probably wanted to ask since she walked over.

"Uh, is it cool if I smoke with y'all? I have to wait for my friend to get home. And of course he forgot to leave a key for me."

Why tell strangers about things they can do nothing about? I looked over at Mario and he shrugged again with the same smirk on his face as before.

"Sure. Yeah, why—"

"Jesus! Here it is. Sorry."

An exceptionally crinkled, plastic sandwich bag was pulled from her purse like a carrot yanked from the ground. Although high-milage, the bag still held its handler's few grams of weed as designed. I didn't see any reason to be rude. When in Rome.

> "No, you're good. I was going to say it was cool if you chilled. You want to sit?"

I was on my fold-out stool but stood up and motioned with my left hand towards it. She smiled bashfully.

> "Yeah, okay, thanks."

While she sat and released her cannabis from its battered confines, Mario lit the back-end of a leftover joint, taking a few long drags before completing the hand-off. Our guest was meticulously hand-separating some flower when she paused.

> "God—I'm Londyn, by the way. I suck at introducing myself."

Her lips tightened on the left side as she kept looking at her weed on her lap. She shook her head once at herself. Was she mad or...I didn't even notice we skipped the most standard of introductions.

> "Wow—no—my bad, also. Uh, I'm Ivan."

I leaned back so Mario was again in Londyn's line of sight. He casually saluted.

> "Mario."

> "And that was Cello and his dog, Aqua, that just left."

> "Wow, so weird. That's my name too."

> "I thought it was Londyn?"

> "Well, yeah."

She laughed nervously before shrugging innocently, then kept going.

> "Aqua's my middle name."

I nodded.

> "Ohh, okay. You sound famous."

Her cheeks blushed pink before the -amous in famous was pronounced. Did dreams of fame and fortune replace those of peace and happiness? Londyn wanted to hear she sounded famous one more time.

> "Really?"

Mario noticed an opportunity, instantly adopting an anchorman voice so fine, Ron Burgundy would only drunkenly approve of it after his second or fifth scotch.

> "Supermodel, Londyn
> Aqua, seen stepping
> through a San Fran park.
> Probably high as fuck."

I didn't know if everyone's eyes could roll and smile at the same time, but Londyn's could. She shook her head like she wanted him to stop, but smiled like she couldn't wait to hear more.

> "I, uh, don't know about all
> that. Y'all not from here,
> right?"

I told her we weren't and how we were each from somewhere different. I want to say she was from somewhere else also, but I didn't remember where. Insanity was the only reason to live in San Fran. Londyn's words. Next year was her seventh in The Bay. The statement she made was clear, but if she knew what it was she hid it well. I planted four-leaf clovers in my garden instead of three (s&) we learned from our trials or were sentenced to execution.[14] That was only the overture to a comically intriguing story.

A wayward train of thought led to talking about friend groups again. Londyn brought up how she couldn't wait for her friend to get home so she could finally take a shower and change. Her previous night consisted of waiting until sunrise for her friend to pick her up from somewhere they decided not to. I recently heard prayer or meditation at sunrise and sunset harnessed minutes of powerful available energy. The orange of the approaching or departing sunlight coupled with the blue tint of the sky was symbolic.

---

[14] (s&) is the current standard keyboard symbol of an *aeonaes (ee-on-nis)*. The punctuation mark is of Aeonilist origin (page 168), representing the comparison of one idea expressed via two separate sentences and styles—figuratively and literally; the higher and lower; the concept and the mechanics. The aeonaes represents a bridge between parallel perspectives, the desolation of opposition, and the clarity of complimentary existence. Also popular in Aeonilist art, the flowing nature of the aeonaes symbol appears often in their calligraphy. In Aeonlism, calligraphy is the visual art of scribes.

Pictured is an accurately recreated, enlarged, handwritten version of the punctuation.

Orange meeting blue represented creating when we spoke.

Abracadabra. Was Londyn not having to see her friend last night a wish granted she only hoped for? The subject shift to the events preceding her flaky friend clearly refreshed her mood. There was a get-together she attended where someone overdosed while sitting directly next to her. That part of the story she delivered climatically, a crowd in her mind gasping at the plot twist while avoiding the edge of their seats. She was no virgin to stories in that genre, she knew where the buttons were and how to push. The pride she instantly displayed at witnessing a sad person almost die was unmistakable, but I guess everyone needed a hobby.

> "This guy was out of control. First he buys like an eight-ball and says he's going to do it by himself. Like, why even waste it like that when you already paid for it, right?"

> "Yeah. Yeah—no—makes sense."

> "Right? Then he's being weird and doing it right off the bar—that was before we came back to the house. But then he was just doing it wherever. He had to wipe his nose like every five seconds, and then he starts crushing-up Speed."

> "Yikes."

> "Yeah, it was after that the guy fucking OD'd."

Mario's right hand inched above his shoulder like a sloth and kept going above his head. I swallowed a laugh I almost choked on. The look on his face was blank to the point it was hard to tell if he knew his arm was moving. His gesture was seen by Miss Londyn, handing her a smile she received like a sincere compliment before speaking.

> "Uhh, did you...did you want to ask me something?

> "So, the guy, he's dead?"

> "Oh...oh, my god. You know, I don't even know. I, uh, I didn't really know him like that. I just saw him around sometimes; that was my second or third, maybe, I think."

> "Oh, okay, okay."

> "Yeah."

"So…"

I felt compelled to rejoin the conversation although defying all logic. I also didn't raise my hand, mainly because each question mentally under review was more absurd than its predecessor.

> "…so this guy does, like, a ton of coke and then passes out and then…then what?"

I chuckled. The San Fran leg of the trip started off with sparklers. Londyn was the appetizer we deserved when trying a new eatery—light, flavorful, leaving a mess all over the tiny plate. And she had more for us.

> "Well no, it was bad. He was like, like seizing or seizuring, I guess? That might not be right. I'm not too much into medical stuff, really. Sorry."

A bashful smile slowly stretched across her lips, and she looked down at an angle making her eye lashes appear longer when she blinked. There was an innocence attached to ignorance we were trained to respond favorably towards. Theoretically it was sensible. How was harmony achieved without emphasizing educating all to the highest level? Otherwise, we were playing a game everyone knew ended the same every time. The desire to cradle the unaware was paternal. It was visible when parents were excused early from everywhere to handle child-related issues, when extra breaks were given to cigarette smokers, and budget additions made for added medical assistance for addicts. We were still a tribe. Helping those who were down before knowing how they got there became tradition, although the how mattered just as much as the why.

Over-assisting was the gentlest form of mutual sabotage.

Once a recognizable inclination to help selflessly was isolated, another enveloping game was unveiled. I didn't know whether it was simply recognized as a possibility, or a premeditated manipulation. The odds of the pattern were played as a way of exposing a shorter route to our desires. Givers and Receivers were realized. Some roles we chose and others were chosen. Hacks were real because math was. Math was a language of measurement and mechanics, our attempt to speak how the universe spoke to itself. It was no different than stories told in the "monkey's paw" style. All of them illustrated the cycle of what was asked for always being received. Aladdin was a prime example. Any story involving wishes being granted showed us the outcome of making our own. There were writers and artists of all kinds telling that one style of story. The expression spoke to the audience and continued to speak as long as the observed pattern was followed.

Energy contained observable cyclical characteristics available for orchestration.

Certain actions were responsible for consistent, instant responses, like pushing a key on a piano. Getting close to a new group of people with calmer dispositions than our current circle, and resources they're generous with, would benefit from said actions. I was no less exempt from susceptibility than anyone else.

> "No, you're fine. I haven't seen anyone overdose, but yeah, from what I've heard they usually end up with a seizure."

> "Okay, wow. Yeah, that's probably what it was then. He was on the floor and everything, and my other friends were trying to keep him still, you know? But it was also like, duh. What did

> you think was gonna happen?"

> "I mean, that's true."

> "Right?"

Did we have to find ways not to care about those who didn't care about themselves? Mario was trying to reignite his dying joint during story-time, and Londyn was just about done rolling hers. Cello and Aqua did a lap around the park and approached from the opposite side of the main path. The conversation was in a natural lull, and with no one talking the buzzing of the hummingbirds was clear. I then realized it was a hum not a buzz, validating their species as hummingbird not buzzingbird. The hum was nostalgic, nearly identical to the sound of cheap stand-up fans in the last stage of their oscillation. Cello added an announcement Aqua barked along with.

> "What's up. Y'all want to smoke?"

He rolled a blunt while he was gone, and oddly, Londyn replied to him first.

> "Ooh, good timing. I just finished; we can pass them both around."

"Or…"

She didn't know Cello. He was a selective smoker and Londyn was a complete stranger who was… well, she was a few things. Cello continued.

> "…or we can just pass this around, and you can have that whole thing to yourself."

> "Oh, but, I just thought like, like I could smoke with y'all."

> "Of course you're smoking with us. We're all sitting here smoking together, right?"

He was a smart-ass being a smart-ass while wearing a Smartaas brand t-shirt, but I couldn't resist joining.

> "Damn, bro, actually never thought of that."

> "See what I'm saying?"

> "Yeah, like we've all had our shit before and smoked together, but with no passing involved."

> "Exactly. We do it all the time and don't think nothing of it."

Londyn was following along silently and more attentively than reasonable, enough so, she was moved to share a realization.

> "Hm. I never thought of that either."

We were full of shit and she was taking us seriously, but…we may have also inadvertently made some sense. Ignorance was married to bliss in our minds, however Londyn's response was an unconscious, yet brilliantly meticulous counter-argument. Ignorance constructed confusion. Ignorance instituted entropy. I saw nothing there worthy to be desired, but that was subjective. I knew what I wanted and what I ultimately needed those around me to want.

Escaped ignorance was sexy.

It was sexy seeking ways to decondition our minds. It was sexy seeking salubrious ways of developing and maintaining complimentary relationships between mental, physical, and spiritual health. It was sexy living in choices decided freely, wisely, and in alignment.

Cello, Mario, and I floated into a weed-inspired conversation ping-ponging into varying directions. A few minutes were spent on the topic of conflict. Conflict arose from shortsightedness. In error, we attempted to correct the extemporaneous misstep for an immediate effect, bypassing experiencing the consequence of our moment of poor time, or situational management. To avoid the outcomes of our actions was to place the outcome on another. Our lack of foresight was meant to be experienced and observed, with the lessons learned applicable towards present growth and future utility. Unaccomplished goals created circumstances watering our well of wisdom. Overcompensation was an act of immaturity pushing us to fix before feeling. Feeling before fixing was how we understood the need to fix, not only the how. Without feeling, we skipped part of an equation where each section was dependent on the former to calculate the latter. Avoiding emotional pain avoided our emotional progress. It was like doing a workout wrong, thinking we were building extra muscle when we were pulling them. Nothing we rushed worked the way we wanted. Inexperienced children did the same, stuffing their clothes in the closet instead understanding the exercise of cleaning their room. The creation of processes to quickly complete necessary, yet unentertaining tasks, was how we kept the majority of our minds clear for pursuits of passion. Streamlining processes were supposed to keep us happier, not yolk us with brainless busy work. Foresight.

Overcompensation inconvenienced interpersonally, and the inconvenience led to conflict.

It was a recipe. Mario went into a whole movie.

> "I know I'm not lying. Think about driving. Instead of being in our lane when it's time to exit we're not. Not prepared. Then we have to get over quick. Three lanes, four lanes, five lanes? Cutting off this car and that car. Now they're mad at us for inconveniencing them for nothing. We're mad at them for making it harder than it could be for us to get over. But *we* started it. they didn't tell us to miss our exit. I figured out why people say, 'Stay in your lane.' Do you know what happens when you don't stay in your lane when there's traffic? Car crashes. And the other person could

be on their way to…to, who knows, uh—"

Cello assisted.

"To a damn funeral."

His head lowered solemnly as he satirically did the sign of the cross starting at his forehead. I played along with condolences of my own.

"RIP to the fallen."

"Y'all stupid for that."

Londyn laughed lightly after Mario's review of me and Cello's mourning, clearly entertained by our strangely enlightening antics. I watched her briefly through my sunglasses as her small laugh returned to its seat thoughtfully. Her eyes fell into a distant stare which could've meant anything, however clearing her throat didn't clear her expression. The masks we wore were alive, they also required rest. Mario kept going.

"But, real shit. And we get around it all by just taking the L. Sometimes we miss the exit, get off the highway, bust the U, and get back on. We take the long way instead of inconveniencing someone else because we

prioritized poorly. It ain't hard."

I agreed.

Looking to others for deliverance from what we created only created enemies.

"It really ain't"

"Here."

Cello passed the blunt to Mario; Londyn was quiet. As her joint left her lips and the smoke spiraled up and vanished to her right, a slap from her left hand popped off her thigh in reaction to something only she was privy to.

"Oh my god, I never even told y'all the end of my story!"

The omission no one was curious about amused her into a laugh emphasizing her smile lines, which sounded suspiciously like an attempt to feel seen for the sake of doing so. I was high enough I would play along with just about anything.

"Oh, yeah? What else happened?"

"Honestly…"

She hit her joint before looking up and thinking.

> "…I guess the rest of the night was pretty chill once that guy was gone. We split the coke he left there, then some girl brought a bunch of nos over. God, I was *so* high."

I didn't know if she was laughing at herself because of how high she was in the story, or how high she was while telling it. I hoped I missed something but thought it best to ask.

> "Oh, okay. So, y'all dropped that guy off after OD'ing and went back to hanging out?"

I chuckled because…wow.

> "Oh no, I stayed at the house with this other guy that was there and waited for them."

It was evident from our reactions we were all waiting for a less blatantly dismal ending to the anecdote. Our narrator was a woman probably in her late thirties who looked ten to fifteen years older than necessary. Birthdays didn't matter much after we could drink and rent a car, but like a car, how we cared

for ourselves internally was externally telling. I still expected people older than I to know something I didn't. We knew what we remembered. What we knew cared nothing of our age, only our competence. It was foolish inherently attaching time to any kind of intelligence.

Immaturity enjoyed no excuse, nor did it have an age limit.

Londyn's story continued.

> "Honestly, it was the craziest thing that's ever happened to me. I don't even know what else he was on, you know? No one did."

> "Yeah, that's uh, that is a little too crazy."

I lied. Londyn's little tale of horror made "a little too crazy" look like an evening of reading by candlelight with a monocle.

> "Right? I barely ever do that stuff. It's just a lot, you know? I'm actually clean now. I didn't even know there were going to be drugs there like that."

That was the part of her not-so-thrilling account catching my attention most: the attempted disassociation. Did we not all have our own internal compass? Could we not feel when the direction we were following led further away from who we were and who we wanted to be? Or was it my friends and I who presented a dilemma? Was the woman's attempt at separating herself from the more grotesque corners of her story a response to the unimpressed reactions she received? Then again, who were we to impress? Complaining about drowning while next to an empty life boat was an option. The experience included the satisfaction of moaning about obstacles while making no real effort to change them. Some lived for it. Feeding our demons satisfied us like feeding our angels, each leading in parallel directions teaching us one lesson through two separate paths. What part of her conscious and voluntary decision was Londyn ashamed of? Fearing exclusion by strangers unable to care about us in any significant way was truly frightening.

I felt like the hummingbird.

The distant look I caught peeking through Londyn before her finale fit perfectly now. We felt bad and did something to feel better before understanding there was nothing to feel bad about.

We carried too much carrying us backwards.

Our grip betrayed us when we held more than necessary. Rambling when overwhelmed by cerebral conversation sounded the same as doing so from feelings of restriction. Londyn was unable to add to the more metaphysical aspects of our interaction, felt insecure, then shared an overly-elaborate experience, attempting to gain immediate validation. Shocking people wasn't difficult, nor was finding the instantly gratifying. We overshared hoping others attributed value to our thoughts and experiences, overlooking how doing so also attracted opinions. Silence spoke softer than scrutiny. There was nothing to say to those not listening. Loving ourselves minimized defending ourselves.

Song: The Dock of the Bay

Artist: Otis Redding

Album: The Dock of the Bay

"I'm sittin' on the dock of the bay/ watchin' the ti-iii-iii-de roll away/ Ooo, I'm just sittin' on the dock of the bay/ wa-aa-stin' tiii-iii-iii-me. "

Mario was already holding back full-blown laughter when I

glanced at him. His left hand was over his mouth in a way making him look like he was just thinking, but his chest bounced dance-move style with subdued amusement. Mario's laugh woke the neighbors. I would personally invite him to every performance if I was stand-up comedian, the rest of the audience would be an oil painting comparatively. I couldn't blame him, what that lady was saying was ridiculous. Were we expected to believe an adult, of relatively sound mind, could end up inside a house knowing nothing about anything previously, or presently going on there? If truly the case, why go? Once the activities of the residence were discovered, why stay? Was the Purposeless Path an endless prayer for more prey? Was that the same road where the "adrenaline junkie" learned to walk? Londyn's belated estrangement to her adventure may have been believable had her giddiness been masked, but it wasn't. Our thoughts, words, and actions were our mind, body, and soul.

What excited us was who we were.

Mayhem was exhilarating, and that's what some of us lived for, yet it would also be how we died. Limited time and space could be spent in, and around,

environments and personalities before the experiences were part of us. There was only so long we could deny what made us feel alive.

Lying to ourselves was our leading cause of death.

All clean laundry was kept together, as was the dirty. At times our memories matched that of a piece of clothing also. The good didn't die young, those who died young died good. I thought thoroughly about that later. We weren't different, just in different places.

SAN BERNARDINO

YOU CAN TRY TO GET AWAY

Did evil have a face? Throughout time and society the idea of one was confidently perpetuated, occupying a central position in many of our spiritual and societal interpretations. Without request—or with—we were born into a world cursing us with an adversary prior to our arrival. The wise ones and gurus of our time sung the same song from every stage and lavaliere microphone. Live audiences and online listeners were passionately reminded how the reality we lived was the one we created, yet we created a reality with a force acting as our enemy? I didn't know what love was or what it meant anymore, but I would attest it was not that. Love erased obstacles, although I didn't know if that mattered or how it would if it did. Our bodies malfunctioned in areas needing support—our lives did the same.

An unexpected voicemail I received at 1:56pm threw my thoughts into a fairground frisbee ride. I was freely getting coffee from a coffee shop on a Tuesday afternoon, an impossibility for me three years prior unless it was a holiday or I requested time off. I worked for myself now aside from a weekend gig. I lived check-to-check, yet with a freedom I was told was reserved for children and the wealthy. Was working for someone else in order to survive the same as freedom? Was freedom a spectrum? What wasn't? Were there seasons of freedom and of bondage? I was purposefully outside of LA hoping a different setting, even for a day, could clear my mind to ponder such mysteries and apply them to my work. It was my first time in San Bernardino and I was perfectly high, my coffee was spiked with whipped cream, caramel, and honey, and it was warm enough to drink immediately. The Sun was out with scattered clouds, and I wore a black, denim jacket, achieving room temperature while sitting outdoors. The mountain range behind me stretched across the horizon with its feet up, while snow-covered caps tilted to shade its eyes. It looked like a painting from the guy with the painting show, brunette afro, and the voice gently massaging your temples.

The photo-studio-backdrop view only required me getting off the train and walking less than ten minutes. The coffee habit was something I started after me, Lennon, and Avery, returned from working abroad last winter. They drank a lot of coffee and smoked a lot of weed, and now I did the same. I saw no set-back with incorporating the customs of others we enjoyed into our own routine. Once we we were done with the insistent socially-constructed educational systems, what other organic education from others did we receive as adults? There actually was another answer: art. Art educated our immortal aspects.

The sharing of our customs—our routines—was grounding, the exchange introducing us to hidden pockets of life with wayward dryer-money pinned inside. "Dryer-money" obviously being the scientific term for money forgotten in pants pockets of all varieties, later discovered during a post-wash wearing. Adopting someone else's awesome thing they did, and making it ours, equaled dryer-money. My mind received permission to carelessly wander because the voicemail I received was from my ex in LA, and I was stalling. It was the third or fourth voicemail they'd sent me in two years, and none of them were pleasant.

I eventually pressed play. It was a very sad and very beautiful voicemail left by one of the saddest and most beautiful people I knew. My eyes often watered when I thought of them, and it was because of instances like that voicemail. Apologizing and repeating themselves—a random selection of slurred words—yet they were sorry and they meant it. That was what the message said. I was sitting on a short, brick fence painted white when the voicemail arrived. It was the kind of message I never thought I would hear, as it was from someone I once called evil to their face because it most accurately described them at the time. I'm sure they didn't agree with my summation. The monologue concluded with, "Just know I'm sorry. And I love you."

> Some accepted apologies, others accepted change.

I listened to the message maybe ten times from start to finish. I sat, I drank my coffee, I listened to the message, and my eyes watered once. After listening to it over and over I realized I didn't know what love meant anymore.

Love could mean anything. Love could be anything. Love was part of our reality, so didn't we create it? We were here to enjoy ourselves which looked different for each of us. Love was enigmatic by definition. The enigma required time, effort, and patience for decryption, but primarily solitude.

Adults would fear the dark as long as children were still given reason to.

Solitude was still the source of nightmares. If we couldn't sit silently without the TV on, or music, or a podcast, we could benefit by asking ourselves why. What was it we needed to confront? What did we not understand? What thoughts were we replacing with those of entertainers? What were we distracting ourselves from? Love could be a distraction. Planets were created in the vacuum of space, and by extension, so were we. Stillness was where life began. It was the reason we were encouraged to pray or meditate in silence and privacy. Solitude was celestial. I was practicing backing-off, letting go, and surrendering. I wasn't asking the question because I knew the answer wouldn't impress me—regarding what love was. My life was filled with lofty goals sleeping at the top of nearly

vertical inclines. I acted as liaison for pink clouds behind blue mountains. Sad hearts behind proud chests spoke an abrasive language. I understood it and translated, yet hated hearing it spoken and wished it never was. Each of us spoke our own dialect. The more we interpreted and shared our interpretations, the deeper we connected and the further we elevated. Being one such translator, love and why it was useful could wait. My work was important to me, I loved it, and plenty was in reach—all crucial for my mental stability. I wasn't bored with the activity which would unavoidably occupy much of my life. It was easier letting go of what held us back when we held onto our passions. We would die the same way we lived, in vain or in love.

My coffee was finished and I was listening to the voicemail again in my headphones. I moved to sitting on a very comfortable chair with a soft, braided seat in front of a square, metal table. Following a brief time there, I relocated inside due to the peace being disrupted by two audibly inconsiderate gentlemen on cell phones. One was playing a war game rattling with automatic gunfire and the overuse of the Wilheim Scream. The other watched a comedian's video-podcast while laughing obnoxiously. Had the show been live, he would have been ceremoniously roasted by the comedian on principle.

Inside, the indistinct, orchestral, washing machine of the customary coffee shop ambience rotated on auto. Granted it was just me in front of my laptop, working in public was still performance art. Audience members filed in and out of the arena bearing witness to my brilliance or blunders. Some shined brighter at showtime. Pressure was a push, and our arms weren't always long enough to be that force for ourselves. The utility of the pressurized vacuum—the womb; the void; purgatory; outer space—was the absolute absence of interference. Why wouldn't an exhibitionist live in us all awaiting their stylistically suitable stage? For most of my life I couldn't understand the obsession with the coffee shop as ideal remote workspace, but an undeniable energy was present I recently recognized. The feeling was similar when working in a diner; I suspected it was the creativity. The more erratic the more energized.

A short, male barista wearing a visor with the store's logo in the center, and hair bleached half-blonde, pressed a lid onto a recently completed order. The inside of the clear, plastic cup was scribbled with ginger syrup, and from top to bottom the drink faded from green into a dark-purple-blue.

"Order for Le'Andre!"

The drink was jaw-dropping. The culinary arts were the most underrated and the most tragic.

Chefs were the architects of flavorful fuel designed for organic machinery.

Each piece was meant to inspire a desire to devour it instantly and entirely. It was a love letter to our ego French kissed into our taste buds. The culinary art form was appreciated by the least number for the shortest time. It was art designed for destruction. Those employed to create in that nature and environment cultivated a transformative catalytic chaos. The air was permeated with the energy of artistry and production, and it was infectious to the open.

Resigned to a seat tucked in the corner, I was another part of the living decor. Being a ghost was advantageous. A warm den of tranquility lived within solitude. Dens were also raided if not properly protected, and the tranquil twisted to taste like a trap. My life's pursuit was to have my work presented on the largest platforms available, yet I was still clawing at the eyelids of an audience unaware I delivered the requested. Being a ghost was discouraging as well. Were there times when it was better not to know who we were because identity came with a label? When who we were wasn't cemented neither was who we became. There was a time for everything. Many enjoyed claiming time did not exist or was an invention of humanity. The measurement of time was simply the record of sequential events. Whether labeled "time" or something else, sequence gently enslaved us. The immortal reminders to prioritize and be patient, with persistence, were relentlessly and repeatedly written into creation. Remembering sugar was more addicting than cocaine was key. All organic appearances were organically informative, while the inorganic additives deliberately deceived.

Part of the LA magic was nothing meant anything, so anything could mean everything.

The person in the coffee shop next to you could be writing a renaissance or a revolution. They also could be listening to a voicemail from someone they knew well enough to know they

may understand each other one day, but that day was on the other side of a mutual and separate rebirth.

> "Isn't that just still clinging to the past?"

> "In what way?"

The two questions came from a pair of thirty-somethings walking in the door who appeared platonic. They both wore all black. One with a black backpack and the other with a messenger bag—Bp and Mb. Bp replied.

> "All of the ways?"

> "Care to elaborate?"

> "There's a lot I could say about it."

> "I mean, we did just get here."

They were in the back of the line with four other people and a Chihuahua waiting ahead of them. Bp chose to elaborate.

> "I just think it's odd that the majority of concepts created by African-Americans have the word black or afro in it. How is Afrofuturism not just non-racist science fiction? Can't

we just get the racism out of the genre?"

"Right, but that's the point, right?

Afrofuturism was created because people of color were getting written out of the future by bigots and small-minded people with access."

"Okay, and now if I come up with a sci-fi/fantasy concept on par with Lucas, Roddenbury, or Martin, it's more likely to get praised only after its pigeonholed. So instead of creators being ostracized for their ignorance or malice, and the genre undergoing some sort of reconstruction, those who were forcibly excluded and forcibly had to create a genre just in order to have their stories told are opting to exclude themselves? I don't—I can't get that. How do we grow collectively like this?"

I may enjoy listening to the conversations of others more than having my own. The line shuffled two spaces forward, but neither Mb of Bp moved as it was Mb's turn to reply.

"I assume you have a solution?"

"I don't know. Probably not."

They both chuckled and Bp continued.

"Like, I get that racism and prejudice and ignorant people inspired 'black' labeled entertainment, but, still? Now? Science fiction isn't called Caucasian Futurism."

A laugh made Mb's stomach spasm as it fought to get out, but was pinned. Mb, one; Joker laugh, zero. Mb made a formal request to Bp.

"Yo, please chill."

"It isn't, right? Please tell me I didn't miss something. You know I don't watch the news and shit as much as I should."

"What is your point, lunatic?"

"I don't know—where isn't there one? We're basically allowing one group of people to have ownership of all major umbrella genres, and everyone else can have a sub-genre?"

"Hm."

"Right? I don't know, it doesn't make sense to me as something to progress forward with. No one in Hollywood or the music industry would dare make a Blaxploitation movie or album right now...and have the balls to call it that."

The line shuffled again putting them two customers from the register, and that time they moved up also. I couldn't hear them as clearly which sucked, I was getting joyfully invested. It was Mb who I guessed was talking next, but I may have missed some of the convo.

> "I think once we get disrespected correctly we get sick of sharing with the other kids."

> "Definitely."

> "I guess, it's like...I don't know.

We can't always be mad at others for how they react when backed into a corner.

> We all have to defend ourselves, right?"

> "Shit, I don't know who else will."

> "Precisely. So, I guess in that sense, I see what you mean but I also see how certain situations leave us *feeling* like we have no options. They're there, of course, but—"

> "They might as well not be."

> "They might as well not be. So, yeah, there's a redundancy to Afrofuturism and black-this and that, but, what it really comes down to is, someone has to do something else that works. Selling the ugly side is what we understand right now. Maybe that will—"

> "Welcome, guys! What can I get started for you?

I loved LA. I wouldn't have gotten to San Bernardino without Los Angeles as initial destination, and I would bet it was similar for most. Mb said selling the ugly side was what we currently understood, and I almost jumped up and started praise dancing. My ex and I showed each other the ugliest sides of who we were, and it was possible our pairing could produce nothing more. My worst was still an improvement for them; their midpoint was unbearable. The experience was brutal, and exhausting, and disgusting, and cinematic, and sexy, and poetic. It was a movie I would have enjoyed watching if I wasn't a co-star. Our relationship was a Greek Tragedy, worthy of thorough review by Aristotle or his constituents.

Knowing ourselves would always precede being ourselves. My ex neither knew that nor wanted to. Why did we wait impatiently for other's eyes to open instead of leaving? We only knew one version of ourselves at a time. Things happened, time passed, and we changed, or we didn't.

Our connection with ourselves was constantly reconsecrated, or turmoil tore us into pieces.

I was the type to think about what I thought about. They wanted to know how to win the game and I wanted to know how to stop playing. It wasn't an easy idea to sit next to, the one about how we were all using each other for an experience.[15] That idea was like folding my laundry as soon as it finished drying, I knew it was best but I didn't want it to be. My ex used me for...the same thing we all used each other for, a want or need. They needed someone they could trust, even if they didn't know what it looked like personified or how to respond to integrity. I needed someone who would allow me to be the parts of myself I buried, even if I didn't know how dark that was or how to repay said privilege. Should those we interacted with need our help, or should they want it from recognizing its value? Was anything else really an equal exchange? Was the opposite not unhealthy?

---

[15] Base Barter Principle: Between two interacting entities there is always a level of tangible or intangible exchange. One's goods are traded for another's services. Although it may go undetected by one, or both parties, and what is exchanged may not be directly proportional, it exists and transpires nevertheless. Even those who give freely expect to trade their generosity for gratitude (see page 263).

Love and desperation didn't coincide.

My ex made me weak and I let them know. Did we love what we loved if it didn't make us weak? Did we love ourselves if weak was all we loved made us? That was more than I wanted to think about. We only learned from we thought about, and the avoided thoughts were often investigation worthy.

Song: Almost Doesn't Count

Artist: Brandy

Album: Never Say Never

"You can't get to heaven...half off the ground/ Everybody knows...almost doesn't count."

The sweetness from the melted whipped cream in my cup was emboldened by the honey and cinnamon tasting of November. It was delicious. Multiple debates with ex-lovers about the mass of brown sugar I added to my food was no deterrent. My support for the use of all naturally occurring sweeteners was unapologetic because their utility was clear. Life was bitter enough. The term was "bittersweet" and not "sweetbitter." After receiving something we didn't want, we wanted something we didn't need. We wanted something we liked we didn't have to work for. Pacification was easier than education. Another reason to recall how addictive sugar was. It was a strange way of attempting to balance the nonexistent scales, but it worked for now. There was no rightful complaint against a proposed solution without first providing a more effective one. I couldn't solve the problems my ex chose to involve themselves in, and that was who they needed when we were together. The lives we each loved were single seat only. Our anger at the inevitability we couldn't fight was used against each other instead. We hated the lifestyle but loved the person. We lived a life of unsustainable extremes. The lows easily induced suicidal thoughts, while the highs made it hard to remember what we thought about. When it was good it was great, but greatness without presence burned bright then burned out. Perfect pictures didn't pose for the camera. Time made martyrs of masters, and then one thing of importance became another. We could have more respect for those making us money than those who made us whole. My ex was apologizing for proving the probability of the possible, a scenario neither of us wanted to be on either side of. I wouldn't even be listening if I didn't find them so attractive, which I was taught to feel about but did little to change. The lessons taught by mortality could be taught no other way, and not every dead thing required burial.

Without them my weekends were boring. I worked every hour I could, saved money, and slept more since I spent most of my down time at home. My ex was my adventure, a sentiment I shared with them two or three times, yet feared how much it meant to me wasn't conveyed fully. The problem was no balance existed between us, and not in the fun way. Those playing both sides lived with none on their own and were loyal to neither. My ex couldn't decide which version of themselves they wanted to be, and I learned to be okay with that. I didn't like being okay with that. It was like losing a bet with your best friend, who was a literal chicken, about whether they could run to the other side of an active six lane freeway. It was an easy bet to win but, you know, it's…it's your best friend. Then you didn't have the chicken and the chicken didn't have you. Attempting to be right for the sake of being right only displayed the limit of our understanding. If doing so made us feel more complete we could benefit by asking ourselves why. As long as we were satisfied with

why we took a direction and where it was going, why stop?

Engaging a new path began with reflecting on our past, our direct source for observing and studying the effects of our choices.

History wasn't bound to repeat itself, seasons were. Winter, Spring, Summer; abundance and lack; depression and elation—all consistently came in different forms. A thorough understanding of the relationship between the seasons and our choices was within our control, and would largely dictate how happy we were. It was similar to deciding whether or not to engage in a wager which only engorged or deflated our ego, like whether our chicken friend could cross the street. When the goal was to prove another wrong we proved ourselves to be. The chicken example wasn't the greatest, but you know what I mean. Scenarios where everyone got what they wanted happened all the time. If both parties weren't benefitting equally, then it wasn't a party. The sincerity of others was only worthy of gratitude. We honored ourselves by only saying yes or no when we meant it one hundred percent. Compromise was not the only way to maintain instrumental interpersonal interactions. Compromise was only needed for misaligned exchanges we were interested in nudging towards contentment. Compromise wasn't agreement, it was settlement. The attainment of harmony was through force or attraction, and it was retracted consistently when forced. The option to attract harmony instead of forcing it to form in front of us was free.

My ex and I should have said no to each other right after we said yes, but we didn't, and now we had a shared experience added to our equations convoluting the math. Not everyone we wanted in our lives could fit. We both got exactly what we wanted without knowing what it would look like. I take back how we "should have" said no to each other only as the word "should" was easier to twist than fresh cookie dough.

A past we were still interpreting was used to inform decisions on a future we couldn't predict.

I found our species surprisingly conceited for one working with so little. I was practicing laughing at myself more, which wasn't easy for an adult who was picked on relentlessly as a child and adolescent. However, I was one

of the clowns as well, like we all could be, I was just working on changing occupations. Perhaps I didn't want to stop the game, I just wanted the why.

If there was such a thing.

I saved the voicemail, took off my headphones, and put my phone in my jacket pocket. For the remainder of my time in San Bernardino I acted phoneless. I was sad I deleted all of our pictures, but if I kept them then I was proving how serious I wasn't about moving forward. The reasons letting go outnumbered those holding on. The keeping of mementos in the midst of releasing unhealthy attachments was an expression of addiction and dependency. We benefited from missing what didn't align rather than keeping it out of fear. It was no different than keeping a secret stash, or keeping the dealer's number, or keeping the patterns of destructive decision making: we were addicted. Addiction was not bent, it was broken like eye contact. A distinct level of maturity was required to break-free from what broke our freedom. Considering eighteen year olds as adults was one of the bolder displays of societal ignorance. From the ages of seventeen through twenty-six we were still akin to a teenager clumsily groping our way through puberty, only the lessons were more expensive. On our twenty-seventh birthday would be our first year of adulthood, since by then we would have *some* life experience worth referencing. Prior, we knew nothing—anomalies aside. Without knowing ourselves we couldn't be ourselves, without being ourselves we couldn't love ourselves or anyone else. Without that knowledge there was suffering and ignorance.

There was no love in ignorance, only servitude.

Ignorance unveiled our agony.

Language was everything, it shaped the way we defined our existence. My ex said he loved me because I was everything he wanted to be. I was twenty-three at the time and they were twenty-two. It was a red flag I chose to paint green, and it wasn't the first, last, or the only. I loved them for who they were, it was only a shame they weren't themselves more often.

MEDUSA SLAIN

HOW FAR IS TOO FAR?

I saw too much of myself in her, making me wonder whether we were related, duplicated, or predestined. The technology and arrogance to hastily create with any available procedure was plentiful. Perhaps there was no choice but to murder her, acting as another star shifted dutifully in the Precession of the Equinoxes. Was I meant to kill her since the first time we spoke? Imagine growing close to someone unknowingly growing closer to kill you, and only finding out with Death's lips close enough to touch your cheek. It wasn't the surprise we thought of when we said we loved surprises or advertised our spontaneity. I didn't think she saw that coming, I know I didn't. There was a charcoal taste squatting in my mouth which repeatedly detailed every useless quality I was cursed with. Every failure reminded me failure was my forte. The only inherent talent I seemed to posses was causing disorder. Was that considered a talent? Everyone played their part, right? What if that was mine? What if I was a disrupter, a catalyst of chaos, one of the mischievous like the Norse god Loki, the Yoruba god Elegua, the Greek god Eris, or arguably the most notorious, Lucifer? The pantheons of the world were only meant to illustrate how the many sides of our internal selves manifested externally. Each mythical figure personified a chakra, frequency, vibration, planetary precession, or part of the body or mind. The gods symbolized the available and necessary pieces of a larger whole. What if I was the one who burned down the forest with a bolt of lightning to clear the way for new life? I never thought about the role of the villainous until realizing residing alongside them would come naturally. If light wasn't appreciated without dark, were bringers of darkness also pedestals of light?

The human body was fragile enough to crack under the slightest push. We lived in asymmetrical vases made of finely cut glass, forgotten as they dangled on the edge of a kitchen countertop. My hands shook uncontrollably, and the fresh blood covering them was a new layer of skin. I kept balling up my fists then releasing them, but they trembled until closed and did the same while opening. I held my breath, shut my eyes, and listened. I was alone in the house now. The only sound in the kitchen was the low, droning hum rolling towards me from the tall, matte black refrigerator. I loved that sound. Something was deeply soothing about it, even now, like it was the heartbeat of the house thumping steadily under my head as I lay on its chest.

How many of our desires were fulfilled by simplicity once we allowed them to be fulfilled simply?

The ice machine kicked on, catching me off-guard, and I flinched and threw my eyes open. I forgot for a moment where I was, then I saw Nakayla motionless and facedown on the floor again. Blood lumbered from her head all over the tile she told me was marble, but I knew granite when I saw it.

> "How Isyss? How is that what you're focused on right now? Jesus Christ!"

If I didn't take a step back I would have real, fresh, human blood on my shoes, yet I found

time and energy to internally debate the quality of the stone I stood on. I knew it wasn't the most efficient use of my mind, yet only after the time and energy was squandered. For unclear reasons unbeknownst to myself, people didn't think I could have ADHD. I guess there was a look and I didn't have it, but my thoughts still scattered like startled insects. Struggling to keep my focus where I needed it never ended. It was usually troublesome, but if it chose to really flare up now it could be my last annoyance as a free woman. Then again, there was no way I was getting away, so I guess it didn't matter. I thought about calling 911, but I didn't feel like it and there was no need to rush. Naturally, Ms. Perfect followed the government regulations and installed cameras all over her home. Ironically, it was only two or three weeks ago when I was teasing her about having them like we were in elementary school.

> "Honestly Nakayla, could you be more of a sheep?!"

> "It's for safety. And you sound manic."

> "You sound like I could make a wool sweater out of your fur. So unless you have assassins after you that you

haven't mentioned, you're just handing over your privacy to the government like an idiot."

"Thank you, Isyss. I'd love to talk more but my fur isn't gonna shave itself. Goodnight."

Now, due to those same nosey cameras, I mentally prepared for a life or death I couldn't argue with receiving.

Artist: Ms. Lauryn Hill

Song: Nothing Even Matters

Album: The Miseducation of Lauryn Hill

" [song intro] Now the skiiies could faaalll/ Not even if my bosssss should callllll/ The world it seems so veryyyyy small-alllll-allll-all/ 'Cause nothing even matters...at all."

***

I saw too much of myself in her. Her demons were friends with mine, they were just younger and less refined with their methods. They fought and dragged us into the arena like slaves turned gladiators. We usually went easier on each other, but didn't that day. Our arguments were petty disagreements easily solved with a few moments of empathy, but we never made it that simple. Why could it be so hard to see what others did? Our misplaced archaeologists' tool kit was missed dearly. It was made to unearth what we both felt, without it we scraped at the surface barehanded. How were we so close yet so distant? The question was one-sided; the answer rendered moot. She blamed me for everything all the time and I knew she was right, but my defensiveness was unrelenting and deaf to restraint. It took a high level of maturity to admit fault, and an even higher level to accept blame. I was too old to be acting like a child, and since I persisted, it was time to admit it wasn't an act anymore.

The verbal advantage Nakayla lorded over me was physically sickening. She was Gangis Khan in a war of words, and I could only control myself for so long before exploding.

We could walk away from what we didn't like, we didn't have to wait for hatred.

Nevertheless, she thought she was so goddamn smart. I always hit her first because I was raised to. Doing what someone bigger or stronger than us didn't like was how we got hit. Every time we repeated the action we were hit harder, the elevated force beating rules into us ineffectively. No explanation, no talking, just a smack to the face making a smile more work than it was worth.

Children consistently shown disagreements were solved with aggression grew up confused by solving them with words.

It was only necessary for animals and children to fight. Animals, because they lacked the capacity to express complex emotion, and children, because they lacked adequate levels of expression. I was the child thinking changing my regressive habits was too much work to try. The result was a dead body two feet away from me on pristine, black and gray granite floors. Nakayla's kitchen was so breathtaking it should have came with masks and oxygen tanks. The island in the middle reminded me of Hawaii, as it was big enough to be a state. A twelve inch oval block of granite matching the floors was its crown, and the edges were hammered by hand. Six slim drawers slid out of the granite with raw, wooden handles. A stocky, beautiful, steel-reinforced,

polyurethane glossed tree trunk sat holding the countertop on its shoulders. I only knew that because I was with her when the salesperson explained why it was worth more than the price tag with mathematical precision. It was a work of art. Six leather bar stools with back and arm rests folded out from the sides of the trunk. The cabinets were all matte black with the same handles as the drawers on the island. Warm, uncovered, LED filament bulbs hung from the three wooden planks stretching across the ceiling at varying heights and lengths. It was like a turn-of-the-century saloon designed by Elon Musk, Thomas Edison, and Paul Bunyon. None of it sounded like it would get along, but each item of decor lovingly encouraged the next.

Opposites didn't attract, compliments did.

The Feng Shui was completed meticulously and purposefully, which was valuable since our mentality was affected by it. Our unconscious mind assumed how we configured our external space represented our desire for the internal. The way energy moved through our homes impacted our movement through life. The energy was embodied by sensory stimuli speaking to us in unseen ways. The use of sounds, smells, colors, textures, and shapes contained benefits far deeper than selling merchandise and exposing toddlers to what their future held for them. The adult mind, even in its most jaded state, was still a sponge. Spaces could be designed and arranged to communicate with us in constant silence and support. The centerpiece of Nakayla's kitchen already sang of a life so far out of my reach, it stopped running because I'd never catch up.

Then there was the stove.

I told Nakayla for years about that damn stove and how much I loved it, and she wouldn't even pretend to listen most of time. It was the Cyrilin Six Series, the one consumer-level stove gourmet restaurants swore by via blood oath. It was designed by Caribbean super chef Cyril Walters, manufactured in Italy, but looked like it was designed by NASA and manufactured in a galaxy far, far away. There were six, gas, stovetop burners with variable power outputs, each cooking to 22,000 BTUs. That meant incredibly quick prep, with more control than most would ever need or know what to do with. The stove's fifty-inch frame packed dual convection ovens with twelve cooking functions all optionally controlled via a mobile app. The cooktop surface was stainless steel, and the knobs for each burner, as well as the handles for the oven doors and storage spaces, were all Black Maple. The finish came in matte black or gun metal gray; the appliance was designed to be an extension of its operator. It was a bargain for restaurants retailing at $16,999, a price too heavy to squeeze into the bikini of my budget. Nakayla knew that. When she finally invited us over and couldn't stop giggling as she walked us to the kitchen, I should have known the stove would be condescendingly waved in my face. In short, her sense of humor was mostly just laughing at people when they felt their worst. As my jaw dropped upon seeing a fantasy cross over into reality, Nakayla laughed until she threw herself into a fit of coughing and choking. She struggled to catch her breath and I didn't care if she dropped it. What was it called when the ignorance of others spilled onto our lives, inconveniencing us severely, resulting in justifiable rage? My anger turned my eyes into pits of boiling lava I swore made my eye lids hotter. The kitchen was a pair of calculated hands shoving me over the edge. It was my dream kitchen, and Nakayla was a nightmare come to life.

***

I cooked the majority of our meals growing up because both of my parents worked long hours at dead end jobs. They made enough to pay the bills, have money for happy hours, and change left over for take-out. Both were high school drop outs, and not the cool kind starting their own boutique jewelry business or putting out chart-topping music. My parents were the kids having kids before knowing what they wanted or how to go about deciding. Consequently, that was why much of my later childhood and adolescence was spent in the kitchen. We grew to hate or love what we were forced into. I loved to cook. In hindsight, it was probably more Displeasing Decision Consolation[16] than anything else, but I didn't mind. Something I should have hated found a way to bring me happiness—it could have been worse. Every social media page I followed was either chefs, cooking appliances, food critics, or recipes. My head received a surgical implant from my parents, a microchip projecting an image of our perpetually empty bank accounts too weak to send a spatula to culinary school. I was also informed scholarships were only for kids whose parents didn't work. Since what they did wasn't work to me, I thought that was their way of saying there was a chance. I was young. I would have been cooking professionally from an early age. I thought what I made was really good, yet was told, like me, it was nothing special. I shouldn't have believed that but I did. As a shy, only child who had trouble making friends and no cousins around the same age, the opinion of my parents was everything.

The world was mind.

Could we not see what parents were responsible for? Most of us had our branches twisted into double double-helixes in their infancy. We did our best from there; making a murderer was easy. Take what was needed from the young human mind, and it would take its life and the lives of others like free samples. No questions asked. The twisted became the twisted. Only those determined to destroy their predetermined paths and start from nothing into the direction of

---

[16]Displeasing Decision Consolation: we can alter our perception of an undesirable decision by creating, or manipulating, aspects of the selection into a more favorable light.
We tell a story producing a false appreciation of what we never wanted to begin with, decreasing the possibility of increasing dissatisfaction and disappointment.
We try fooling ourselves into settling. Happily. Was there beauty to be found in torture? (see page 263).

the unknown found freedom. The authentic freedom we imagined more than lived was as close as our present pattern of inhibition. Luck was the other alternative—stumbling into an unlikely, overtly aligned circumstance without request; a miracle. True miracles were overlooked more often than overstated. When wouldn't that pattern have existed? Was parental trauma not part of the parental experience?

The creation was always the mirror exposing the cracks in the creator.

When the creation did otherwise, were those not anomalies? The anomaly was part of the pattern, it didn't represent the pattern in its entirety. Genius represented universally dispersed potential, not the potential all would unlock. As cliché as it was, it all started at home. Every aspect of life was a story. Whether the stories were what we told ourselves or what others told us, they shaped and reshaped our value of life and our place within. It didn't matter if the stories were real or not.[17] With my parents holding the pen, no story I was part of read like a happy one. When my father suffered a heart attack shortly after eating the best Jerk Chicken I ever made, me and my cooking were blamed for almost killing him. That began anything I did making everything worse. Instead of pursuing what I loved, I was working with my mom every weekend from the time I was sixteen, and every other day once I graduated. It was joy-stealing. My mom was the caregiver for Mr. Lucky Anders, a ninety-three year old man in a wheelchair with a glass eye and one foot—the left one. He lost the right one in the jaws of a disapproving crocodile while attempting to secure one of their children for captivity. I thought his injuries were justified. The fire we played with played back. Waiting on that old man was not where I needed to be. I closed my eyes when I needed them opened the most so I could pretend I wasn't where I was. No one told me how our paths and choices copulated in creation of our experience. It was no different than the creation of anything else. Going somewhere

---

[17] Falsehood Theory: A lie is the truth had circumstances been different. It is a believable alternative to a provable fact or sincere point of view. All that separates a lie from the truth is a thorough imagination. Lies and truths occupy the same space: stories we choose to accept or deny (see page 263).

was the only way we got anywhere.[18]

Mr. Anders was the first person I killed.
Technically.

Naturally, I cooked for him too and knew what he could and could not have. However, after having to work two doubles while my mom was recovering from self-induced alcohol poisoning, I was tired and struggling to focus. I was eating some left over noodles I made the night before, and Mr. Anders innocently asked for a bite. I chuckled, shrugged, and helped a few noodles into his mouth with an extra pair of chopsticks.

It only took seconds for the asphyxiation to begin.

The way his eyes bulged it looked like there were thumbs inside of his head pushing them out. First I thought he was choking and tried giving him the Heimlich Maneuver, but then I remembered the damn peanut allergy. How could I make Asian food without sesame oil? He was dead by the time I got the epipen out; I figured I would be dead soon by lethal injection. I

called the police right away, they came, asked enough questions to write a bible, but they believed me when I said it was an accident. In the eyes of my parents, their baseless doomsday prophecy of my food and I displaying our lethality was fulfilled. Killing someone was much faster by hitting them in the head with an iron meat tenderizer.

What we needed most was usually in arm's reach.

Nakayla was proof. It was no less of a mess than cooking though, ingredients were everywhere.

> "Not so smart now, are you? Hm? Nothing? No slick comeback? Okay, then. I might like the new you."

I then grasped what I did and it was funny. Murder wasn't funny, but the whole lead-up and the fact it actually happened...well, it would only be getting less funny with time. For years I wished the peanut allergy Mr. Anders was cursed with was Nakayla's, where some random extract could accidentally make it into one of her meals. My happiness counted the minutes til she was

---

[18] The Journey of Genesis: Journey of Genesis: no direction was arbitrary. For us to arrive anywhere required movement. Standing still led nowhere; going anywhere led somewhere. The path we began led to the path where we were needed (see page 263).

gone, yet cried for hours at her absence. It ruined everything. It was the kind of sadness filling lakes with tears and canyons with heavy hearts.

***

When ashamed I got angry and lied about anything making me look bad. Trying to be a "better person" taught me something I wasn't.

> There was no such thing as being a better person, we only became more or less of who we chose to be.

I didn't know if I was becoming more or less of me and gave up on trying to figure it out. The rules we placed on ourselves, and pretended we agreed with blindly following, were brainless. We were born into, or gave birth to, families of strangers we grew to familiarize ourselves with over time. These people weren't chosen. Our parents, children, siblings, aunts, uncles, were all forced onto us. Even if we chose to make a child, it was still culturally looked down upon to simply give them away if we were unhappy with our dynamic. Adoption was obviously a thing, but still. Kids were made without permission, so we didn't get to

wash our hands of them without leaving a permanent residue. The instruction was to love family because we shared DNA, or risk being ostracized, considered ungrateful, or in possession of a psychological disorder in need of medical treatment. My parents loved their kids and each other like a chore. Their example showed me love was an uneasy interaction never as satisfying as envisioned. Love was trading an hour of misery for a minute of happiness. My sole personal precedent poisoned my soil. I loved others the same way I was, and it made perfect sense to me. Unfortunately, even what we were okay with could yield outcomes of the opposite.

I always said I wanted kids but never thought I'd actually have any—I was a mess. My diet sucked, I never exercised, drank too much liquor and too little water. I smoked cigarettes when I drank and when I was stressed, and depending on my mood, enjoyed a recreational powder a few times a month. Apparently my body had the determination of a Navy Seal. My perfectly healthy, baby girl, was born with bright eyes and a laugh tickling you under your chin. I found out too late to abort, and for awhile I was okay with the fact I didn't. I was twenty-three and on my own, but for the first time I felt like there was someone in the world who sincerely loved me in the purest way. As time passed, I discovered purity was a phase passing like time did. I didn't know where I went wrong. I didn't know if it was because she grew up without a father, I didn't know what happened I didn't know about, but something made her a terrorist. Her big breasts and eyes, full lips, and small enough waist quickly displayed their dexterity. To say she became insufferable was an inexcusable understatement, and it didn't help she was an okay student when she wanted to be. Education only mattered for so long though. The friends she made senior year were all thieves and drug dealers, and they showed her how her body was worth even more than she was getting for it. I went through her phone and saw it for myself. When I confronted her we fought, and I ended up smacking her around pretty good. She called the police on me and eloquently told them she feared for her survival; I received an extremely stern warning. The two cops which arrived were both male, and I would have thought they were in the presence of the goddess Venus. An offer made at the feet of her alter was the only deed absent. They clearly didn't know Medusa was said to have once been beautiful. Nakayla

getting anyone she could to do any and everything for her became her life. She was a Pied Piper of the opposite sex, she was cocky about it, and it made me nauseas. Nevertheless, her game ended the same every time. Single-handedly she would create a situation where her life was in danger—or she was about to be homeless—then run back to me crying.

> Insincere charm was a rainbow, mesmerizing, yet only momentarily.

So, I would love her, and I would help her, and she would play me too, and we would fight, and she was a terrorist. Another arrogant, vindictive…*person* who thought their actions wouldn't create consequences. One-dimensional people treated people one-dimensionally. I guess she thought she was so pretty she could talk her way out of anything. Whatever she couldn't talk her way out of, showing a little extra cleavage or flirting a little more forwardly usually did the trick. When neither worked she walked away. However, there were repercussions and karma was real; Causality was a law of the universe. She used her way from one guy to another, capitalizing on each of their particular applications. Some were protection, others were convenience, a few were an escape, but they all needed to spend money. Why didn't she have any female friends? There was nothing she could squeeze out of them. Keeping her focus where it would benefit her the most was how she got her kitchen. My dream kitchen. Abe bought it for her, just like anything else she asked for, because she did everything Abe liked in bed.

> There was a difference between what we worked for and what we deserved.

Abe was one of those fake-smart idiots born tucked into money like the cheese in stuffed-crust pizza. He never took the time to learn skills like how to read out loud or not to start a fight (that his security or the police wouldn't have to finish), but even he didn't deserve her. Conversely, Nakayla deserved every one of those little pointed things on the tenderizer I bounced off her head. Monsters were born to be slain. The snakes were cut free from the head of Medusa; dead snakes were harmless. The beautiful evil was vanquished poetically and the world could now rest easier. I hoped they understood the service I performed, looking part of me in the eye and removing

the eye-soar from the face of the Earth. I acted heroically. I hoped I was honored as a hero, as a deliverer of what some saw as darkness—a pedestal of light. I was her karma just as the crocodile was for Mr. Anders. The fire we played with played back

.

I killed my daughter. Someone needed to.

Dear Nakayla,

My beautiful baby girl who I saw so much of myself in, I'm glad the part of me amplified within you is gone. Life for those you've crossed is now more fair, honest, and caring than it has ever been. I would hope another found the courage I did to do what was necessary if I didn't. Whatever the cost charged to me I will gladly pay it with interest, and my life.

Love you forever baby,
Mom

NAKAYLA
NAKAYLA

Final Journal Entry

It was funny being excluded for being seen as different, and the funny part was most important. We were all unique, literally, every single one of us, yet we were also the same. Life was accomplished when we saw ourselves in others and others in ourselves. That was something bigger than we needed to talk about, the work just needed be done. If we could find ourselves, then be ourselves, we would see what the universe saw. I just wanted to enjoy the view with whoever wanted to do the same.

There was a story I heard about a hummingbird and a peacock.

A hummingbird landed on a peacock's feather and couldn't help commenting on its beauty. Curious, the hummingbird asked the peacock which feather was his favorite. The peacock, having only seen his feathers in the reflections of lakes and puddles, remarked he saw none more special than the next. The hummingbird examined the feathers more closely. They remained strikingly beautiful, yet her initial perception of them was altered. The longer she looked, the more their uniqueness faded before her gaze. Shortly after she flew away, no longer impressed. Bored.

That was the joke. Our divinity was hidden when our essence was. The eye of the beholder held beauty, and at times it was held away from the beautiful. When did the most desirable path become the road most trampled?

Who taught us rarity wasn't the only thing we shared?

Who taught us to hate what we were? Who taught us to live lesser?

I was fine being excluded for being unique by someone who was the same. That shit was hilarious. When the aliens invaded we would run together as the human race once more.

Hopefully I'd be dead long before then.

ALIGNED

TO THE PATHS
WE CROSS

Themeface of Union Station switched at certain angles. The building knew it was a passageway, the chameleon the chameleons passed through as exit or entrance. Depending on the day and the lighting, the station was a microcosm of the city's marbled mystique. The Polar Express for the wandering adult-adventurer pulled into LA every hour like it was Christmas Eve at the North Pole. It felt like any day could be a holiday. Dreamland was a sleepwalker. Knit dreamcatchers reached for nightmares above restless beds, while human dreamcatchers hoped to capture and kill the deconditioned concepts casting progression. Differentiating between bums and billionaires was difficult since both dressed identically. It made perfect sense. Neither the independently wealthy nor the independently destitute were obligated to follow another's dress code. Although on opposite ends of

the financial spectrum, the lifestyles they cultivated allowed them to be the lone contributors to their survival. It was painfully poetic. The silent grandeur of the perspectives were perpendicular, however it was the way the homeless dressed which inspired the rich. Those with less to lose did what they did first and most authentically. The dirty kids shaped Los Angeles, which was why the city was so lax about them living outside wherever they wanted. Those who didn't understand that, or weren't open to doing so, would probably be happier somewhere else. Everyone in LA was supposed to be there. No one arrived accidentally, but no one was begged to stay—Kobe and Nipsey excluded. The nomadic life wasn't for everyone and neither was the Angelonous (an-jello-nuhs). An Angelonous lifestyle, of course, being one lived in Los Angeles or according to its customs and cultural principles. Those living on the street made choices at breakfast most wouldn't survive by lunch. Their raw appearance was a reminder of reality's artistic indifference regarding medium or material. Obvious inspiration abounded, and those with access were taking notes quicker than bank thieves. The layers, the oversizing, the rips, the holes, the paint—down to the palette—

were hardly reimagined in the creation of bubblegum, affluent-only, hyper-capitalist approved versions of the organic. Pastels and bleach stains symbolized faded vibrance from living unsheltered for upwards of twenty-four hours per day. Rays of California sun painted on whatever was worn the same as California painters. The colors weren't style choices, they were battle scars.

If those beneath the stars looked up for inspiration, perhaps the stars looked down for theirs.

It was why wealthy patrons paid so much for fine art and why it was undoubtedly worth it. The price point attached to art pieces eclipsed what the average person made in a lifetime because they were a single divine expression. It was almost like owning a life. There was a reason why only some street-artists became multi-millionaires. Many begged patrons to buy whatever was thrown in front of them, few syphoned their souls into tangible tokens hoping others felt touched by the same transcendency they did. The untethered creator created from a cosmic dutifulness ignored only to their own detriment. A divine expression was created out of

self-alignment, purpose, or understanding, often ignited by what we interpreted as especially painful, or near perfect. That caliber of creation made deeper, intangible connections available. Divine expressions were mirrors. Divinity was the mirror we all recognized ourselves in once we knew who we were. The people pouring money into paintings, sculptures, fashion, cars, and jewelry, were buying "high-end", or what could be called "high-frequency" items. Cash was currency and currency was energy, so a high-currency exchange was also one of high-energy. It was the act of raising our frequency, or the intensity of our frequency, by the external acquisition of the divine rather than via a metaphysical or spiritual path. "Hype-beasts" were simply those determined to add to themselves from the newest external sources with the highest vibration. It worked for some. The rich and non-rich were each equally equipped with many ways to remain where they were. I was quietly listening intently.

The clothes weren't the only dovetail between the have-alots and have-littles. Blurred lines were seen through fogged lenses in romantic lighting, coerced by the similarities in the cryptic conversations. Manic mumblings and questions asked anxiously for themselves to answer could be regarding millions, or meth memories. Meth memories being the varying stretches of time in a drug addicts life they imagined living. Both sounded the same. The visions were grandiose, outlandish, and appreciated only by those of a similar mind. My admiration for the closeness of genius and madness beat my fear of it to the finish line by a breath. The lines we crossed with purpose transformed us, making us different unintentionally, a process producing uniqueness. There was a difference between being unique and different. *Unique* originated from the Latin word for one. *Different* was a descendent of differing, or "to set apart." Unique brought us back to ourselves, to oneness. Different brought us somewhere else, apart.

Different was a tourist destination for the directionally divided.

The flight home was always hardest to catch.

***

Union Station on a weekday morning was a blender on the fourth setting. Sitting by the big staircase that stretched upwards to the second floor, after an already long night, was where the unexpected inspiration to analyze my overall mental condition inserted itself. Lots of people cycled through, lots of complimentary and polarizing frequencies. I didn't get laid, I drank more than I wanted to, and I was running on three hours sleep—a trifecta of kicks to the shin delivered by my free foot. I was anxious to manifest my next aligned employment opportunity, working for myself while helping others how I could. Bartending was cool, it was just time for another direction. The only difference about that particular Saturday morning was having to be up at six to leave by eight. I would usually sleep-in a few hours longer; I think I got to the station five or ten minutes before nine. I would have been there sooner, but I wanted to improve my consistency with meditating prior to social engagements. The differences I noticed were exciting. I thought slower and more thoroughly, speaking less to those who only listened to collect information or listened lazily. Marijuana & Meditation was my new peanut butter and jelly. I outgrew squirting ketchup on my mac and cheese, but PB&J was right up there with curry and chick peas. The food we ate was as important as what we did with it. How could we help others if we couldn't help ourselves? If we thought we were helping we weren't, and we chose to believe that or not. What each of us required to find alignment was seldom the same. There was no real way to know what someone else needed or needed to accomplish. We knew what worked for us and what others said worked for them, otherwise there was only inference. Without the difference determined, we continuously tripped over our feet while wearing shoes two sizes away from ours. All required guidance. Puzzle pieces fell from the sky we tried catching, matching, and connecting simultaneously. If action wasn't taken to step back, and up, so we could step forward, we took on more than allowed us to move anywhere.

***

I was okay with not being behind the scenes spiritually, but I was led to help and chose to listen. The *corentice* resonated as soon as I heard the designation. They could be tarot readers, holistic and energy healers, psychics, crystal wrappers, doulas, breath-workers, teachers and guides— the weirdos of the west. The *corentea (ko-ren-tay—plural)*

studied the patterned flow of energy within a given medium— the current—understanding the character of the energy shifted with the medium. Energy was directionless on its own, the medium provided the possibility of direction. Corentea was seen as a Surrenderist approach[19], experiencing and interpreting the currents of energy more than manipulating their motion. They understood healing crystals, numerology, and past lives; psychedelics and marijuana were used for everything from channeling messages from the ethers, to enhancing orgies. Once you crossed paths with these people you realized they were the special ones—if you looked for special. They were looking for ways to help because an aspect of their experience understood the necessity.

Abundance was given so we could give abundantly.

I heard it labeled The Burning Man Religion, but I didn't know what that meant and couldn't afford a ticket to the festival. I also heard it called New Age, but none of the practices were new, so the connotation there lost me. The spirituality so many sampled

---

[19] Surrenderist Futurism: A Surrenderist assumes that present events forecast an unalterable future. They let go, allowing the probable outcome to proceed presuming they cannot, or should not affect it. Surrenderists encapsulate fluidity, peace, and acceptance. Patience (see page 263).

borrowed components from Buddhism, Hinduism, Taoism, Alchemy, Wicca, Pantheism, Gnosticism, and Paganism. The connection to the Abrahamic faiths as influencing "new age" wasn't one I heard often, but maybe I just wasn't around those people. I didn't think many thought about that stuff anyway. Regardless, I continued to be amazed at how clearly everything influenced everything else. I enjoyed looking into the origins and etymologies and realizing the connections. It was like playing a song and translating the emotions of the notes. No matter who I was around from the community, the conversation included the terms most-teased: vibes, signs, energy, frequencies, crystals, astral-anything, birth charts, lower-self, higher-self, life path, and, of course, anything referencing astrology as valid. The complete list was longer. The teasing was diminishing as more reported consistent results able to benefit anyone.

The processes growing and building us collectively, broke and rebuilt us individually.

Too many told us we were awarded for avoidance. Where we learned and where we practiced what we learned were

separate. Barricades weren't always blockages. The line separating the walls of fire and the walls of stone was blurred. One burned our weakness away as we walked through, the other forced our feet to be through with dead-end direction. Today I hoped for fire.

I was here to meet a Possible. The ancient texts called them a syzygy, a frequency [within a person] who was a metaphysical compliment. Astrologically, the same word described a planetary alignment—the parallel was clear. Theoretically there were three of them: a higher and lower compliment, and a twin. The higher satisfied the mental chakras of communication and awareness; the lower satisfied the physical chakras of adventure and sensuality; a twin matched our frequency, giving us what we usually gave to others. Together we furthered one another's ascension rapidly. Einstein stated all in life was vibration, and fortunately we could alter ours. Entire adult lives were spent sifting through simmering sands for soulmates for that reason. Something in us knew there were multiple ways to walk in our divine vibratory tone, and that was one of them. The fountain of youth was real and came in many forms. The quest to remain young forever was analogous with forever remaining aligned. Tremendous insight quietly perpetuated itself while we yelled over the answers to our inquiries. Individually, we saw those who ascended everywhere all the time—the seemingly superhuman. The Einsteins, the Cleopatras, the Carrys, the Hicks', the Teslas, the Hitlers, the King Jrs, the Jacksons, the Jordans, the Winfreys, the Watts'—there was a spectrum. Those Frequencies walked in their divinity without introduction or explanation, leaving footprints next to the mythical demigods they followed. They tapped into part of themselves everyone wouldn't, and what it was called was different depending on our demographic. The most common term was genius—although it was beyond that—and it was not reserved for the internationally recognized and rich. Mechanics fixing anything touching their hands, manipulating the inside of automobiles unknown to them with ease, mentally made structural connections in their minds others couldn't. Fulfilling that caliber of potential was available to all, yet the necessary sacrifices involved rightfully deterred the impulsive and the unready. Those choosing to live in their divinity were historically known as aeons, as they were emanations of Source Creation fulfilling various operations of the universe. There were no good aeons or bad aeons. All acted as part of the *AefeA* (ee-fay)—the singular cycle beginning from the point of cosmic creation—and the *AeforeA* (ee-for-ay)—the discernible cycles created within which mirrored the AefeA in varying degrees. Some built, others cleared space for the builders. *AezaleA* (ee-zah-lay) was the "genius", talents we seemed intrinsically connected with because they expressed subconscious environmental responses.

Genius wasn't a gift we were given, it was one available for discovery.

Discovery was a way of life for aeons, striving to ascend past acts of anger or ignorance to live harmoniously in understanding. When anger arose, wisdom was excavated through exploration. Apologies were offered swiftly, for anger was an unnecessary instructor of last resort. All was done to further all. None was devalued to confirm the value of another. Divinity was defined in many ways all describing the same. All carried divinity by birth, few by rite. From that basis, part of Aeonilism was said to be shaped, a perpetually expanding interpretation of expressed universal interconnection. The philosophy was more grounded in practice than it was in description. Existence was permeated with observable patterns with guiding properties. More was seen when we knew what we saw. For instance, one such pattern was that of the miracle. A miracle was not impossible, it was an improbable, making it an anomaly, making it part of a cycle—as all anomalies were. Were there any recorded miracles of glasses of water turning into horses? No, because, how? However, the natural Ocurrents of a river flowing red like blood was scientifically explained simply. Why? Because the rules governing miracles governed everything else. The miraculous part of a miracle was the thing happening when wanted, not something outside the laws of nature gnawing into the realm of reality for a moment of glory. Miracles were statistically in the game, meaning we could depend on them to happen... when probable. Understanding the interconnection was part of Aeonilism. It was an old idea making a resurgence as all sensible ideas usually did.

The first Aeonilists were the scribes capturing the vibratory power of our voice between finger and instrument, making it so the eye saw what was heard. They were the initial ones to act as aeonaes.[20] Questioning the wilderness until it questioned them in return, Aeonilists were folded inward infinitely from all sides until all sides were one.

Growth wasn't painless, it was timeless.

Achieving the highest level of consciousness earned many titles across the parallel disciplines. The terminology was arbitrary, of course, but our brains were small and we needed tricks to retain information. In Aeonilism, AeieA (ee-yay) roughly transliterated to mean "the connected understanding" or "one, connected." The "i" in the center of AeieA symbolized the connected one, the Eye of Harmony. Observers of interconnectivity. One would achieve AeieA, then they would recognize the depth and breadth of aeonaes. It was no different than enlightenment, ascension, alignment, crossing the abyss, being delivered, or saved. Then the message was forwarded. Progress through preservation. Humbly, the scribe was positioned behind the message and the messenger, and the Divine was above all, hence their names were known by few. It was

---

[20] aeonaes: (see page 124)

said that would change with time as all did. They were the holders of the Perpetual Pen—their first and primary symbol.

The diamond-shaped insignia was organically inspired by divine geometry, as seen in the Golden Ratio, the Fibonacci spiral, and every human face. Aeonilism closely observed the patterns made present throughout the finger print of creation, as they were said to be guides offering clarity. A triangle occupying the top portion of the diamond signified the pen facing upwards, receiving guidance from the above. The inverted pen brought the guidance down to where all could grasp, grow, and gain. As always.

The universal wisdom aided all on their journey, guidance to be respected and utilized respectfully, yet authentically. Follow the energy. A myriad of paths and purposes presented themselves once we prepared.

Preparation was a personal process for each of us.

Altering our path for those still preparing erased our progress.

The more progress preserved, the more progress perpetuated.

Time was dethroned as dictator of our direction; our compass pointed freely to collective cohesion. I would confirm my Possible knew that as well. The partnership of Possibles required both to be self-aware in near totality, or openly expressing an educational interest. If student and teacher were not both recognized as educators, neither grew. Those who taught in purity gained the regard of those respecting wisdom and the pursuit. Was judging others by their potential instead of their practices not a sign of having much to learn? Would that not place us at the mercy of another's ignorance? I surrounded myself with those enthusiastic to learn from each other, and my life radically transformed shortly after. My syzygy assisted my ascension or was excluded from my experience, and I would be treated in kind, respectfully. I could paint the town red with plenty of friends already—a saying I always enjoyed for how it illustrated the red energy of our

Root Chakra running wild. My favorite of those idioms was *purple haze*. Purple was the color of the Third Eye Chakra, if it was hazy then so were our thoughts. Didn't the Third Eye govern our ability to grasp our surroundings? The lens of our mind was periscopic. When balanced we connected the dots, when unbalanced we connected nothing and thought we did. My last Possible was now one of my closest friends, easily the best man in my wedding were it to happen tomorrow. Fortunately, these meetings weren't strictly based on romantic potentiality. My cousin could be a frequency presenting mutual benefit and an opportunity to ascend.

It wasn't one of those meetings though.

Our date wasn't until nine-thirty and they wanted to do coffee. I didn't want to do coffee, and I should have just said that but I did not. My problem with speaking up for myself was more a problem of speaking my mind. Symptoms of unresolved fear swore us to secrecy. It displayed itself in various ways and that was one of them. Fear stopped us from honoring ourselves, and I would need to understand what that part of the AeforeA meant for me before becoming a corentice. I would like to say I

hoped to arrive at that point in my life sooner, and I did, but I also didn't. There were times we regressed in order to relearn. Meditating and working with energy worked so well for me I thought I outgrew it.

Our lungs didn't outgrow oxygen.

I was almost back to the point where what others thought of what worked for me changed nothing. Why would adults argue over opinions? Honoring our word made us deserving of all we found exciting. I was almost thinking like a billionaire.

Clear stigmas still surrounded spiritual practices claiming physical effects, and the stigma spoke loudly to our arrogance. Why would the Earth not naturally carry the ingredients to aid what was born from it? I marveled at the ease seen in life once the veil was dissolved.

Life was easy by design. The unwise conditioned us to believe otherwise.

A global cycle was started we were still figuring out how to replace. I understood what the problem was—if there was such a thing—and most other thorough-minded individuals did as well. It was energy work; broader alchemy.

Energy moved when it was refocused.

Stopping the flow of energy was never an option at our disposal. Energy couldn't be destroyed, what made us think it could be halted? When energy was refocused there was change, so refocus was how we changed cycles. Only the past was absolute. The future and present evolved simultaneously.

***

Getting especially high before an introduction to someone new was something I did. For years I thought I was just shy, but it was deeper than I knew. Whether it was a cookie or a carrot, what we ingested altered us physically, mentally, and spiritually. The energy of environments and individuals were ingested also. Some were made more sensitive to the absorption while some did it to themselves, but it was what that sensitivity represented which eluded most. We were eternally objects of involuntary osmosis. What if one of the voices heard by the schizophrenic wasn't their own? The power of the mind was still in the experimental stages, where more knowledge of it meant more knowledge of

everything—and vice versa. The creation of the Energetic Spectral Frequency Correspondence (ESFC) helped tremendously. It organized the parallels between the varying interpretations of energetic measurement and made it accessible in one space. Chakras crossed with Solfeggio, Qi crossed with Prana; Buddhist, Hindu, Daoist, Aeonilist, Scientist, Christian, Jew, Gentile. A previously disjointed concept gained clarity. It was my Throat Chakra and frequency 741 that was out of balance and had been. The Throat Chakra was also the vibration I was currently most aligned with, my Home Frequency. I felt like it may change over time, but I was still exploring further. The energy center and corresponding part of my mind was opened by cannabis and alcohol, as other elements did for other areas. There was a measurable science, it wasn't illusion and parlor tricks. What "charging" a crystal actually meant confused me until the ESFC. Light, heat, and sound were sources of energy, the basis of suggesting to leave crystals in sunlight, moonlight, sound-baths, or to simply sleep with them. Those were all processes transferring heat, light, or sound into the object—energy—which the user would theoretically interact with as it was released. Wrapping crystallized stone in a conductive metal then amplified the frequency with the addition. I charged my copper-wrapped crystals when I polished them. Rubbing the stone and metal on a cleaning cloth built enough friction to feel the heat against my skin. Science. The question of the spiritual and metaphysical as placebo was also interesting. The Placebo Effect was one of the most definitive. It proved the power of the mind as well as the unseen. Didn't we all long to create in three-dimensional space without lifting a finger? How was the mastery of tricking our minds into radical action not a superpower? Was the ability to mentally separate from ourselves in order to encourage and direct ourselves not extraordinary?

> The human mind, barbarous and persuadable, was a wonder of the universe.

Perhaps being filled with wonder was also how we lived as one.

Artist: Outkast

Song: Vibrate Higher

Album: Speakerboxxx/The Love Below

"Every boy and girl, woman to man/ When you feel you done about the best you can/

Vibraaatttte/ Vibrate hiiigghhheeer."

She was late and the station was crowded. It wasn't the nineties. Being tardy wasn't cool it was irresponsible. Everyone knew when they were going to be late, they just decided how much respect and responsibility they felt like exercising. We didn't forget to be considerate, we remembered to do what we wanted. I couldn't be too mad at that. Were we obligated to be who we were for anyone outside ourselves? If we weren't doing what we desired, how did we know who we were? Whether momentarily or permanently, we viewed ourselves as part of a whole or part of nothing. Our perspective was demonstrated through our actions. Fifteen minutes late, no text, no call. Maybe she wasn't a Possible, or even one inclined to arrive when she agreed to. Ghosting would probably never be an action of the past. Ironically, ghosting would probably never disappear. Nevertheless, I turned into a ghost if they didn't show up in the next ten minutes.

Wasting time only compounded wasted energy.

Certain circumstances proved pessimism was a waste as well, like readying ourselves to leave a location before we usually would, only for the tardy person we're waiting for to stroll along simultaneously. Not only that, but strolling and clearly not taking the process seriously. She wasn't dressed for a date, she was dressed for...the gym. The twenty-four hour gym where we could waltz in looking our sloppiest during the dead hours between midnight and four in the morning. We scarred each other in romantic relationships by choosing not to communicate. External relationships were optional. The undertaking of understanding ourselves was already more than enough work for most of us. She started talking before I could stand up to greet her.

"So, where are you from?"

"Hello."

"Are we doing that?"

"What? Being civil?"

I laughed. God, if I wasn't high the interaction would be a headhunting contest. Her tone was jaded green, and impatiently yellow.

"Sure. Hello, how are you?"

"Fuck, not so good actually. I was supposed to meet someone here for a thing. Don't you hate when people are late?"

"We only hate from unexamined experiences. From what I understand."

Her posture straightened like a flower finding the sun, while her hands rested behind her back like petals. I cleared my throat and stood, resting my hands the same as she. I overstepped, and she called me out on it with an elegant reminder. My ego was still decaying. I replied humbly.

"As always."

She nodded and payed me a generous courtesy.

"I'm from Chicago—by the way."

"Really?"

She thought about it.

"Don't believe me?"

It wasn't that, something just didn't match. Her hair was in two Dutch braids ending together in

173

a ponytail, and the frames of her black sunglasses were shaped like cat eyes. She was smart enough to wear them like I did—the sunglasses; mine were aviators. The eyes betrayed us all. Copper rings were on every other one of her fingers plus her thumb, each with a different crystal attached. Her style raised curiosity with a trail of footprints leading around corners cloaked in daggers, saying nothing regarding where she was from. By the time she was at the "go" in Chicago, her head was in a sweet spot where I could see her eyes lingering too long at something distant.

Betrayal couldn't hide itself if we knew where to look.

Because of that my questions multiplied.

"Born and raised?"

"Oh, no. And I actually live just outside the city."

"Okay, nice. Where at?"

The smirk appearing on her face laughed internally to a joke it wouldn't share, but at least it pushed her cheeks up into soft circles under her eyes.

"Have you been to central Illinois?"

"I've never been to anywhere in Illinois."

"Well then, even if I told you, you wouldn't know where I was born, raised, or lived, would you?"

It was a challenge, which made sense because everything about her was. She was like a Rubik's Cube with a figure molded by the hammer and chisel of da Vinci. However, it was that damn smirk and the glimpse of her eye holding passion hostage which clung to me unwaveringly. I tested the waters.

"Afraid I'd drop by for a visit?"

"You don't know me, but Fear happens to be my middle name."

"Your parents should be happy you didn't murder them in their sleep for that."

Her lips twisted with confusion as she gently itched the back of her neck.

"They let me pick it out."

All I could do was chuckle; she was funny and rightfully proud. I swear I could see her eyes through those sunglasses—I knew I could. I couldn't tell which they wanted more, to see or be seen. She let a small smile slip free for a second, running her fingers around her ponytail like it was a dance. Whether she was doing so purposefully or not, she was a natural magician. Subtle movements sent invitations deserving of pressed seals of red, melted wax. I didn't know where I was being invited and I didn't care. I forgot about her being late. I really needed to do better, but she also knew the Frailty of Hate[21] and how to present it. Each interaction with each other or our environment was an experiment, and our brains subconsciously recorded the data. Our minds then waited patiently for us to use what was accumulated.

Wisdom was the outcome of choosing to examine the patterns in our experience, then creating an avenue to comprehend them thoroughly.

Only once we pursued wisdom did we have anything worth saying, and only once we were asked was it said. I needed someone who knew enough to know the value they brought to an interaction, while knowing everything around us imparted everything needed. Sitting with that knowledge brought the warmth of wiser ways, and I was okay if others found that unimportant. I wouldn't pay to convince someone of what they could find out was true if they tried.

The excess energy to pull another up to a plateau most clawed their way through conquering was held by few.

Clawing our way up the cliffside was necessary for each of us, we found ourselves there if we chose to. Not everyone did. I needed someone who was found, and I wasn't going to forcefully attempt to elevate anyone spiritually. That was colonization. I continued to converse.

"And your twenty-one, right?"

"Four."

"You're *forty-one*?"

"Huh? No, I mean—"

---

[21] The Frailty of Hate: hatred arises from unexamined experiences, increasing and perpetuating regressive behavior. (see page 263).

"I'm kidding."

"Right. Age matters to you, then?"

"Maturity does."

"Doesn't it to all of us?"

"Does it?"

"Hm. Yeah, that makes sense.

She touched the palm of her hand to the top her head, then reached back with both hands and pulled her hoods up. She wore two hoodies, one smaller than the other and cut above her naval. The second one was longer and went down to her knees, with a larger hood than the crop. My hood was also on and covered down to the top of my sunglasses. She zipped her larger one down just far enough to show the choker she was wearing, a single orange-red stone wrapped in copper. I pointed.

"What's your pendant?"

She glanced down and held it.

"Oh, it's uh, an opal."

"Does it glow?"

"Yeah, it gets highlighter-orange at the right angle."

"Very, very nice."

"Thank you, thank you."

She smiled and bowed before shoving her hands into her hoodie pockets. The crystals we wore closest to the throat would most directly effect that chakra. I was interested.

"Has it helped?"

Her right hand left her pocket and held the stone again.

"I feel it has."

"Some more creative language?"

"Hmm…"

As she thought, her hoodie zipper was lowered until each side went their separate ways. I assumed we were both wearing all black, but it was nice to confirm. An Aesheam[22] mala was wrapped around each of her wrists just like mine.

Laying over her chest and down to her stomach was another longer necklace resembling a rosary. It was two Aesheam twisted together with one crystal at the bottom of each. I interrupted her thought and pointed again.

"That's called a, uh…"

"Aenheam. Interesting you have the malas but don't know what these are."

"I've seen people call it different names. Don't be judging me."

She smiled and shook her head playfully.

"I should ask you your thoughts on that.

"But do you care?"

"Would you be offended if I didn't?"

"Only if you pretended you were."

She shifted her weight to her left foot and held her Aenheam with both hands.

"And you're thirty-four?"

"Yeah."

"Getting old, no?"

"Oh, so age matters to—"

---

22 Aesheam (ee-shem): A mala bracelet or necklace which is handmade by the owner exclusively. 108 knots are tied into a single cotton cord, with the 108th knot being tied around a small crystal of the owners choosing, wrapped in a material of the owners choosing. The last knot may also simply be tied with the free ends of the cord to close it. This follows in the similar tradition of Buddhist and Hindu malas due to the universal numeric significance—nine as the highest single digit. The creation of the mala is a meditative practice for the creator, focused meditation. It is recommended the mala is created in a peaceful atmosphere where the creator is able to reflect on whatever necessary, while their body is occupied with a simple and repetitive task. The importance of the task is momentum. Momentum is the fuel of creation. The fuel of creation is the fuel of life. Creating an Aesheam is a way for one to practice divine procedure. One connection built on top another. It was worn as a divine reminder.

"I'm kidding."

She winked at me. I nodded and muted most of my smile.

"Well played."

I golf-clapped as celebration of her execution. She might be chill, but most were when you first met them—even if they showed up late. She looked around at the station and scanned-over a few people as they passed by. It was obvious even with her eyes shaded; she wasn't subtle. She brought her attention back to me.

"So, what's up? Think we're doing this?"

"What?"

She rolled her eyes and smiled too widely.

"I can't tell if you're joking."

"Are we *supposed* to be doing something?"

"Don't you wanna know the obvious shit like my signs, and what I'm called to do, and what my diet is, and—"

"Goddamn—okay—I get it. Can we not...have a conversation? Like, were you forced to come here?"

Her, and a heavy attitude I didn't foresee, firmly stepped a foot closer to me.

"Was I forced—wow. I'm, uh, sick of my fucking life and dealing with the same shit day after day. That's what forced me. Do you know how many people I've had to watch get handed *everything*? You don't. I deserve better. I'm meant for better and I'm sick of wasting my time, so, I'm changing that. And this can help me. Maybe you. Maybe someone else. I don't have time for small talk. What'd I miss?"

I knew a lot of people claiming they liked surprises, however none who explained why. I responded.

"No one deserves better. No one deserves anything.

That's why we have so much to be grateful for. Your word choice is interesting."

She folded her hands in front her by her waist and I duplicated. Most of the station's crowd cleared-out, so there would probably be a lull before the next influx of bodies. It couldn't have been 10:30 a.m. yet. My unnamed counterpart wanted to know something about me.

> "Is this what you do? Needlessly correct people?"

> "Do you have something against education?"

> "Is that a question? Aren't you like a fucking piano teacher or something? And you think you can *school* me?"

> "I love teaching piano— smart-ass. And that would depend, again, whether or not you had something against education."

> "I don't, which is why I would willfully forget anything I even *thought* that you taught me."

> "Cool. Then there's no real reason for us to continue communicating then, is there?"

> "If you're serious about why you're here then we can fight right now. Again, *I* don't have time to waste."

What she referred to was an online-trend in conscious spaces, and too many were saying it worked. Public combat, like the gladiator matches of antiquity, uniquely stimulated us to release something instilled via societal conditioning. Something buried. People were experimenting with the method and reporting they were getting where they wanted to be faster than imagined. It made sense. On our Journey of Ascension we all experienced crucifixions. Arranging a fight in public would just be doing so publicly, an attempt to shock the self into alignment. After the fight it was supposed to be over —all of it—but it never was. It was messy, which was why it wasn't anyone's first choice unless they were desperate. Very. I was not. At all. Getting hurt in a real way was part of it.

I didn't like games based on the game of the life. I played with mine sparingly.

I stepped back and folded my arms behind me. She scoffed.

> "Wow. I mean—oh, my god."

She tilted her head almost horizontally and looked me up and down.

"I actually didn't hate this—the…choice of attire."

She winked again before resuming.

"But *now* I get it. You put the look together so well because—"

"Christ. *Please* say over-compensating. Pretty-mother-fucking-please."

"Perfect—you already know. Saves us from the awkward reveal."

I rubbed my forehead while chuckling. The retelling of an epic was nearly as good as reliving it, and I couldn't wait to share with anyone who would listen. My turn.

"Okay, and let me guess, I'm over-compensating for my dick size which you think defines me in some deep, meaningful way, right?"

"Your…"

She laughed with her mouth closed while her shoulders laughed with her.

"Comedy. But, what's that saying? It's, uh, something about coaches…coaches and playing—yes. Coaches wish they played the game as well as they taught it. I think that's it—close enough anyways. I don't know—or care—if your dick's small. I'm guessing it's your creativity, originality, and talent level that needs an upgrade."

Ascension was the cyclical journey of walking deeper in our divinity. The journey took longer for many of us because we chose to act out of alignment to satisfy requests from the ego. The ego wasn't bad or wrong. The ego thought of the present only and of itself only. Without the ego we would be dead. The ego yelled to save ourselves because it was too valuable to die, and by extension so were we. Without the ego we also lived in unending contentment. I would ponder the parallel perspectives later; the philosophy could wait.

A fear of loss was a fear of gain.

I knew when a fight was being picked as casually as a chocolate bar in a dollar store checkout line. I didn't care though. The drawback of loving to teach was loving to teach even when we shouldn't.

"Bitch, I don't know who the fuck you—"

Slapped before I could finish. Loud too. The rings made a difference, and their chime was audible. I didn't have to look to know people were watching and waiting to see what happened next. The drama wasn't just on screen, it was always showtime somewhere. The momentum was now with my anxious opponent.

"Nope! Couldn't the fuck be talking to me! Not when you ain't even doing shit for me?! Who the fuck are you, anyway?!"

Her hand darted towards my sunglasses. She made contact, but I grabbed her wrist before she followed-through, squeezed, then pulled her arm diagonally down to my right. She was noisy for no reason.

"Uhhhaaaahhhh!"

A group of three police officers twenty or thirty feet away slowly turned their heads. They looked over their shoulders first and then turned completely around. The im-Possible tripped over my foot, and was aiming to head-butt the concrete step I was sitting on earlier, when I grabbed both her hoods and yanked back. Her right wrist was still in

my right hand, so she spun weird, couldn't balance, and dropped her phone when she landed on her left side. More being loud.

"What the fuck! Let me go, psycho! Ugh!"

She kept pulling to get out of my grip, so I let go and she slammed her wrist on the floor.

"OW!"

I fixed my glasses and looked through them to check on the cops. The outburst was enough to rouse one's interest. They didn't move, just watched. I crouched down next to her and used my inside voice.

"Can you get off the ground? We *both* look dumb."

"*You* look the fuck dumb! Get away from me!"

"Just *get up*. Fucking cops are everywhere, bro."

"I said get the fuck *away from me!!*"

Alternating feet sprung towards me at random, I batted them away, then stood up with my hands raised chest-high. The authorities joined the game.

"Miss, are you okay over there?"

"Yeah, c'mon, guys—what's going on?"

I couldn't be mad at the police, they would've looked ridiculous for not saying anything. She was on the floor quiet so I spoke.

"Yup, we're good. Thank you, thank you so much."

I addressed her sternly.

"Stay on the goddamn ground, then. Don't care. Have fun with that shit life your so desperate to change or whatever. "

"I hate you."

Hate. I shook my head; I was warned about people like her.

Those who hated in haste found life hard to love.

I replied.

"Right. Good luck with that too."

We transmitted energy to others driving them away from us but closer to themselves. Wonder lived in everything. I turned to head for the exit; I wasn't even mad. The integration of new frequencies into our field was trial and error. Sometimes they didn't work, other times they did. It was odd how we harbored anger at probability. Did we understand the variables we perceived weren't the only ones of consequence? What exactly did we think we were owed and where was it coming from? What we planned, calculated, and coordinated was one cog in a system of one billion. Nothing was owed to us, giving us everything to be grateful for.[23] Literal contractual obligations aside, there were no exemptions. Family, friends, romantic partners —we didn't owe them and they didn't owe us. No one needed a reason not to do something. No one needed a reason to say no, and there wasn't anything required to be explained or justified. Part of us didn't return when we gave more of ourselves than we kept. Expenditure was required for every activity down to the smallest.[24] Our level of health and energy dictated how experiences were interpreted. Eating required energy from our bodies to break down food,

---

[23] General Ownership Phenomenon: (see page 92).

[24] Base Barter Principle: (see page 142).

which was why eating could be physically exhausting. Our perspective changed under fatigue. The more sensitive we were to our energy, the more wisely and effectively it was utilized. A phone call required energy. A recharge was needed to restore us to one hundred percent for another interaction. Otherwise, we lived in confusion wondering why we lived inconsistently, capturing and losing ourselves in a race with neither a winner nor a finish line. How many times have we called someone and said "I'm so glad you picked up. I really need to talk." We often didn't ask or offer a choice. The unintentional removal of the optional nature from our exchanges slowly eroded our relationships in near untraceable ways. Another level existed one degree deeper, wearing a patient smile living on the slow waves of a watchful heartbeat. Nothing owed us anything. Not the bottle cap falling on the floor top-side-down, or our sandwich *almost* getting nudged off the table, or a coin toss falling heads up to match our wager. We weren't owed anything going our way. Ever. The volume of daily grace we received and overlooked like it was an expired gallon of milk was enough to turn one sour.

I was maybe five steps away from the Possible when I was shoved hard in my back. My footing was quickly lost in unfamiliar territory, and I fell on my chest like a mattress tipping over. The wind was knocked out of me. I felt the amethyst pendant I was wearing shatter. I was fighting off the creeping, murky lava moving from the corners of my eyes to the center. I couldn't blackout right now in the middle of Union Station. On the floor. But I guess when we blacked-out the floor was usually the destination of choice. I felt like my arm fell asleep, but before it did, it sang a hypnotic lullaby to the rest of body too soothing to be ignored. Footsteps ran past me, then ones sounding the same going back in the same direction. I think. The ones who needed to stay usually ran, but they would end up in the same places they ran from.

Nothing lost was needed to move forward.

I got up and found her ID a few feet down from where I face-planted. She didn't have a purse, so I guessed it fell out of her pocket when she fell to the floor. Her name was Lamor Andrews, I was sore, and I understood why I was where I was. I walked the long way out so I could avoid the cops, who graciously pretended like they saw nothing. How we lived was based on how those lived before us. From Adam and Eve in the Garden eating from the tree of good and evil, to Jesus and Mary when he turned water to wine. Motivation wasn't always an encouraging speech delivered by a distinguished actor. Holy books all over the world recorded the same; the pattern had nothing to do with gender. The feminine and masculine grandly complimented the other both internally and externally. The masculine energy dove into black holes and returned with lost light when walking divinely. The feminine energy pushed the masculine to transformationally walk in their divine vibration where their feet would drag til knees were buried. The colloquial saying, "Behind every great man is a great woman," stemmed from the same expression of feminine and masculine energetic dispositions, not gender. In my case I was pushed literally, which I accepted over no push at all. Nothing we needed to feel whole came from another person. However, if we asked for what we couldn't yet provide, it came how it could until we were where we needed to be. Probable bruised hip aside, I didn't regret how my morning started. Regret was only

felt when we dishonored ourselves. Regret was what stapled us with guilt, and sin, and shame. Honoring others came with honoring ourselves because we were mirrors. The rules we followed could always be changed. Self-awareness was the beginning, self-destruction was the pledge to commit.

The optimal treatment of others, and ourselves, was contingent on first understanding the difference between what we were aligned with and what we were used to.

Speaking and acting in ways, which only felt one hundred percent right, could be easier said than done, easier done than believed, yet was always perfectly necessary. Everything I came with was still with me, I didn't get arrested, and although I was favoring my right side, I could still walk. I was practicing replacing the word winning with another one—learning. Winning was a survival instinct. Those who searched for competition already lost, but they would learn.
As always.

II LIGN

TO THE PATHS
WE CROSS AGAIN

I ran until I got to the parking lot across the street. Two charter buses were parked preparing to take passengers out of state, and the crowd was large enough to disappear into. Step one was getting away from the station and out of sight, just in case that asshole was mad enough about the blah-blah to play victim. I probably would have been. The green bus on the right had a paper sign taped inside the front windshield. Handwritten in black marker on a white, regulation-size piece of printer paper, were the words "Vegas Bebe!" Why not? Vegas was amazing. The good times in Vegas were so good, I ended up moving to LA.

The other bus waited for their driver; the driver waited for his coffee from the taco truck about twenty feet away. A third bus pulled into the small parking lot with a scrolling sign displaying South Dakota one letter at a time. It was all black with black tinted windows, and the silver stripe going down the side looked like superheroes could surf it. The bus to Vegas was the standard white and green with lightly-patterned grey curtains. The appearance of the vehicle can differ drastically from its destination. Levels of decadence still swam beyond the boundaries of monetary affairs. Experiences still existed exceeding all offers to the point of insult. Freely gifted thanks-givings carried heavy price-tags left undisturbed. Exploring our passions was paramount at a time when how we aided others' survival directly effected our own. Did the extinction of the barter system extinguish the socio-economic necessity of self-discovery? Entire currencies existed unimpressed by decimal points, and that was problematic for those acting in ignorance in positions of large-scale leadership. God forbid we moved forward by looking back. No intangible, untransferable funds would get me onto a bus, but they could grant audience or access to people and places rubber wheels didn't. What could

I exchange for shade? The Sun was out, and the heat was bolder than usual for how early in the morning it was. Ironically, I drove myself from Boston, to live in LA, to stand in front of a bus for Vegas. What a trip.

A woman stood to my right, a few steps from the sidewalk, wearing thick, elliptically shaped sunglasses with white frames. The blue, canvas shopping bag on her right shoulder went down to her knee, and the white one in her left hand almost touched the ground. Her right eye was covered by a black eye-patch, with her head under an ill-fitting, red and black, one-braid-in-the-back wig. Aside from the wig and eye-patch, the woman wore plain, slightly baggy, straight-legged blue jeans. Her brown, low-top sneakers used to be pink, and her black tank-top fit closely around the bulge of her stomach hanging over her pants. An elderly Mexican couple waddled up the sidewalk like a pair of penguins, standing a few feet behind the woman who was half-way through a cigarette. The two attempted to share a beverage, but the man couldn't gain leverage to lift the lid off the styrofoam cup. A soft backhand from the woman hit his forearm, and she pointed at the drink which was handed to her without objection. Her thin thumbs, in equally thin, fuchsia-colored gloves, pushed up on the lid and cracked half off. A few drops of what resembled hot chocolate dove from the cup, splashing to the ground near the other woman's foot—the one with the eye-patch. Eye-patch whipped her head around and looked at the ground, then to the couple, then smiled tenderly before turning back to face the street. She looked back over her shoulder at the couple and smiled again, faced the street, then turned back to them once more. It was dizzying to watch. Eye-patch said hello by waving like she found love-at-first-sight on day one of preschool.

"Hey, y'all look happy. Are y'all happy?"

The man looked at the woman, and she said something to him in Spanish before replying to Eye-patch in Spanglish.

"Oh, si, jes. Thank you."

The woman nodded and smiled politely at Eye-patch and handed the cup to the man. It was clear she didn't speak much English, but Eye-patch continued as if they were old friends catching up in the waiting area of a hair salon.

How did we ignore those we interacted with while in the process?

"That's cool y'all, that's real cool. I'm single, you know? Going through a break-up, or whatever. This guy I liked just left me here. Can you believe that shit?! Excuse my language, y'all—sorry."

Eye-patch tapped the ash from her cigarette, took a drag, and went right back into it.

"Y'all stay together. Don't date. Most don't know how to act once you show them you like them.

He left me right at this damn corner. We get in a fight, and he just kicks me out the car and takes off! Seriously. And I'm the one that fixed the breaks on that motherf...on the car, you know? But he ain't want love, he only wanted what I could do for him. Y'all wouldn't even know nothing about that, huh? I spend everything I got to help him and now I'm the one left out here? Man, fuck LA. I'm going back to Vegas.

Excuse my language, y'all—sorry."

It was called the city of angels, baby, not the city of love. I heard people from parts of Bakersfield sounded like they could be from the south; I wasn't expecting Vegas to be her final destination of choice with her twang. Then again, Vegas was for everyone.

A ten minute delay in departure time was yelled towards the two buses from the taco truck. Those grumbling to themselves about the setback clearly didn't see the mutual benefit. I would always wait happily while the pilot of my motor-carriage adjusted their caffeine level for maximum cockpit alertness. The two hoodies I was wearing made more sense when I left the house, but they were way too much now. I would leave in a minute anyway; I tried to think about something other than how hot I was getting. On the tips of my toes I looked to the other side of the crowd where no wandering police officers were visible. Now was usually as good of a time to leave as any, but then I started thinking about the mess inside with what's-his-face.

Work needed to be completed, by myself, but also by all of us. More accurate descriptions were created, but it was the old terms we used requiring clarity. Most of them were straightforward. Sin and Karma were two different words describing the same cycle, and neither was related to a mysterious universal law of good and evil. The characters of Good and Evil were supposed to motivate us, not define us. Karma and Sin described living in self-misalignment. Karma was created. Our karma was based on what we believed was worthy of reward or punishment. How often was it asked why bad things avoided bad people? The amount of information we encountered outnumbered our numbers, yet we self-righteously assumed we understood the purpose and connection of each breathing puzzle piece. Weren't all critical components characterized by imperceptible movement? The assumption any knowledge we possessed would remain irrevocable was unsupported. Knowledge was a form of energy. Energy required a framework to be utilized for any formulation. Energy existing outside of a framework was chaotic. For thousands of years the words karma, sin, and crime, globally agreed on unclear speculative definitions. Karma described perceived accountability, which was interesting because proximity mattered. Holding hands with the guilty held us to sharing their

fate. Our karma may be a car accident, in which case we should drive alone. Stifling our perspective wouldn't expand it.

> Good and evil were one hundred percent subjective, meaning the power associated with them was the same.

I wished I was narcissistic enough not to feel bad about the Union Station thing, but I wasn't. I started fasting every other day a couple months ago and it helped painfully. Fasting fed our minds before our bodies. How deeply did that connection go? What about those who involuntarily went without meals for extended stretches of time? Did they inadvertently overstimulate their own minds? Was it not only what we ate but if we ate at all? The excitedly swollen appetite of my deconditioning opened my eyes to my own faults abrasively. My appointment with karma was made as soon as I chose to listen to the voice guiding me. It was the man at the front desk with the silver hair, matching beard, and eyes sharper than an iron tongue. God had one voice but we had two ears. The two sides of the brain interpreted the world differently; the "angelic" and the "demonic", the conceptual and the mechanic, the right and the left, the above and below. Aeonaes. Where was there ever contention? Didn't we see what creation saw once we saw through opposition? Dichotomy existed without alternative and we navigated or floated aimlessly. Either choice was okay and with their own unique results. An emotional response, to others making decisions we would not, signified a personal area out of alignment. How could we be bothered when we understood necessity? What were we mad about?

In Buddhism it was The Wheel, the observable motion of universal nature. The Wheel was directed by necessity, and how The Wheel proceeded in its direction was directed by decision. The Wheel's velocity changed based on choices, enabling Existants[25] like humanity to play a contributing role. Realizing our desired outcome while observing the Nature of Necessity was how we communed cosmically. Survival was the only language all life spoke fluently. First we survived, then we lived. Listening deliberately granted access to Necessity's instruction of

ascension or intensification. Growth wasn't always becoming something else, sometimes it was becoming something more. Our depth of vision was determined by our diligence (s&) we saw what we looked for.[26] Apparently I was looking for a fight, unable to see an option where I avoided having to hide my face from searchlights. Our enemies weren't our only adversaries.

Some battles were fought to remind us war was fought first.

I loitered with the group of travelers until the bus driver closed the luggage door on the side of the vehicle.

> "Miss, I still gotta scan your ticket. Or do you got one of the paper ones?"

I wasn't paying attention; I could have left five to ten minutes ago. I answered the question I shouldn't have been there to be asked.

> "Huh? Oh, no, I'm leaving. Thank you, though."

> "So, uh…"

---

[25] Existants: (see page 95).

[26] A sentence containing an *aeonaes*, Aeonilist punctuation (see page 124).

He shrugged, then saved himself the trouble.

"…okay, cool."

The fingers on his right hand formed the peace sign, he turned around, and tapped the side of the bus twice before stepping up the stairs and in. I watched it drive away and then walked to the corner to wait for the 60. It was going to be a long ride back to Long Beach.

***

I didn't live the SoCal life movies were made about. The postcards and TV advertisements were recorded somewhere I didn't have directions to. I hadn't been discovered nor was I Homeless In LA. I was just a girl with a goddamn dream. I didn't act, sing, dance, or do sex-work. Nothing against those majors, they were just oversaturated and over-stressed, and I didn't have the stamina. A cousin of mine sold her sexual services for a few months and paid her student loans off last summer. And mine. The environment was what stopped her, otherwise she would have seen how high the money could stack before her mind was lost. Getting under every kind of influence was needed to get through a weekend of seeing clients at a

hotel. The most she saw in a day was twelve; she remembered five. A plane ticket to Fiji was promptly purchased after the loans were settled, and the next time I saw her was a month later. I would have killed to go to Fiji, but my cousin almost did the same. Her life was a movie I would consider paying the twenty dollars to see in theaters, but I couldn't be the star.

Some rewards I wouldn't chance reaping, to ensure no chance of reaping the grim.

The bus arrived, I entered and walked to the back, right-corner, tripped, and fell into a dreamless sleep. Almost two hours later I woke up four stops before mine —which I loved. Falling asleep one place and waking up in another was what I imagined time traveling was like. The ten minute walk down Market to the building where I rented my room felt like twenty. The darker it was, the slower time felt like it moved. Every third or fourth streetlight was broken like the scene found in every third or fourth horror movie from the 1980s. The landlord lived in the space across from my room, and I say "space" because calling it a room would be like calling my asshole an astronaut. Maybe in time, but she still needed·to clock more flight hours and raise the consistency of her antigravity maneuvers. The landlord and the girl stacked two dressers on top of each other creating one wall, the second was a ten foot, beige, floor-to-ceiling office cabinet. The thing looked uncomfortably wedged between the ceiling and the faded-brown laminate floors. Parallel to the wall opposite my room, out to about eleven feet into the center of the common area, the thing stood fossilized. I ignored it when I moved in because I needed somewhere to live quickly, and bullshittingly enough, not much has changed for me there yet. The common area also wasn't much of one, it was half landlord storage space, half "bedroom". The building was a one-story daycare center which the landlord, Jeremiah, converted into an apartment building. He said he personally filed for the property to be commercially rezoned, but I doubted it.

Doing the bare minimum returned the same.

Everything was gross, but it was cheap, the utilities were included, and I was finally out of Huntington Beach. My speed-walk was incorporated for the duration of my travels, as the one thing on my mind was

undressing and showering. Technically, two things. I didn't know if I was sweating a lot but I felt like I was, and the stickiness from the fight clung to me like someone I was ready to break-up with. Feeling sticky sometimes was pretty good, it was proof we interacted with something which could have stuck around. It was proof some sense of stability still existed.

As I walked into the building, echoing off the walls, was the recycled laughter of a prerecorded studio audience. The landlord's girlfriend never left the house, and in my humble opinion she...well, I was going to say she lacked any visible importance. I could be nicer. Nevertheless, the girl kept Jeremiah's ball-sack wrapped around her waist like a championship wrestling belt. The only thing worse than a woman being a bitch to another woman, was that bitchy-bitch also being a lazy one. I squeezed my keys so they stayed silent while I walked in. After the kitchen, the laundry-dryer stack, and the bathroom, was my bedroom. I got in, locked the door, and immediately started peeling off my hoodies like I hated them, but stopped. A tarot reader told me to sage my myself more and it made sense. I didn't just do something because someone told me, Sydian was right about a lot—the tarot reader. Options in my life I wouldn't have seen myself, or would've taken me much longer to uncover, were interpreted and shared with me. I didn't know much about the workings of tarot, but I didn't hate it. Sydian did what they were supposed to very well. Two mantras they shared with me introduced me to the clear power of words. The first, "My internal voice speaks only eternal wisdom and divine guidance. I am listening closely," was to help me trust myself. The second, "I am unable to be distracted by erroneous thoughts. The quickest path to my peace and prosperity in unimaginable and overwhelming abundance is clear. I am pulled towards it all-ways," was to assist my focus and growth. Sydian also told me my relationships would unfold how I wanted—"How I wanted," that's all they said. It was a message as powerful as clear intention.

I started wearing all black two months ago and didn't feel the need to change. The black was worn purposefully. Initially I didn't know why I was drawn to the achromatic, but after coming out of meditation a few weeks ago it was clearer. I remembered watching a guru online speak about wearing all black, and he highlighted the absorption factor.

Black reflected no light which meant it reflected no energy. All was absorbed. I was in a place in my journey where absorption made perfect sense, and I was glad I heard what was shared with me. The sage was suggested to cleanse myself of the access energy bound to linger. Whether or not a tarot reader knew what they were talking about was irrelevant. Guidance did not need to understand its utility, the guided did. A message to protect ourselves may be delivered by whom we needed protecting from, or delivered only so its application was contemplated. What was heard on our path which shouldn't be?

How we listened was how we lived. What did we know that wasn't heard?

To ourselves, to others, to the silence, to the noise, to the universe, to our fellow aeons, all were worthy of our ear. A conversation began at humanity's awakening, and the same conversation was still taking place. Joseph Campbell coined it The Hero's Journey, and the film industry called it Save The Cat. There were reasons why the same story was repeatedly told in ancient civilizations across the world mathematically incapable of sharing cultures. It was why whether we studied Sumerian texts, The Tanakh, The Gospels, The Book of the Dead, The Dead Sea Scrolls, The Quran, The Bible, or the Ayurveda, if we knew what we were reading, the connection between them all were strands of one web. The Bible fascinated me most because it combined practices and wisdom from more cultures than realized or recognized. Or admitted to.

Couldn't we look to the stars and watch celestial paths spin the same as our own?

I was told the Druids understood and shared this information with whomever sought. The Cosmic Conversation was the only one, and together we were at the center. I desperately needed to understand that connection, which was why I was learning to shut up and listen.

I kept the hoodie on so I could cleanse it. I lit the bundle of dried leaves I kept on a shelf-thing I bought and built. All my witchy items were stashed there. I moved the sage around my head nine times, and did the same just below my waist. Aeonaes.

"Shit!"

The window should have already been opened. My landlord and his girlfriend were still...unaware of many things I was already acquainted with. An aluminum can sizzling with aerosols sprayed indoors as a deodorizer was healthier to them than burning incense, which was fine. What wasn't fine was if they smelled the sage it would be a whole problem I would have to deal with. I knew it was a power-move meant to minimize me, but as they were collaborators to my survival via our housing agreement, it was wise to be considerate. The window slid opened like it had a running start, smacking against the other end of the frame. I shook my head before using my sketchbook as a fan for the leftover smoke. The window would've been opened at some point regardless, it was hot outside and the building was always stuffier than flu season. It was terrible on the humid, rainy days when I was forced to sweat or drown. Today was another cookie-cutter SoCal afternoon: no clouds after eleven in the morning, with a light breeze cooling the shade. Another beautiful day I would be spending at work, but at least I wouldn't be—a TV laugh-track interrupted my thought as it exploded from outside my door.

"Hahahaha!"

"H-hey, Jerry. Can I borrow you're microwave? M-mines been on f-fire for two days"

"Hahahaha!"

Yeah, I would rather be at work where it was more peaceful, which pissed me off deeply enough to only notice occasionally. Between the loud-ass TV, the overly-ambitious attempts at trying to sing loudly-as-hell down the hall, and doors being slammed every ten to fifteen minutes, my apartment was a living migraine so excited about being a migraine it did summersaults. The door-slamming attacked my sanity with a grin since it was so easy to avoid. The lone entrance and exit was guarded by a metal screen door on hinges covered in rust. The hydraulics probably broke around the same time Elvis first heard Roy Hamilton sing. When the door slammed, it was metal on metal and sounded like a sledgehammer hitting a thin sheet of steel. The four other adults in the building could easily prevent the disruption with an extra second of patience ensuring the door closed silently. I was the only one who did though.

Excessive noise-making was a cry for attention, a deficiency of purpose and fulfillment expressed.

Those who disrupted were without direction. I needed out because I needed peace, and earlier at the station just...wasn't what I was trying to manifest. Before the sitcom concluded I showered, dried, dressed, and was ready. A beer ad played louder and more obnoxiously as I locked my door, heralding one last poem prior to my exit.

> "If you weren't taking advantage of your life...how *weren't* you being taken advantage of?"

A progressive rock guitar-bass riff rolled out an unmistakably cliché set of chords as a climax. No mercy. Thanks, TV, I'll go kill myself now. You win.

***

The carnival was already underway by the time I was supposed to clock-in. I wanted to quit working there. I couldn't quit tonight while still attracting the new opportunity I needed, and my savings account wasn't strong enough to carry me triumphantly out the door. The stupid part was it wasn't even a bad gig, the management was just all over the place. It was my second or third time freelancing with my art, and it was so close to being chill. A couple hundred a night on Fridays and Saturdays to do illustrations for five hours was cool. I set up at a restaurant in Long Beach right in the middle of everything on 3rd and Promenade downtown. The place before it did Mexican seafood; they did Italian seafood. The pier being a short walk away was probably the primary reason for the consistent nautical aesthetic. The food was on par with Italy's, which wasn't an easy accomplishment anywhere. It was an organic and house-made pasta restaurant on one side, and almost a patio coffee-bar on the other. Contemplating the two equally classy options while strolling though the main dining area, ceiling mirrors peering down overhead, I was in the sexiest place to ever employ me. I thought I would love freelancing more, but it wasn't as different as I thought. I didn't literally clock-in but I had a start-time, meaning I could also be reprimanded for tardiness. My arrival time wouldn't be an issue either without the management discrepancies. The drunk one with no life worked the most, which made the drinking make sense when I thought about it. I knew her name, and it was Lissy, and Anton was the other manager. He made it very clear he did not respond to Tony. When he wanted to flirt and talk before my shift, he didn't care what time I was ready; if he didn't it was a problem. He gave me some shrooms and two hits of acid for free maybe three times, then he started acting differently. My aunt told me something easy to remember before she departed dearly. Perhaps it was best we gave in advance for the favors we would surely have to repay. She didn't talk like that at all, so she said it more like, "Be nicer. You're probably gonna act like a bitch soon." I could tell Anton didn't have an aunt like mine. When I was feeling my best one night he accused me of being a drug addict; he was entitled to his view. According to him my energy was overwhelming and I needed to "lay off the drugs."

What we chose to share was opened for the audiences opinion.

Consciousness was a spectrum. The spiritual, magical, and scientific sought to understand the movement of energy used to encourage or undermine. Was what each did with the energy any business of any other?

Witnessing divinity still inspired apprehension. The unrecognized voice of a gift was met with closed ears fearful of a curse. Ignorance was the one-man-band of inquisitions, witch trials, and crusades. Messiahs were still murdered in the afternoon, convicted as common criminals for no longer carrying the cross of conditioning. The Christ of the Bible wasn't the only one crucified. I kept a low-profile around Anton after his comments. One of the easiest ways to protect our energy was by recognizing who it excited and only sharing it with those similar. He wasn't all wrong though, there was absolutely such a thing as too much. Thresholds were real and necessary. Overwhelming or being overwhelmed when sharing or receiving freely happened easily. Growth was a journey happening in seasons as all did.

The heat of Summer wouldn't suit us if we were dressed for the chill of Autumn.

It was the same with Lissy. She would definitely be upstairs, supposedly doing payroll, while sneaking shots and watching right-wing extremist news sources. That wasn't hearsay either, I was an eye witness to her buffoonery. She never talked about it or mentioned it, and was cordial with me to the point of being genuinely funny on occasion. That was perfect. I wasn't trying to work there for the rest of the month let alone the rest of my life. I understood the Necessity of All[27], but I wasn't offering support to bigots. I guess I wasn't at that point in my ascension yet. If I took a shot or a bump with Lissy, then I could start the show whenever I wanted. The shit she talked my face off about wasn't anything she'd remember saying by the end of the night—that made two of us. But again, if I wasn't doing what she wanted when she wanted it, a previous non-issue became one. I did get to say I worked at Elixae though, which I unapologetically brought up in conversation just so I could say the name in association with my own. Other than the management, I was over the atmosphere of intoxication. I drank at work just to speak the language of the drunk, which wasn't the reason I wanted to indulge. Alcohol was celebratory or therapeutic, not coffee. I would be working from home by

---

[27] Compasis: All possible is necessary. Nothing happens without all (see page 263).

the end of month because I knew why I needed to be, I just didn't know how. So, for another night I was at work. Lissy was present and doing exactly what she always did, exactly where she always was. The song and dance loved to sing a tune.

"Hey, hey!"

My enthusiastic greeting made her flinch, almost losing an ice cube from her rocks glass as a result.

"God! Getaway, devil!"

I came up behind her and gave her a hug over the top of her chair while she faced her desk. My arms were embraced warmly before feeling the sting of a swift, playful slap warming them literally. I almost yelped.

"Jesus! Uh, why?"

Lissy's giggle was giddy with drunken euphoria, and she swayed side-to-side while humming *Pop, Goes The Weasel* and holding my hug longer than wanted. Then she was curious.

"How are you, miss Lamor?

"I'm very well, and how about yourself?"

"Better, than, ever. Take a shot with me before another *bullshit*-ass Thursday?"

"Well, remember it is lanséa, now?

"That's right, that's right— my bad—still getting used to it. Ee-on-say. lanséa. I love that for you, girl."

"Thank you, thank you."

I curtsied, holding the end of my hoodie where the zippers connected in each hand while spreading my arms. Lissy was quick though.

"Look at you, cutie. We definitely got to pour up to that."

"Aww—well, uhh…"

I clicked on the backlight to my phone and checked the time. By twelve minutes I was late, and I smiled hard without separating my lips. I knew she was going to say it even though it was obvious how uncomfortable I was.

"I mean, you definitely don't have to…"

The sentence faded like the colors of dusk, and she watched bored by the death of its vibrance. The backlight on her phone was woken up also, as she too, checked the time. Go-go-gadget-carnival. What was it the oracular beer commercial was saying before I left the house? I guess we all had a turn to take one for the team. Or did we? Whatever.

> "No, no, you know I can't let you drink solo."

Lissy's right hand raised an almost-empty glass, holding it like the Statue of Liberty, while her left reached for the bottle she poured her same drink from.

> "You're good-people, lanséa."

It didn't take much for people to say we were good people, yet it always sounded sincere.

Perhaps being good-people required only an earnest attempt.

Naturally they could be lying to manipulate me into being their backup, or sincerely glad to have me joining them in their loneliness. I didn't know how much of a difference there really was. It was easy to be good to others, knowing the appropriate time was the trick. A shot glass, belonging downstairs with the rest of the glassware, was plucked from Lissy's desk drawer

like a ripe rose and filled a half-inch from the top. How she held it out for my retrieval almost made me think I forgot my cap and gown at home. Her preparation level was scary and sounded like it.

> "Okay, what's the toast?"

> "You toast. It's your party."

I laughed nervously and she shook her head before correcting me.

> "No, no, no, that's why I *don't* toast! Crazy. C'mon, what is it?"

> "What are we, uh, toasting to—okay…"

I looked around the doorless office as if Lissy wrote witty one-liners I could use for a toast on the walls. I raised my glass higher.

> "…okay, I think I got it."

> "Everybody, shh!"

Her performance of managing the eager and imaginary audience was a little funny. No one was all bad. Her shot was repositioned to Statue of Liberty mode as I approached the crescendo.

"To falling in love—"

"Yes—finally!"

"…with ourselves."

How her throat cleared the room I almost saw the imaginary attendees awkwardly exiting as quickly as possible. The initial enthusiasm was retracted and her glass lowered to about her shoulder. Four or five slow head nods oozed their way up and down from Lissy's neck. Her eyes held contact with mine longer than I wanted which I tried dismissing.

"I told you I suck at those things."

I chuckled and let my shot swing towards hers; Lissy tucked her glass away like a loaf of bread.

"Wait, wait."

"Girl, I gotta get back to my —"

"To boss bitches. To boss bitches getting whatever the fuck they want whenever the fuck they want it."

She closed her eyes and drank without touching glasses. Upon them opening, she squeezed them tightly together and blew out the heat from the alcohol. Her glass was shoved at me like mothers did to kids who needed to learn how to wash dishes correctly, and I grabbed it before realizing what I was doing. The painfully standard, black leather office chair she sat in spun half-way around to face her laptop. Keyboard keys started tap-dancing before I could stack the glasses together. Lissy addressed me, but opted to keep the back of her head as spokesperson.

"Have a good shift, love. Let me know if you need anything."

Artist: Dr. Dre

Song: Talk About It

Album: Compton

"I don't know everythinnnggg/ But one thing, one thing I do know/ One thing, one thing I do know (I know, I know, I know)/ Is one day I'mma have everythinnnggg/ Is one day I'mma have ev-ry-thinnnggg."

I left without responding and took the stairs down through the kitchen and into the dining room. The bar was straight ahead, and I walked over to drop off the dirty dishes. Allik was behind the bar with Adam's stupid ass. He was washing his instruments while Adam played a game on his phone. It was obviously a game because the volume sounded like it was on steroids. Allik looked over his shoulder at him like he was considering the best place to hide his lifeless body—both of my hands were free if needed. Or a shovel. Allik untwisted his face when he noticed me, nodded courteously and smiled. The two stacked empties were stood on display in my opened palm; he chuckled and shook his head because he already knew.

> "Weird. How'd you get those?"

> "Get what?"

He pointed and smirked.

> "The two gl—"

> "I don't even know what we're talking about."

I shrugged, put both glasses on the waist-high bar, and slid them towards him while looking to my left. He caught the pair while looking to his right, and slid them off the counter and down into the sink in one almost uninterrupted movement. Confusion comedically found a home on Allik's face while his eyes moved suspiciously from my left to right hand.

> "Wait, you didn't just have…wow."

> "What's up?"

I played right along, acting genuinely unaware of why he would be confused by nothing being in front of me.

> "I swear you had two shot glasses when you got here."

I opened both hands, turned them over, looked behind my back and then back to him with tight lips and a fake-offended face.

> "That is weird. Where would I get shot glasses from?

> "Ay, I'm doing a double tonight. And now I'm seeing shit? I need a shot glass for my goddamn self."

I laughed; Allik could be funny sometimes, much funnier than Lissy. He was the weird, cute guy at the club or wherever, who was paralyzingly shy. The weird ones were the most interesting. Say one word to them, and they opened up like the little door Alice crawled through to Wonderland after drinking the Drink Me potion. They were the type wanting to talk to you, yet said nothing thinking they needed to master small-talk, which they didn't. Did anyone? I worked at Elixae for almost three months before we spoke for longer than five seconds. Luckily, the tall man looking at the small monitor I brought with me playing a slideshow of my work didn't take as long to show interest. He was also wearing sneakers I was aware could pay my rent for at least two months. I naturally assumed gaudy fashion displays relayed a message from one to another of disposable income ready for disposal.

> "Allik, I gotta go see if this man wants to give me money. Blessings, blessings, blessings. May your tip jar overflow."

> "Same to yours."

He put his hands together, closed his eyes and bowed. I returned the gesture, then started to speed-walk to my table before stopping myself. I was working on representing who I was more accurately, especially in public. What opportunity required us to rush?

When we were ready it was time, and it would not be time until we were ready.

Our only responsibility was continuing the forward momentum of pursuing purpose and understanding, like walking confidently towards one who awaited us. Slowing down gave Mr. Money Shoes time to turn and face me approaching in a manor as relaxed as his own. He smiled politely and pointed to the screen.

> "This yours?

> "The art or the monitor?

He smiled.

> "The uh, well, I was thinking the art, but, hm, the monitor actually ain't in bad shape."

He dropped down into a crouch like a guillotine, running his index finger over the monitor's base to continue his inspection.

> "Little dusty though."

His laugh was both quicker and harder than mine. I was willing to bet it wasn't his first stop of the night, describing about half of the customers who came in. I smiled and half-jokingly pointed out how he could get a monitor from any online store, but each of my pieces were commissioned and completed in minutes—blah, blah, blah. I really wasn't saying anything "blah" at all, it was just the same phrase I said a million times to redirect the conversation back to the art. Josh was his name and he was cool. I respected him deeply for buying nothing once he realized it wasn't his style. I still faked interest in the work of others until lately, presuming my attention alone was at least a temporary joy for the creator. How sympathy and empathy were expressed said nothing about where it was directed, and everything about the director.

Being fake defeated the purpose of being alive.

The purpose of being alive, of course, being to do whatever we wanted. The grander purpose of being alive was finding how we could help. Help is what we would all need. Josh sent my website to a friend of his he thought might like it. Not the worst start to the night. Last week a girl and her mom stopped me while unpacking just to let me know they bought two pieces from me they loved. I didn't remember them and felt bad, however they made my

night instantly. It wasn't about receiving external validation, it was the receipt of sincerely excited energy over a creation I brought into the world. No emotion was higher than excitement. Our inexplicable enthusiasm, grabbing our hand and running ahead of us, confirmed divine expressions. I didn't even know if art was it for me. Illustrating could just be leading me somewhere else, a point on my Journey of Genesis[28]. I felt like there was a role for me in the spiritual community, but I didn't know what that was or how to find out yet. If I was born into an ancient BCE tribe, I obviously wouldn't have been the village digital artist. Technology changed, but the tribal roles necessary to be filled did not. Were we born when we were because our birth in another time would've been purposeless? Was each instance of life brought into being when needed? The Universe only knew survival, and we knew no more than it did. That simple. Friend, spouse, lover, boss, partner, parent—the roles were personally present, fulfilled by ourselves or our elected. How did we know if what we did was where we excelled? How did we find fulfillment? Right on time

---

28 The Journey of Genesis: (see page 155).

Allik sent over my nightly neat pour of La Mente Anejo tequila, and I gulped half of it immediately in two takes. My brain deserved a break too.

The rest of the night went quickly. I sold seven of my five dollar 4x6 prints, and the new Bluetooth printer I was using worked perfectly. A group of four, drunk Parisian men with five o'clock shadows hilariously requested I draw a dick. I agreed on the condition they each bought one, and they all paid before I picked up my stylus. My favorite. I used to get mad when customers asked me to take time to create something a frat house college freshman could draw them for free, but it was a challenge now. It was like scrimmaging against the junior varsity team in high school, you couldn't allow the kids to win.

Obstacles excited me once realizing strength awaited on the other side every time.

Strength or death. That was a poetic way of saying I drew a lot of dicks since I started doing customs, and they were pretty easy to get creative with. Everything was easy to get creative with, only more effort was mandated. Instead of finding our own authentic style we took the authenticity of others and called it our own. It was easier to appropriate what wasn't ours, however the pursuit was ultimately regressive. Regression was my only real fear. Almost true, I also feared demonic possession only because nothing about it made sense to me. Wait...never mind, demonic possession was off the list. I just now realized it was an energetic sensitivity combined with a severe internal power imbalance. Possession took place from within. I thought the part about the entity entering us was the mysterious one, but it wasn't. Being possessed by a spirit was not the same as having one within us. We ingested spirits of varying magnitudes into our bodies daily. Wasn't "spirit" another term for a form of energy? Did possessions historically occur in more rural areas due to the energy being more available with less obstruction? Drug addicts and those with severe mental illness were said to often display the same symptoms as the spiritually possessed. Was that considered coincidence?

The scientific and spiritual explained the same concepts in ways differing perspectives could comprehend.

Why couldn't a stimuli-spike in a precise area of our mind awaken expressions in the base languages we've built others from? Our mind's creative processes were still dripping with enigmatic sauces. What did we know about it logistically? The brain's production was more understood since we understood little of measuring ethereal elements. Through the mind the spirit realms were accessed. The spirit who possessed a body was the one allowed to. The unconscious mind being recognized as a chasm of unknowns could be regarded as one of modern psychology's most casually known facts. We didn't understand what happened when, or how, it was stimulated. There were powerful placebo-like effects attached to the relinquished consideration of personal or interpersonal safety. It could be argued parents were possessed when finding the power to lift an SUV to save their child pinned beneath. Wouldn't it be interesting if fireworks went off in similar areas of the brain in both instances? What if the fight-or-flight response was activated

and couldn't be turned off? Could control be given to a demon then taken back at will? Did we not see how the fables of myth and legend spoke immortal instructions to us? Every exorcist heard growls from the demonic to get away from their host. The Holy Spirit came as joyful and uncontrolled praise, the Unholy as fierce and chaotic defense. As above, so below. Were we open spiritual possession once the control we fought to hold onto left rope burns on our palms? not balanced? Wouldn't degrees of possession exist as there were with all else? At times control could be partially lost, other times everything was. Could certain forms of mental illness not be classified as low-level possession, with certain possessions measuring as low-level mental illness?

Didn't we all feel the push to do things we couldn't explain our motivation for?

I forgot what possessed me to rabbit-hole myself, but I wanted to know what possessed me to deal with Lissy and which 'ist'—therap or exor—was best suited.

After the dick pics it was just a few self-portraits, one of a couple and another of a timid girl with oversized pentagon-framed glasses. The highlight of my evening was a gentleman fervently dancing with headphones on in the bike lane just outside the restaurant. He was a rounder, baldheaded man, who's white dress shirt and navy-blue dress pants both fit baggy. He held a white, wooden cross, maybe four feet tall, while he danced and spun around like he was advertising a close-out sale. Two words were painted on it in red, "Jesus" vertically and "saves" horizontally. What was the man saying about his faith? Did the peace it brought him push him to spend time dancing in the street waving a cross? It was 2023. Was he hoping to effectively communicate a message? Then I remembered how possession worked.

The cross itself didn't symbolize "Jesus saved", which is why nowhere in the Bible did it recommend wearing one or tattooing it on our body. I thought it wise to discuss my hypothesis with my grandmother to confirm it carried validity, and she graciously confirmed it did. An understanding was shared with me regarding the energy attached to the cross many carrying them didn't have. The cross in Christian theology was represented in three ways, not to say these were the only three or were sequential.

First, it symbolized being lodged in the cycle of the toughest part of growing—the crucifixion. The cross being an instrument of death, a form of chaotic energy, an instrument of transformation; an instrument clearing a path for new growth.

Second, a lot was happening during that time in the gospel account. Some say it was the messiah dying for the sins of mankind, and that may be true. I didn't know about that part. Part of what was taking place was the messiah proving he was willing to die in honor of his divinity. Wearing or carrying any symbol without living in symbolic alignment made it a curse instead of a blessing. The curse was reminder of our choice to do other than what we agreed. A curse was simply the outcome of willful disobedience. The cross only blessed if we were willing to die in honor of our divinity as it signified. The unwillingness to walk in alignment allowed the crucifix to enroll us into a life of crucifixion. All ancient symbology worked the same. Magic described producing measurable psychological effects, which became tangible through associated action. The scientific and the spiritual weren't arguing, they were interpreting.

> The religions of the world weren't arguments, they were explanations of one idea meant to make sense to many different people.

Third, we could be inheriting the character of the crucifix, becoming the instrument bringing painful transformation to our environment. It was the ultimate symbol of conviction in every sense of the word. The pain was transformative in how it strengthened and revealed more of ourselves if we chose to ask and listen. The ability to ask the question separated the human from the hamster. Bold inquiry returned bold insight. Why did we die? Because we lived. Dying a death where we honored ourselves instead of our conditioning only made us wiser and further aligned. The further into alignment we moved, the less we acted or lived in ignorance.

> The pain we caused only produced more of the pain we aimed to avoid.

Ignorance closed our eyes to the obvious. There were also times when our wisdom could be used selfishly, with the understanding of what we gained being at the expense of an energetic equivalent.[29] The crucifixion—the sacrifice—was the precursor to our Resurrection and the original necessary ingredient. It was closely followed by the Tree of Good and Evil. Good and evil distracted us from recognizing the utility and distinction between those who created space, and those who created from it. Some needed a push, and some of us were pushed to assist. The crosses predating western practices were mirror images, representations of the Grand Compliment—aeonaes.

"Hey, are y—"

"What-the-holy-fuck!"

It was Allik, the ninja, silently appearing and jolting me out of my head. Lissy probably felt the same when I popped up behind her upstairs. He jumped with surprise at my response almost as much as I did at his question. He wanted to laugh.

"Sorry, I didn't mean to, uh...did you say 'what the holy—"

"I have no idea what I just said because I feel like you scared my skin off."

---

[29] Base Barter Principle: (see page 142).

We both laughed.

> "Goddamn. I don't think I want to know but, what does that feel like?"

I stared at him unresponsively and blinked twice deliberately. He laughed again before replying.

> "Had to ask. My skin's a homebody. Never goes anywhere."

> "Well, knock or something next time before entering my office so mine doesn't either, okay?"

He got the joke and shook his head.

> "I was seeing if you were okay, crazy. You looked like you were sitting here watching your—your whole damn life pass by."

I rolled my eyes then shrugged.

> "Something like that."

His tone changed.

> "Everything okay?"

> "Yeah—yes. Just…just ready for a, uh…"

I was going to tell him I was ready for a change, but why? I didn't even know what it meant for me yet. Not everything we knew about ourselves was for others to know.

Self-discovery became self-deprecation when invitations were extended to our internal dialogue prematurely.

I walked myself into more unnecessarily painful situations by doing so then I wanted to remember. Keeping Me to myself wasn't personal, it was peace of mind. Walking before running was useful because getting ahead of ourselves built broken foundations. Running was a form of walking, an exponential fractal expressed through motion. I delivered my revised response.

> "…just ready for a nap, seriously.

More than one thing could be true, but Allik was more connected to his spiritual side than he was aware. He slowly nodded with a side of mild confusion; he knew something was off.

> "A nap—I hear that, definitely. But you're good

other than that though, right?

"Me? Yeah. All, uh…"

I picked up my tablet from the collapsable stool to my left, and scrolled over a few images until I was satisfied. I turned the device to face Allik.

"…you know, all masterfully executed dick pics aside."

"Wait, that's…"

He started to lean closer for a better look but broke down in laughter before he made it. Adam looked up from behind the bar.

"Damn, what's so funny?!"

Adam couldn't see anything from how far away he was, and Allik's back was also facing him. I whispered to Allik anyway.

"I'm pretending like I didn't hear him."

"I don't even know what we're talking about right now."

I smiled too big and didn't try stopping myself; Allik smirked proudly in return. I loved a quality call-back. It was one of my favorite ways someone showed me they cared about what I shared with them, the other was when they asked me what I meant by something. I was getting extra distracted.

"Well, before Adam runs over here or something, let me hit the road."

"Good plan."

A friendly hug was exchanged, just a hug, yet it added a little more warmth to the tequila in my stomach. We both let go, and I watched him—a little too boldly —walk back towards the bar. A wave from the alcohol came over me and all I could think about was sex. My lower-chakras bubbling like I just struck oil could mean mischievous evening —fine with me, just not right now. I stopped staring at the way Allik moved, put my tablet in my backpack, and unplugged the monitor I thought I unplugged like ten minutes ago. I needed to raise my vibration. The vibrations, frequencies, and energy of the body lived in a literal way in the plasma and electrical signals in perpetual motion within us. The vibrational increase I needed was the blood currently doing the Cupid Shuffle in Club Vulva, to sober-up and call a ride to their quiet, suburban home in North Clearthought. Our "higher-selves" lived there comfortably.

The higher-self did not exist as a separate entity. The higher-self was a term referring to us. Me. You. Everyone. Anyone. Who else would it be? I thought about it. Who was the higher-self we referred to as if part of us was separated? Following that line of thinking, our conscious selves were the lower-self? No. Absolutely not. None of that resonated at any level as sensible or reasonable. I needed to stop doing that. I needed to stop mislabeling myself. My higher-self wasn't giving me guidance, my higher-self wasn't sick of my dead-end habits, I was. Would a spectrum reading left to right, rather than up and down, clarify neither held more significance than the other?

Everything else was the enemy, and the enemy was so clear it was stupid. Evil was anything limiting our understanding. Ignorance was our only adversary. The people teaching what the devil was didn't understand what the devil was. The word devil came from the word Satan. What did Satan mean? Obstacle. Many of us based most of our lives on what was good or evil, right or wrong. The embodiment of evil was an obstacle.

> Obstruction was a voice in our minds praising the power of instant gratification without mentioning the slow regression.

Only after indulging the obstructive did we see how far back it moved us, and how much work was necessary to return to where we were. Obstruction could also be a person, environment, or situation. If we were an obstacle for another, we were their Satan. Was the epitome of sin being a barrier against another exploring how to most thoroughly live divinely? What else could be worse than being satanic? Referring to the actions—I didn't know much about Satanism as a religion or philosophy. I knew why my mind went where it did although I was pretending like I didn't. It was more considerate to run away from someone than to be their obstacle without understanding that responsibility. If we truly stood out of the way of all others, would we be left standing alone? Alone in our oneness; content in our complimentary, cosmic connection to consciousness. Harmony. Loneliness was a word we would forget we learned, as to never need to forget we learned it. Was

I looking for a fight at Union Station, or a chance to be fair? It wasn't always about the big picture. The moment was seized before the day was.

***

It was 12:53 in the morning when I checked my phone—no notifications. The kitchen was closed and the bar would do last call in like ten minutes. A couple leaned against the far left of the bar with their tongues waving all over each other's faces, and a mixed gendered group of five or six members laughed and sipped their waters. I finished my tequila and the rest of the ginger ale the timid girl was nice enough to get for me. I offered to draw her something else for her kindness, but she smirked at me so ridiculously I paused like a video game to rethink what I said. I still wasn't used to people being nice for no reason, and reminding myself of the symbolism was often needed.

God spoke through pointless acts of consideration. All of the gods. Any of them.

The Universe, the Source, the Creator, the Most High, Yahweh, Yahawa, Allah, Elohim, Zeus, Jupiter, Ra, Shiva, Vishnu, etc.

Humanity was one organism channeling and speaking versions of the voice of god.

The more we thought the less we did, and sometimes less was more. Other times it was just less. Right now less was less, as Adam's annoying voice shrillingly announced last call early, so my regular amount of over-analyzing was left in the waiting room. The trains weren't running and the next bus wasn't for twenty-five minutes, but I rather be at the bus stop with the over-talkative, randomly assembled clan of characters than around Adam. Inevitably, he would attempt starting a conversation I didn't want. Adam was a prime example of someone who chose to live the life most did. Some played the game, some watched, some coached, others wondered why the game was played to begin with. I tried participating in a conversation with him about something of consequence, however it was shorter than the ball point of a ballpoint pen. No eye contact, no questions, no opinions. We didn't speak the same language, which was fine, but he was the one who initiated. Was he trying a new cuisine he could immediately smell wouldn't agree with his palette? I could always be boring, but I knew that wasn't true. Boring was one of the few things I wasn't. Boring was also subjectively defined so...regardless, I wasn't worried about my level of intrigue. He would either adjust to a more eclectic taste or I would simplify mine. I didn't like his demeanor enough to learn his language, and I never saw him interested in trying to learn anything. He was sexier than Allik which was why I tried talking to him. Tall, muscular, light beard, dark and curly hair—whatever. There was a type I attracted which worked with me disproportionately. Adam was an example of one frequency I was drawn to for reasons adverse to my growth, yet momentarily satisfying. Momentary satisfaction benefited us also, but there were times for those interactions and now wasn't one of them. I wasn't bored enough, and I wanted to know what that meant for me. It made sense Adam worked where I did. For now. Growth.

Trying to change our dynamic with people was like trying to change the chemical reaction between two elements. It was possible but not worth the effort. There were plenty of other elements we could naturally react well with. There were no wrong ways to express our divinity, only expressing more or less of it. Dance, sing, make love, make war, make peace.

A place and time for all, even in places and times where cohesion wasn't understood.

What resonated guided us, even if we were guided into the darkness.

My guidance told me it was time to finally get my ass home.

SAINT MOE

THE VIBRATION OF CONVERSATION IS EDUCATION

I stood in the smoker's section outside of the departure gate for Air France. It was hot enough I still didn't need to wear a shirt under my denim jacket, and for that I was eternally grateful. At a little over seventy-five degrees in the shade, I was that temperature's number one fan, waving a giant foam finger for it to continue singeing the scoreboard. Moe connected me with the Paris gig, which changed my life before anything really happened with it. First-class everything to speak at a theological conference about my stupid spiritual theories no one cared about. I thought my analysis was inspired, but after more than a decade of attempts, I was overdue to love something I put together for once. If we knew the odds were one in a million, the only question was

patience. I was going to Paris for the second time, my first time as a featured speaker. I think Moe was able to get me in the door because they thought I would shit the bed anyway. Guess who had them them sliding off their seats? I loved being doubted. A crown of thorns was always worn before a crown of reverence. There was no alternate route leading to the same destination. All detours were created synthetically.

Additionally, my findings weren't stupid, they were just boring if you didn't know why they mattered. When I assembled them for my first paper it was passable, but even through the staunch goggles of science, the revisions were pretty damn well presented. Moe loved it and told me to just be patient—blah, blah, yada, yada. Most people said something similar about my work if they liked it, but he actually bought the journal I was published in. Most didn't do that. We talked a lot even before the whole speaking engagement connect, but it was still a happy surprise when someone bought something I worked on when they could've bought anything else. Moe's son was also the same age I was, and he bought his first house about a year before I converted to Burger Crown, leaving McDunn's. Burger

Crown's hamburger was $1.68, their competition's was $2.56. Unless I was celebrating, my fast food budget was $2.00 per day. I was no where close to buying a gourmet pizza let alone a house. I wanted his son's success to be motivating, however it was easy to feel like I would never catch up. But who was I chasing? The owners of the lives we coveted didn't know we existed and didn't need to. I wasn't chasing Moe's kid.

Was the goal getting what we wanted, or getting what others did that we didn't?

The hardest thoughts for me to navigate were those of comparison, the variables involved were never forthcoming. Some things were easier said than done, and sounded better when thought of than said. I didn't remember how I met Maurice and I didn't need to. Who we met was more important than how. He mentioned his last name once, but I forgot it and never brought it up. Things like people's last names were usually irrelevant also, at least while they were alive.

I loved LA. It took a lot for me to get there, and Moe understood despite being born and raised in The Valley. He told me it was different out there, more spread-out with nothing to do but shop. Westminster Avenue and the Venice boardwalk was the intersection he relocated to. The front door of his building was maybe forty-five steps from the sand, which was where we first met before everything with the Cednas[30] happened. I was down there because I bought all my art and jewelry from the beach; The Venice boardwalk was a goldmine. I wished I was creative enough to have something to sell there, but my brain didn't work that way and that didn't bother me. My art appreciation was my art work. I browsed or bought crystals and art from one table primarily, and soon I was cool with the artist and would go just to hang out. On my off days or after work I would head down, smoke, talk some shit, then head home for something to eat and a nightcap. Carmic Crystal Creations was the homie's brand, and his name was Cello. He wanted to keep a C theme because of his name, nothing gang related, a point still worth specifying in LA. Maurice knew Cello which was how I met him. I

[30] Organically occurring instances of duplicate DNA in completely unrelated carriers; naturally born human clones.

guess I did remember the story. Per his last call, he would be here within the next fifteen minutes, and when he arrived I would thank him for the millionth time.

We were forever indebted to those reminding us we were worth believing in.

Our inaugural conversation was one I politely interrupted midway through.

> "Hold on, hold on, hold on."

I put my phone in my back pocket and Cello put his Chihuahua down.

> "Yeah man, can I request a replay on that one too?"

Maurice shrugged casually and laughed, and I remembered to stop being rude.

> "I'm Icarus by the way—forgive me."

The apology was exaggerated purposefully and he got it.

> "Icarus? Like from, uh, Greek mythology?"

> "Same one."

> "No shit! That's who you're named after?"

> "My dad named me, and when I asked him, that's what he said."

He laughed again. Maurice laughed a lot, and it was what I would imagine an old movie star's laugh would sound like. Traveled, Carefree, and Wise were his titular starring roles. The laugh always rolled out in a bouncing set of four, smaller, conjoined chuckles pushing the others playfully. The rhythm was so consistent it sounded rehearsed, but obviously wasn't. I didn't know many genuinely happy, older men, as a result of most not living the life they wanted. Maurice was the opposite. Imagine if Buddha was a sixty-nine year old surfer who looked fifty-one, with a mane of silver hair like an albino lion. I was thirty-four when we met, and he was easily in twice as better shape than I was.

> "I'm Maurice, man, good to meet you."

> "Definitely, bro. But what were you saying?"

> "Oh…"

He chuckled humbly.

> "If God can't fuck up then neither can we. That's all."

He shrugged without removing his hands in his khaki short pockets. Cello and I both laughed and I responded with comical confusion.

>   "Did you just say, 'That's it,' bro? Please break that down, sir. If you have the time, of course."

>   "Would love to, man, my pleasure. So listen, I was born at night but it wasn't last night. If we're made in the image of some god, or the universe, or the source, or whatever it is, then whatever we're doing is apart of The Plan then, right? How could we fuck up the plan of whatever created everything we know of?"

I started calling him Saint Moe shortly after his sentence came to a close. When Cello and a friend of his were going on a road trip up north, he gave them a one hundred dollar gift card for supplies. He was sainted after that. The mosaic of Saint Moe hung in a stained-glass window, the light shining through next to the images of my other personal West Coast legends. He joined the OG Mixx, from Long Beach, which was a prestigious classmate. Moe and I clicked and started talking at least once a week, and it just became a thing that happened. I would go to the boardwalk and hang out for a few hours, and inevitably he'd show up at some point. I didn't need his number, no one did. The engines revved almost as soon as she arrived and the timer reset to zero, ready to record an old World Record broken by the new. We spoke like team members in a three-legged race. These were some of the more memorable conversations.

1. Trying

>   St. Moe: Listen man, try everything you can. Life is about trying things.

>   Me: Yeah, definitely.

>   St. Moe: No, seriously man.

Not being where we wanted didn't mean we weren't closer.

>   You know? But we had to try different ways of getting things done to figure the things out. We discover ourselves by interacting with new environments and people, and taking note of the current ones.

Me: So you've never been somewhere and just completely regretted it?

St. Moe: Well, of course man, at the time, but, I don't think there's anything…no, there's nothing I can look back on and say, "Fuck that, I regret that experience." I have all my limbs and they work. My mind works. Sometimes we don't know how bad we have it until we're introduced to better. Other times we don't know how good we have it until it goes bad.

Me: Don't know what you got til it's gone.

St. Moe: Classic.

Me: That line always made me think about relationships.

St. Moe: Really?

Me: Every time I hear it. If we know we don't know what we have until it's gone, shouldn't couples spend more time apart?

He tilted his head to the left as he thought.

St. Moe: I'm trying to think if I've heard that worded another way, but I don't think I have.

Me: Don't be trying to prove me wrong just to do it, Moe.

He laughed.

St. Moe: No, no, I mean I think you're onto something. *I* get it, anyway.

Me: Right? Maybe? I don't know. I mean, I have no idea.

St. Moe: Yeah, I got'cha.

Me: It's like…I've always thought effort was so important for everything. Like, when someone close passes away it teaches us the value of life. It sucks, and it's terrible, but it's effective.

Are we saddened by death, or how we act like it doesn't exist until it does?

I think we're sad we don't try harder. Loss, and the associated feelings, force us to ask these questions.

St. Moe: If you don't mind me asking, did you lose someone close?

Me: My mom, yeah. You?

St. Moe: Sorry about that.

Me: All good. Thanks, though.

St. Moe: But yeah, my dad.

Me: Condolences.

St. Moe: Thank you, sir.

Me: For that reason I'm glad I thanked my grandmother before anything happened to her. I was born in North America because of her. Even with its very particular arrangement of bullshit, here is a big head-start over some other places, right? I could've been born anywhere, bro. And then probably would have to *find* my way over here. She deserved to be thanked. A million times.

St. Moe: Is she…

Me: Oh—no, she's better than ever. Off gallivanting in Jamaica somewhere.

He laughed.

Me: She'll probably live to be two hundred years old or some shit. I'm going to see her for Easter so I can get fed and talk her face off.

St. Moe: Well, all the luck to her—to you both.

I closed my eyes while grabbing the bridge of my nose. Even with my sunglasses on I felt like the sentiment was expressed; Moe responded to my body language.

St. Moe: Uh oh, What'd I do?

Me: Am I a dick if I say, "She doesn't need luck"?

He laughed.

St. Moe: You don't like luck?

Me: Isn't there some quote about luck and preparation working together?

St. Moe: Man, I know what you're talking about, just not the exact wording.

Me: Okay cool, we both know then.

Moe and I chuckled; I continued where I left off

Me: If I can be prepared and lucky, I'll take it. "Both"

is my favorite multiple choice answer.

Getting both was getting Heaven and Hell at once.

Get some of the high, and some of the low. There's always a bridge between the above and below—an aeonaes. Surviving the bottom to sail at the top was the full spectrum experience. But yeah, there's a line sometimes, the anomaly, I get it. Chance: the unseen aspects of the cosmic equation in action. Makes sense. I don't know, maybe I'm just not that lucky.

St. Moe: Honestly, I think you said it. Luck and preparation remain close. And getting "both" is what we live for.

I shrugged.

Me: What about you? Were you close with your grandparents.

St. Moe: Got close with my grandmother after my grandfather died. Just tried to be there more, you know?

Me: Yeah, of course. I did the same after my mom passed—me and my grandmother spoke a lot more. Definitely get it.

St. Moe: Exactly. Shit, I even taught her how to play poker.

I laughed.

Me: Yo, that's fucking hilarious.

St. Moe: Yeah, man, so we had some fun. And she kicked my ass in cards. She still had it.

Me: That's really cool.

St. Moe: Yeah, both of my grandparents taught me a lot in their own way. My grandmother used to tell my father a bedtime story he then told me. Do you…

Me: Obviously, Moe—yes. Tell me all the stories.

He tapped his temple twice with his index finger, nodding barely. His throat cleared, and I felt I should've hailed for the usher once more before the show began. Clearly too late now. Moe was ready.

St. Moe: Okay. "There was a child just like you, with parents just like you have, living in a city just like the one you live in now. And that child was special. They weren't special because they were born more unique than any other, but because they chose to be what the world had yet to see: themselves. There was also something they didn't know, being ourselves and loving ourselves were synonymous.

Being ourselves was the easiest path to choose, although not the easiest to see through til the end.

Loving ourselves meant doing what we loved, even if we were the only ones who loved what we did. Love could mean being by ourselves, sometimes for a long time, but that was when we explored who we were without interruption or influence. Alone was the sole location of true self-exploration. Only then could we find those we could help see clearer while they did the same for us."

Me: That was a bedtime story?

St. Moe: He told me that more times than I can remember.

Me: You had a, uh…you had a wild childhood, huh?

He laughed.

St. Moe: I've been lucky, man. I've lived a really good life.

***

2. The Garden

St. Moe: Were you raised religious?

Me: I was, yeah. Christian. You?

St. Moe: Catholic. Did you keep going to church and everything very long?

Me: Oh yeah, until I was around…twenty-two I want to say.

St. Moe: Okay, then you'll probably dig this. I'm not very religious anymore either, but I thought this was pretty cool. What happens when we tell a kid not to do something?

Me: They do it.

St. Moe: Everyone knows that, right?

I chuckled at the obvious set-up.

Me: Uhh, yeah, I'd say that's, I guess, pretty common knowledge.

St. Moe: Okay. Do you think God would know that?

I smiled and raised my chin in intrigue.

St. Moe: Not bad, right?

Me: I'm listening.

St. Moe: Okay, so The Garden of Eden. The story goes that God *tells* Adam and Eve specifically to leave this one tree alone, *along with* why it would be fun if they don't. Sound right?

Me: So what does that mean?

St. Moe: Great question. Here's another one. Did God want people to be knowledgeable? He told two children what not to do because he knew what we

all do. Think about it. We know the rules say God wouldn't tempt people because that's what the devil does, but I'm pretty sure God could've kicked a snake out of his own garden if he wanted to. Not that God could ever be small enough to belong to a gender—which people obviously created.

Me: Goddamn, Moe!

We both laughed.

St. Moe: It's really the perfect example of what we go through. Didn't that story just show how the masculine and feminine interacted within us? Replace the names Adam and Eve with Yin and Yang, and how does the narrative change? I saw a story of elements fulfilling their individual roles and together discovering wisdom. Grand compliments, acting in synergy at levels unknown to us. With that wisdom they knew enough to survive in a world on their own. We are told where the tree with the fruit is if we're listening. From there we choose to take a bite, or take a hike. The forbidden places have gifts for us we will give greatly to possess.

Let's imagine they say no to the snake and stay in the garden. Then what? They wouldn't even know they had genitals. The garden of Eden went as planned. As everything does. As always.

I laughed at the candor, suddenly seeing the deep connection between confidence and consciousness. St. Moe was like Buddha meets Fonzi.

Me: As always?

St. Moe: Oh, yeah, man. As always. My uncle said that shit all the time. What's happening is what's always happened. Everything is always going as planned.

Me: Who's plan though? Yours? Mine?

St. Moe: There's only one of them.

Me: Moe, for the love of… for the love of getting laid, please don't say it's God's Plan, bro.

The old movie star smile made a classic cameo, then stepped out of the frame as the next line was delivered.

St. Moe: Would that be the wrong answer?

I thought for a few seconds.

Me: I mean, I know what that's trying to convey it's just…way overused, and usually used incorrectly.

Moe presented his fist for me to fist-bump in agreement, to which I obliged happily.

St. Moe: We're editors.

Every kind of thing in the universe has been created, then we create re-presentations to accommodate the intellect of the age.

We just got here. What's to argue with? Why wouldn't we be repeating what came before us? What else would we know?

Me: Not a big fan of that but okay.

We both laughed.

Me: Like, goddamn. That just sounds so…

St. Moe: I don't know. What's so bad about it?

Me: Moe. So what, we're just on some eternal hamster wheel?

St. Moe: Everything is.

Me: And that's fine with you? That everything is going where it's going regardless of what we do?

St. Moe: Is that what you heard me say?

I thought about that, letting my eyes physically search around for information I was looking for inside my head. I saw actors do it so much in movies, I did it involuntarily. I was done digging. I found nothing.

Me: Can you say it one more time?

St. Moe: Every summer isn't the same every year. Some are hotter, some last longer. All of existence is the same way. All happening happens in seasons. We see that when we look. There's a theory, I'm sure you're familiar with, that we live in a simulation, and I see

where it comes from. We live in a fractal. A system based on the perpetual momentum of one patterned cycle built on top of another. That is the example we are meant to follow. Repetition is a universal language. The universe only knows what works and does it over and over.

Survival through growth. Growth through survival.

Anomalies aside. (Which, really, could probably also be mapped-out with a large enough range.) The fractal is a pure expression of the universe, the thumb print of creation. And we're part of that. That's it.

Me: Interesting.

St. Moe: I think so. I didn't always know this by the way. I was probably around your —how old are you?

Me: Thirty-four.

St. Moe: Okay, so I was about your age, or maybe a year or two older. I spent my thirties cleaning up my twenties, and my forties cleaning up my thirties, and now I'm finally cruising a bit. But yeah, I was a little older than you when this finally really, *boom*, you know? The lightbulb went off and I had to get to work fast.

Me: Where'd you start?

The time he took to think was brief in length, yet dense as inner cities.

St. Moe: I read a lot of philosophical fiction. Our general schooling taught us generally. We were taught how to survive, not how to grow. I have my own definition of Philosophical Fiction that makes sense to me. They were narratives taking place entirely in the head of the narrator or the antagonist, or entirely about the thoughts of the narrator or antagonist. I needed that. I was always the type to be too far into my own head, but now I could do it productively. I could get something out of it, you know? I needed to practice observing myself, observing others, and taking note of the cyclical patterns.

The discipline to stop and observe was the difference between creating Heaven or hell for ourselves.

Or, like you said, getting both if both is your thing. As we observe, we see we have to rewrite our understanding of the most basic concepts[31].

Me: Like what?

St. Moe: Yin and yang aren't opposites, they're compliments. That's what dichotomy is—two, created from one—which is fundamentally different than duality—containing two. We call the selfless utilization of our gifts "good." The selfish we label as "evil." None was in opposition, only acting to fulfill an aspect of all. Where could the opposition hide?

---

[31] Stabilization Assimilation Law: Some are pulled to question every action, thought, and inclination regarding what it means to be alive, dead, human, or otherwise.They express a disconnect regarding what is viewed as acceptable of our species on the most elementary of interpersonal, societal, and cultural levels.
The maintenance of daily mental stability is then achieved by exercising a level of adherence to the standardized practices and perspectives. The responsibility of those who question is knowing when to do so (see page 263).

Me: I don't know if I'm there in my journey yet, bro.

He chuckled.

St. Moe: It doesn't happen all at once. It took me awhile to be okay with war being necessary.

Me: Necessary for what, exactly?

St. Moe:

War is a form of communication.

It should obviously be the very last one we throw on the table, however it exists now because it's still needed. War speaks to our animal, not our intellect. It was one of our options we kept around because, like in all conflict, winning feels good. And sometimes losing does too. War was one of the languages of the lower chakras, like Philosophy was of the higher. It's what you guys are calling your higher and lower-selves or vibrations, now. The higher understands the concept of an experience, while the lower understands its

texture. Neither is better or worse, only different paths with different outcomes. But no one wants war, right? How can we effectively communicate without speaking a mutually understood language? That's it. But yeah, it took a while to be okay with the fact we're literally just not collectively there yet. We're still growing, or at least have the ability to do so if we want. But everything has a limit. Who knows where ours is. Or was.

***

3. Day-jobs

St. Moe: What are you getting into tonight?

Me: Nothing fun, Moe. Working the weekend; hating clocking-in; the usual.

He laughed and patted my back, which I imagined was probably screaming hopelessly in mime for encouragement.

St. Moe: Ay man, nothing wrong with clocking-in.

Me: I know *you* don't clock-in, Moe.

He laughed again. His sense of humor was an archer. The punchline was in his possession before it could sneak out of its sparring gear.

St. Moe: No, I don't anymore, but I did. Most everyone does at some time, and we have to do it. I think we should, anyway.

Me: For what?

St. Moe: Once you figure out what your purpose is and why it's your purpose, then you can work for yourself. Work for someone else who knows their purpose, and why, until u do. If you can. At least then you see what it looks like. There's nothing wrong with that. We aren't failures or lame, we are making money to survive while we develop ourselves and ourselves. Once we grow and find purpose, working under others is a waste of our time. Definitely.

Me: So how do you know when you find your purpose?

St. Moe: It goes back to trying. You try each thing that makes you happy, and you see if you can make money doing it. You see if you *like* making money doing it. Then you go from there. Hell, you even try somethings that make other people happy. Why not try something helping someone else? It's not guaranteed to work, but nothing is.

Me: That's true.

St. Moe:

The way we help others that makes us feel like ourselves is often our purpose.

Me: Damn, bro. That last thing you said.

He laughed.

St. Moe: Did I say something wrong?

Me: Bro, you know you did *not* say anything wrong. I was just having the same conversation with someone else.

St. Moe: About which part?

Me: Helping people. Like what does that really mean, you know? Where we think we're creating ease we could be increasing difficulty. What if I say something insulting and someone slaps me in the face, but the slap deters me from saying the insulting thing again? What if that's the only way the lesson is clear to me? Like what you were saying about war that one time.

St. Moe: Hm. Almost forgot about that.

Me: I remembered. But something there makes sense. I think about some crazy shit too, Moe.

He laughed like he wasn't surprised and I was appreciative.

Me: We assume help only comes in the ways we like.

St. Moe: Definitely. We don't see help as subjugation we see it as salvation.

I liked when people assumed I knew the meaning of higher-accuracy words like subjugation. Casually academic interactions were a very cool, and very subtle flattery. I was pretty sure I knew what it meant from context, and when I looked it up later I wasn't too far off.

St. Moe: And there are different ways that shows itself. Growth isn't a priority when we are loved at our lowest. In that scenario, it was love that stood in our way.

Me: Goddamn, Moe. Love is the bad guy now?

St. Moe: Luckily there are no bad guys or good guys. Some break the soil, others plant the seed, then others harvest. There was building to be done before the building began. We played our role by simply being here, but we expanded our role by choosing to follow the guidance.

Me: That's an adventure on its own.

St. Moe: And if we want to step into a more connected existence it started by not looking back.

My progress was paralyzed chasing what was running away.

Me: So you've never went back for something you left behind and been happy you did?

While he thought I took the time to do the same. Did I really repeatedly waste my time thinking I was turning around for something of benefit?

St. Moe: We can't move backwards in time, not that I personally know of. I've went back and did things and had a good time, but I also made more work for myself.

Me: It balanced out then?

He smiled.

St. Moe: You're absolutely right. And that's exactly why it wasn't worth it.

Me: So you wouldn't do anything that felt like going backwards just for a good time? You wouldn't have fun for fun's sake?

St. Moe: Oh, I absolutely love having fun for fun's sake, don't get me wrong. I won't have fun at the expense of my goals. I wouldn't want to pay that price even if I could afford it. For some it makes sense —I get that. Hell, it's the same reason I'm not into audiobooks.

I chuckled.

Me: Bro, what could possibly be wrong with audiobooks? I'm halfway through one right now.

St. Moe: They're a step backwards for me, man, no way else I can look at it.

Me: Okay, how?

St. Moe: There's a meditative element to reading that's lost when we don't have to sit and focus our minds. When do people listen to audiobooks? At the gym, while driving—

Me: Multitasking.

St. Moe: There you go. Multitasking deviates our focus, and is either a symptom of greed or poor planning.

> We're already running on the fumes of a long lost attention span. I'm trying to keep the little I have left.

I want to be *forced to* sit and block out the rest of the world, and maybe stop to look up a few words, or read some funny dialogue over again, or highlight something insightful. We are more involved when we physically read.

> Reading is how we practice listening to ourselves. Reading practices presence.

Didn't we need more ways and more time to practice that instead of ways to avoid the work? We want everything for nothing then wonder why everything we want alludes us. No antidote was found without first tasting the poison.

***

4. Therapy

Me: I'm probably going crazy, Moe. I might need professional help.

He laughed.

St. Moe: Just make sure you don't get ripped off.

I grinned.

Me: Ain't that your generations thing? Not to trust the quacks?

St. Moe: Oh, one hundred percent, but I personally love therapy. Everyone should see a therapist, life coach, shaman, clarif, alchemist, corentice[32], or whoever works, you know? As long as whoever you're seeing tells you why you're fucked up and not the other way around, then you're not getting ripped off. Trained therapists and psychologists especially.

I laughed, although it probably would have been funnier with my own therapy experience as reference.

Me: How would that even work?

---

[32] corentice: (see page 145).

St. Moe: Easy. There's the reason we think we're depressed, or anxious, or whatever, and then there's the real reason our specialist has to decode from the midst of our encrypted experiences to show us. Both of you are usually equally surprised where the root hides. Not surprised because it came from somewhere unusual, but surprised at the connection between the root and everything growing from it.

Me: Have you went?

St. Moe: Therapy?

Me: Yeah.

St. Moe: Yeah, of course.

Me: What'd you think of *your* experience?

St. Moe: Honestly?

Me: Definitely.

St. Moe: It made me realize something I've since realized is true in most situations.

What pleases our naked eye is often different than what pleases our clothed one.

Me: And what does that mean exactly?

St. Moe: Great question; it's simple. Our public and private interpretations of the same thing may differ, which is worth considering when having to pass judgment.

Me: Hm. That is worth keeping in mind. I guess for me, I end up asking the same question. How similar do two things need to be before we say they're the same?

St. Moe: What does *that* mean?

Me: I guess I just can't see therapy being much different than talking to someone I already trust. Like it's hard imagining them telling me something I legitimately didn't know.

St. Moe: Hm. My therapist taught me something else I didn't forget—not yet, anyway.

I chuckled, intrigued.

Me: Bro, you got awhile before I see *you* forgetting anything.

St. Moe: Shit, I hope so.

Me: But what else did the uh, the therapy sesh put you onto?

St. Moe: Stop listening to people who don't know nothing.

I laughed.

St. Moe: Good one, right?

Me: Definitely a good one.

St. Moe:

The inability to objectively analyze our experiences and recognize the neutrality of their nature means one thing. We shouldn't be giving advice, we should be getting it.

Advice from someone who knows what they're talking about, you know? So, yeah man, I dug it. Of course we want to think we have the ultimate insight into ourselves, but we are here to-gather.

He interlocked his fingers from each hand and squeezed them tightly.

St. Moe: Not together, to-gather. To bring existence closer, to share space, perspective, and wisdom.

Me: It's what we're doing right now, bro.

St. Moe: Exactly man, yeah!

He grabbed and gripped my shoulder before tapping it and putting his hand back in his pocket. Taking fatherhood seriously was attached to a distinct character, I understood that from talking to Moe. I didn't know what caliber of dad he was. His kids could think he was Superman, or Clark Kissmyass. Parents and their kids could easily hold opposing views of the others conduct. Then again, the same could be said for a lot.

The feminine energy of creation was no different than the masculine energy of instruction. Energy was neither attached to gender nor stagnant in it's state. Once we chose to answer the call, we answered it wherever and whenever. A father would father those receptive of said energy regardless of who they were. Moe walked in his divinity. Our connection to both the largest cosmic phenomenon and the smallest instances of almost nothingness were intrinsic and simultaneous. God played the same arrangement of notes up and down the scale creating individual symphonies. Divine steps were taken once we no longer labeled what was, and what wasn't created divinely. Inexplicable wonder was equally distributed throughout existence. Each creation was full of wonder —wonder-full beyond measure— which we appreciated or did the opposite. Freely we could consume the same entree of broiled brainlessness we secretly spoke condescendingly of others for considering to be real food. Insight and ignorance were both equally necessary paths, in ways seen and unseen, producing distinctly different outcomes. An awareness of the environmental balance between adoration and objectivity, standing close enough to finish our next heartbeat, was revealed through the Necessity of All.

Closed-minds were left behind closed doors when we conversed with those who took time to think, and thought about the thoughts they chose to share.

***

5. *Relationships*

> Me: Where the girls at, Moe?

> St. Moe: Man, I was gonna ask you the same.

> Me: You're single?

> St. Moe: Oh yeah, man. I might have to come to that bar you were telling me about.

> Me: In OC?

> St. Moe: Where you used to work, right?

> Me: Yeah. Damn, forgot I told you about that. There are, uh, a few art pieces that used to walk through from time to time.

> St. Moe: Oh, I bet. And thankfully now I'm not bored.

> Me: Not bored?

> St. Moe: Oh, yeah. You know how it is, man. You go to find some chick because fuck it, what else is there to do, you know?

> Me: Been there.

St. Moe: Right?

Adding another person to the life you're bored with does not make it more fun, it makes it boring for two people.

That simple.

Me: Adding another person to the life you're bored with…okay, yeah.

He laughed, probably because I repeated part of what he said like just saying it would grant me one of three wishes instantly. I wished. The entertainment experiences only understood once felt were most coveted, yet the lessons taught that way shook us loose from lethargy without a window of warning.

The purpose of life was growth, as it did so without direction.

Just like dying. I thought of that every time I saw a flower bend towards the sun.

St. Moe: I had to think about that for myself too, of course. People want babies —not teenagers, not adults. We're not taught to really think about what we're asking for. I love my kid

more than anything, but I didn't want an adult when I thought about having him.

I laughed. The circle of life sounded more like an oval. Or an ellipse.

Me: Yeah, I can't do kids, so I'm glad you and all the others can. Doing God's work out here.

St. Moe: Ay, it ain't for everybody. The first trick is the hardest. Don't have kids with someone who will fuck up your life.

We both laughed.

Me: Please tell me you have the cheat code for finding that out.

He thought about it, and I moved to the edge of my seat, respectfully.

St. Moe: I remember telling my uncle this. Fun fact, he changed his name to Linus Ace. Nice, right?

Me: Linus? Was he, uh, like a Charlie Brown fan?

St. Moe: Ironically he hated it.

Moe laughed. I was shocked.

Me: He *hates* it? Jesus, I love that shit. I watch The Great Pumpkin every year.

We both laughed.

St. Moe: I know, right? We had to wait til it came on TV to watch it, and that was before we got a TV with a remote.

Me: Wild times.

St. Moe: Tell me about it.

Me: But what about your uncle?

St. Moe: Oh, yeah—Linus.

Me: I really hope he was a rock star. Or porn star.

St. Moe: Basically a combination. He owned a bookstore.

I smiled a Shepard's smile.

St. Moe:

I would rather die alone than foolish.

I said that to his face after his wife cheated on him for the millionth time. And he replied, "But how will you live?" He was a bit of a monk.

Me: Monks are cool.

St. Moe: Yeah, they are.

Me: I used to think I would die of boredom being a monk, but I thought about it, and I'd probably never be bored.

St. Moe: Think so?

Me: Definitely. The way monks commune with nature and each other has to be at a level most never reach, or only reach momentarily. Cultivating their cosmic connection and assisting their spiritual ascension is their life. They do that all day like it's their job because it basically is, right? It's our job to do the same thing, we just neglect to. I fully expect monks to levitate above their mattresses when they fall asleep.

Moe laughed.

Me: Right?

St. Moe: Yeah, I can see it.

Me: I'm like hold on...okay, not sounding all that bad when you really think about it.

We were both sitting and the ground and he stood up.

St. Moe: I gotta stretch these legs.

Me: Actually, yeah.

I stood also.

St. Moe: But yeah, man, it's just...we just keep an eye out, you know?

We've all been around people who make it easy to be around them. Those are the ones who won't fuck your life up.

It's a process learning to love peace over possibility. Or great sex.

Me: You know how to do that too?

Moe thought quietly for an almost uncomfortable length of time. I considered interrupting, but decided not to rush him.

St. Moe: I know we have to honor our time as energy.

Me: "Honor our time as energy."

St. Moe: Yeah, man. A lot of things slowed down for me and got a hell of a lot more peaceful when I started doing that. Not only doing it but understanding why I was doing it. Knowing why we do something is the only way we'll stay dedicated.

Me: So, why'd you change how you honored your time?

St. Moe: Well...it's like eating. If someone was like hey, do you want to not-eat today and instead watch me eat in your face, I would quickly and confidently do anything else.

Me: Yeah, fuck that. I love food.

St. Moe: And I love peace and having the energy to do the things I want when I want. It wasn't always a bad diet or a chemical imbalance draining us, it was often our choice of where to expel our energy. I had to make changes. I show no love to those showing no gratitude.

Doing otherwise steals energy from us we had to work to restore. Over time, that kills you. I had an ex I *chose* to keep going back to. Sound familiar?

I laughed.

Me: Possibly.

Moe smiled.

St. Moe: Of course it does, because it sounds familiar to everyone. Okay, assuming the average relationship rules are at play, none of our exes force our return. We make a choice, and then we're mad the consequence confirms what we already knew. There's no reasonable way to blame someone for acting with consistency.

Me: Is this some, "Turn the other cheek" shit, Moe? Because I have never really been a supporter.

He laughed.

St. Moe: Perfect example—I think this should work with you. When's the last time you got in a fight?

Me: Like, a fist-fight?

St. Moe: Any physical altercation. The *when* doesn't matter as much as how. The last time you were in a physical altercation, could you have left before it started?

I didn't have to think about that and I wished I did.

Me: Could I? Easily.

St. Moe: But you made a choice.

Me: Not one of my favorites.

St. Moe: And you probably already had a feeling it was coming.

Me: Definitely.

St. Moe: There you go. If someone wasn't housing, feeding, employing, or educating us, they were an option easily dismissed instantly. As stupid and cliché as it was, we had to live and let live.

Me: Do you know what that saying means? I feel like it can fucking mean anything anyone wants.

We both laughed.

St. Moe: It's absolutely one of those, but I see it like this. We live our lives and allow others to live theirs. That's how we live and let live. And if our lives and our decisions begin to effect the lives of others—

Me: That's when it gets complicated, right?

He used both hands to maneuver his hair into laying flatter.

St. Moe: We can always step out of the way. It shouldn't ever get complicated.

Life is supposed to be easy. Anyone telling you different is lying to your face whether they mean to or not.

Me: Should I tell them you said so if they ask?

He laughed.

St. Moe: They probably will, so yeah, tell'em they can meet me at the beach.

I started laughing first and then Moe did as well, shaking his head before pausing.

St. Moe: This thought crossed my mind a few times. What if there was mandatory adult education teaching us how to constructively express our pain? Just a what if.

I took a second.

Me: Less fights on the beach?

He smirked.

St. Moe: And probably less fights in here.

He tapped his right temple with his left thumb.

Me: I'd be okay with some more peace of mind.

St. Moe: Wouldn't we all?

We create ourselves purposefully or passively.

Might as well get in on it meaningfully and diligently.

***

6. Podcasts

St. Moe: So many people I know told me to get into podcasts—and they love them—and I just can't. I don't know why.

Me: They are pretty good. Just…overall informative.

St. Moe: Man, I know! And that's what everyone says, just how much random info they get they would've never looked into, and it's great, and they're great—

Me: Yeah, that nails it.

He laughed.

St. Moe: I think I would stop talking to people if I got too deep into podcasts.

Me: I mean, they're not *that* good.

St. Moe: No, no, not even like that. Just…I *see* why they're so popular. Podcasts satisfy our need for learning through conversation. We find time to converse with one another on an intellectual level so infrequently, we listen to other people do it for entertainment. Or was it more a laziness thing? Why have a conversation when we can listen to someone else's?

Me: Okay, Moe, on that note—

St. Moe: What's funny is I really don't know. Are they at least sexy?

Me: Podcasts?

He roped me in, right there. I was almost going to sit that one out.

St. Moe: Yeah. If they're sexy in some way no one has told me, then I get it. Sex sells for a few real psychologically and philosophically sound reasons. Part of that is sexiness, you know? Sexy is cool.

Cool is cool once it stops giving a fuck about being judged, and only gives a fuck about being itself at its healthiest and most authentically expressive.

That's fucking cool.

We need more sexy nerds.

Me: More what?

St. Moe: Sexy nerds, man. We can't just choose to take care of our body *or* our mind. Obviously we *can*, but why not both?

Me: Told you, Both is bomb, bro.

His finger waved once towards me, then held its position pointing. A sign of just how bomb Both was.

> St. Moe: You sure did. And there you go, sexy nerds working on their mind and body so we knew both was possible. Who doesn't want to be smart *and* sexy? The Sexy Nerd Club. Isn't *that* what cool is? Maybe not the name but, you know? What's cool is sexy and it's that easy. We're conditioned to see our bodies as our sexiest feature when it's actually our minds. Our bodies are sexy as hell, but our minds control the body. The body moves as the mind does. I just realized this just now, by the way. No cowboy wisdom, promise.

Moe laughed at himself in a distinguishably genuine way. The laugh said, "I would be laughing at this even if I didn't say it."

> Me: Moe, get away from me, bro, I'm hungry and I'm going to get my damn food.

His laughter rolled on smoother than the good deodorant sticks. I cut him off a lot of the time and I could tell we both understood why. He tumbled down rabbit holes like children tumbled down hills on spring and summer afternoons. He walked towards the souvenir shop next to the Venus Hotel while I went and picked up my fries from the fish & chips spot. I didn't get through half of them before Moe popped back up. I grabbed a few fries, dunked them in the Sauce Twins —ketchup and mustard swirled— and stuffed them in my mouth like they were illegal contraband.

> St. Moe: Really quick, had to tell you this, bud. You see these guys stapling flyers or whatever to the trees? I really can't wrap my head around it.

Way too many people are comfortable abusing trees.

> They're literally a source of oxygen. Very confusing.

I stopped chewing and smiled at Moe closed-mouthed while shaking my head. He laughed.

> St. Moe: Peace, man. Enjoy. Those look delicious.

He walked across the street towards his apartment building.

***

7. Us vs. Them

> Me: It's them that are the funniest to me. The ones with the five hundred dollar shoes who think that says something impressive.

> St. Moe: Doesn't it?

> Me: What? Having no concept of the value of money?

> St. Moe: And more than enough to spend on whichever girl will let them see her naked. Its usually about pussy even when it isn't.

I laughed.

> Me: Bro, that's fucking so funny because I heard no lies told.

Moe paused.

> St. Moe: Well, you know, I guess I should correct that. We live in different times now, you know? So I guess it comes down to getting laid. Whatever that means to us. We can deny it if we want. Replace 'getting laid' with 'peak physical satisfaction' I guess, if you want our asses covered.

> Me: But that even—

> St. Moe: Even the guys spending the ridiculous money and the girls who buy right in. That's their thing, you know? I was there once. I remember. They were great times and then they stopped being great, so I did something else. But yeah, most of it was pretty much a waste, but you try it. I know you've spent the stupid money on *something*.

Was that something we all did? I bought high-end versions of daily-use appliances and electronics to complete my required hours of Retail Therapy. It was like getting a new toy and a new tool; Yin and Yang. But then I thought back a few years, back before I knew anything.

> Me: Yeah, there's been some shit. Basketball jerseys oddly enough.

We both laughed. I shook my head at my past-life nonsense.

St. Moe: There you go. And it makes sense at the time until you realize it doesn't anymore, right?

Me: Sounds about right.

St. Moe: I promise man, you seem to have your head on your shoulders so you'll dig this.

Me: Okay.

St. Moe: If we are getting wiser as we get older, we get more careful playing Us vs. Them. The dividing lines look more like marks made on the wall showing how tall we're growing over time. Some just aren't as tall as the others yet. It's like forgetting June comes before July. We even say it all wrong.

Arrogant people are not stuck up, they're stuck down.

That's how the small stuff like that can change the whole way we see things. Speaking of July. Am I personally okay with celebrating the independence of a country still protecting domestic terrorist organizations, as long as they hate groups the government wants dimmed, discounted, or destroyed? Not really. Do others have the right to disagree with me and celebrate whatever they want peacefully as I celebrate what I want peacefully? Yes, yes, and yes.

Me: Okay, then I have to ask —don't shoot the messenger.

St. Moe: Uh-oh.

Me: So, what about the racists, and rapists, and serial killers, and all of the other bad people? You're not against them? We shouldn't stand against them?

St. Joe: If you want the real answer, the truth is we don't know what or who to stand against. We're guessing. Common enemies are created to bring about quicker change. What happens when the energy of many is focused on a single goal? Things happen. And if enough of us say, "Hey, we don't like this," then we keep standing against whatever it is. Slavery used to be legal in America; segregation used to be legal in America; public executions; human experimentation—it's a long list, man. It took time for us to globally understand the penalty for cheating on your husband maybe shouldn't be death, maybe the two of you should just try the relationship thing with other people. It took time for us to globally understand enslaving other humans might not be best.

Me: Is that not the saddest shit you've ever heard?

St. Joe: It is. But it says a lot about many of us.

Hurt people cause harm to others because they know how to feel powerful, but not whole.

Some inflict pain because it's all they know, some spread love for the same reason. And either way this doesn't change. None of us remain committed to anything not done for ourselves.

I let that sit.

Me: So what's the fucking bright side?

Moe laughed.

St. Moe: Looking for a bright side is something I personally see as an issue. It brings us back to the small classifications—the light against the dark. As if the light and dark weren't both needed, each doing what they did how they did it to keep the wheel turning. We were looking for the nonexistent and wondering why we couldn't find it.

Me: Then what should we look for?

He thought momentarily.

St. Moe: We look for what feels right and enjoy it once found. We make life as easy for ourselves as possible. Not easy in the sense that we do nothing, but easy as in...yeah, doing what feels right. Doing what makes sense. We can try to fix what we enjoy, but we don't try to enjoy what can't be fixed or doesn't want to be. What can't be fixed we leave behind, and we look for the next opportunity for enjoyment. Clearing the distinction between selfish and sensible is often the soothing our minds are missing. Life is designed to be our joy, although all won't speak to us in that way. We're in a cycle where it takes work to keep our joy. But look where we are? Drinkable nutrients fall from the sky and rise from the ground. The plants heal us. The plants improve us. The plants grow the stuff making us grow. We have a shield around the living being we grew out of that made us, and supports us so They can experience themself. It was ultimately the same reason we had kids and the same reason we created anything. The art of creation allowed life to make a piece of themselves into a separate, self-contained entity with interaction capability. The apple didn't fall far from the tree, you know? Could we blame the Earth for wanting to see its own reflection?

Me: Can I ask you a personal question?

He laughed.

St. Moe: Shoot.

Me: How do you know all this? Really?

He grinned. Then the grin grew into a laugh growing like Jack's magic beanstalk.

Me: Bro, am I even ready for this story?

St. Moe: It's a very long story, but the short version is very short.

Me: Hit me with the cliff notes.

St. Moe: Man, I tripped a decent amount of good acid, in some densely vibrational places, with densely vibrational people. In hindsight, it was work and experimentation, attempting to unlock these parts of my mind conditioned to remain closed. It's not something everyone can or wants to do, nor is the effect the same for all. Some experiences were more beneficial than others, which was also part of the experience. I put a lot of effort into not overdoing it either. I set intentions, I meditated, and I always asked for wisdom in one way or another. We can get what we ask for and we usually do, yet our expectation of how our answered request will appear causes the hand reaching for the other to miss.

We have to say what we mean if we want what we say to happen.

Do we want to move somewhere new for the scenery, or are we moving to find ourselves? To start a new life? To find inspiration? Clarity was of more benefit than caution.

Me: I feel like I should be recording this.

Moe laughed.

St. Moe: I'll need a secret identity if the audio gets leaked.

I wondered how one would solve that.

Me: What if in the beginning I say "I am not talking to St. Moe, I am

talking to someone else." Would that work?

St. Moe: Perfect. It's like I was never there.

***

8. Clones

Me: Seeing people dress like you is weird, right?

St. Moe: I don't think anyone dresses like me.

He laughed.

Me: Moe, don't act like you don't look stylish, bro.

St. Moe: Man, I just wear whatever the girls are into. I never really got fashion.

Me: Really? Fashion is low-key important.

St. Moe: It is?

Me: "Importance" is relative, but a lot of people just don't get it—like you said.

St. Moe: Enlighten me—please, sir.

Me: Okay, uh…let's say…okay, what's the most basic definition, right?

Fashion is one of the ways we say something without saying anything.

Fashion is how we tell a story about ourselves using clothing and accessories.

The second one makes sense to me as a one sentence way to describe it. I really didn't give a shit about fashion either until my view changed.

St. Moe: Hm. Never thought about that.

Me: Right?

St. Moe: Yeah…yeah, so let's say, you. What is your style saying?

Me: This wasn't supposed to be about me, Moe.

He laughed.

St. Moe: I thought it was about everyone?

Me: Well of course it is, yeah.

St. Moe: Or, explain my look.

Me: No, no, it's cool—you're right. Everyone.

He waited.

Me: So I'm wearing all black. The color palettes we're drawn towards are telling. I would interpret wearing all black to be the act of giving nothing away. Nothing I'm wearing has any visible brand names or logos either. We brand-watch too much. Too much for me, anyway.

Brands are a blunt and unreliable instrument used to judge someone's worth.

St. Moe: Absolutely, man. Well said.

Me: Thank you, Moe.

St. Moe: So what made you go all black?

Me: Honestly, it wasn't planned. A lot was going on at the time. I used to wear more color but it was just… it felt like another task. Black with black is simple. Then when I realized the symbolism I continued.

St. Moe: Very nice.

I shrugged.

Me: Just putting some effort into understanding more, right? Being less dependent, more informed, more aware. Colors, sounds, and organic material all emit measurable frequencies vibrating at varying rates. Our environment speaks with us constantly because we have the means to understand.
Communication can be interpreted as involuntary. Humanity isn't the only version of life using language. But I get it at the same time, right? Everyone's trying to build a brand, and live comfortably, we just go about it immaturely as fuck.

St. Moe: There you go. And I think that speaks to how much room we still have to evolve. Most of the adults act no more maturely than their kids do. But it's evolution, you know? We start somewhere and we end up somewhere else.

Me: No, that makes sense.

St. Moe: There's actually a name for that process or philosophy, it's called The Journey of Genesis. The path we plan to take leads to the path we need.

Me: Did you study philosophy?

Moe laughed like he was at his favorite comedians first televised stand-up special.

St. Moe: I like you, Icarus. You think I could be an academic philosopher— that's a first-time accusation.

Me: Ay, that sounded studious as fuck from over here, bro.

St. Moe: I just know a little bit. This girl I dated for awhile was pretty deep into that stuff.

Me: Always about getting laid.

Moe and I laughed hard, as I applauded at the return of his new catch-phrase.

St. Moe: As always. So because of her, I know that one, and…Christ, there's another one she never shut up about.

Me: I bet she'd love that you can't remember it now.

St. Moe: Oh, yeah. She was *so* much fun.

He rolled his eyes and I chuckled.

Me: Did you tell me about her before? I feel like I remember you mentioning an ex.

St. Moe: She's the most recent, so it was probably her. God, amazing in bed though. Ex-gymnast with red and black hair that was buzzed at the back, you know? And then always braiding her hair or twisting it—

Me: Sorry, Moe, were you telling me about something she always went on about?

He smirked.

St. Moe: Did I get sidetracked?

Me: Barely notic—

He snapped his fingers once triumphantly, and it sounded like a golf ball being hit off a tee.

St. Moe: I got it! Sorry to cut you off.

Me: Bro, do not apologize. Tell me the secret!

St. Moe: Far from a secret. I forget the guys name, but the other concept was Compass.

Me: I've never heard that word before.

St. Moe: I'm sure most people outside of Jalise's *particular* circles would. Jalise is the ex.

He rolled his eyes again.

St. Moe: But yeah, Compass I thought was interesting because it speaks to…well, it speaks to everything.

Me: And it's a philosophy?

St. Moe: Yup.

Me: One to rule them all, huh?

He nodded.

St. Moe: Probably the closest to doing so.

Philosophy taught us how to think, not what to think.

I probably should have studied it. Shit, everyone probably should.

Me: Hm. We're taught how to survive instead of how to grow.

St. Moe: There you go. Anyway, Compasis basically means "a step together." None happens without all. Basically each step taken in time being taken by everything in existence at once. The universe seen as one organism.

Me: That is interesting.

Moe nodded again while I let that sink-in also.

St. Moe: But that actually goes back to people dressing like you, or really copying anything.

Me: It does?

St. Moe: The evolution. There is only one way to evolve, we either make ourselves uncomfortable or it's done for us. If me, or you, or anyone does anything resonating deeply enough with people they're compelled to mimic it, it's there's now. Plagiarism was the highest form of flattery because it contained the most utility.

Mimicry signals our time to evolve.

The same thing will happen with spirituality, the occult, religion—all of them. All of spirituality is going to end up going mainstream. The process is moving right along. People are already buying and selling metaphysical benefits without purpose. They buy the experience of self-discovery from someone else and assume that's the end. The shortcut to freedom and illumination is imaginary. There's nothing to be bought. We have to walk the steps ourselves. That's what the people they're paying did. In practice, I suppose that's where spirituality and psychology differ. But that's why so many people aren't growing, and worse, they think they are. Many healed themselves just enough for the strength to carry bigger bags of money. Consciousness will soon have a street-price. And that's okay. It's what the West does: remove meaning; monetize everything. We'll just have to dig deep again, and at that time, the dilution of our connective thought and action will be the inspiration.

Me: None happened without all.

St. Moe: There you go.

***

9. *Landlords*

St. Moe: You rent, right?

Me: Unfortunately, bro.

St. Moe: Roommates, or…

Me: Roommates, but I have my own room.

St. Moe: Oh, okay. How many to a bathroom?

I chuckled.

St. Moe: Oh, boy.

Me: Very "oh, boy." Four guys.

St. Moe: Where do you live, a frat house?

We both laughed.

Me: At this point, I would take an actually frat house over this place.

St. Moe: Yikes.

Me: It obviously could be worse—I've lived in worse—but it's just annoying and I'm excited to get the fuck out of there.

St. Moe: Shitty roommates?

Me: Yo, you would think that's what it would be, right? Nope. The goddamn landlord.

St. Moe: That's different.

Me: You pronounced bullshit wrong, Moe. It's bullshit.

He bent over laughing that time. That was one of my funnier comebacks.

St. Moe: What's wrong with the landlord?

Me: Are you in a rush?

He laughed again but was able to remain upright.

St. Moe: Aw, man! Okay, go for it.

Me: He walks around with no pants, just tighty-whities.

Whenever he wants. So before I stopped using the kitchen—which is connected to this also but kind of separate—I'd catch his balls waving around all day because LA gets hot and the building has no central air.

Moe bursted into laughter, pushing up the frames on his sunglasses to dab the corners of his eyes.

Me: Yeah, bro. And he's not even like old and senile, no, he's like in his forties or some shit. He absolutely knows better.

St. Moe: Can't really think of an excuse for that, no. I mean, did it get *that* hot?

Me: It got hot, bro, yeah. But I managed to beat the heat with my pants still on.

Moe shook his head.

Me: I survived. Look at me? Good as gold.

St. Moe: Yeah, you look good for living in an oven.

Me: Thanks, Moe, I try. And that's just *one thing*—one.

St. Moe: It's not worse than the balls waving at'cha, is it?

Me: Of course it's worse, Moe.

St. Moe: Yikes.

Me: The guy leaves food out all over the kitchen. Then he's surprised there's roaches everywhere and mad that I "complain so much" about them.

St. Moe: That's what he said you did? Complain?

Me: Yeah, bro. I was done right there.

Why debate the narrow-minded who enjoy their narrow space?

I realized later his response pointed to a narcissistic disposition also, but like days later.

St. Moe: Okay, okay.

Me: But yeah, he leaves food out overnight and I bring it to his attention and he blames *me* for the roaches. It's my fault because he says he's been leaving food out all along and never saw any bugs.

St. Moe: Are you serious?

Me: Very. That was actually when I realized how delusional people could get. Like, I knew it was possible, but I never saw it in person or to that extent. It was still within us to disassociate our actions with the clearly associated consequences. The truth was a choice.

St. Moe: Scary stuff.

Me: Scary, fucking, stuff, bro. But yeah, I stopped talking to him after that once he personally attacked me verbally in that same discussion Re: the roaches.

St. Moe: Wait a minute, were the roaches so bad you stopped using the kitchen?

Me: Partially. The landlord demanded I take out the community trash from the kitchen, as well as taking the large trash can down to the curb on trash day. The large can is used by the four guys, the church next door, plus random people from the next building over. It's his job, he's just lazy as fuck.

St. Moe: Icarus, you live next to a church?

Me: Yeah, Moe. I live next to a goddamn church.

A rolling chuckle jogged out of him sounding like it could be called rocky road ice cream.

St. Moe: Man, you're keeping all the gems to yourself.

Me: My apologies.

I took off my glasses and rubbed the lenses clean, then returned them to my face.

Me: But yeah, I said fuck that. I wasn't taking all these people's trash out, and I wasn't using a kitchen where a grown man was fine with roaches living in his microwave and air fryer.

St. Moe: Tell me you're joking.

Me: Bro, I wish, I wish, I wish, I was joking like Dave Chapelle be joking! But no, no I'm not.

St. Moe: Man, I am so sorry. If I had the extra sp—

Me: Nah, it's all good. I'm getting the fuck out of their.

Something is going to come through soon, and I'll be out!

St. Moe: There you go.

Me: But that's not it, Moe.

St. Moe: With the landlord?

Me: Oh, yeah.

Moe closed his eyes and shook his head.

Me: I definitely found a dead mouse on the kitchen counter where I used to chop up vegetables before cooking.

St. Moe: No.

Me: Yeah, bro. A whole dead mouse, but I hadn't been using the kitchen for over two months by then, so I legit didn't care.

St. Moe: Wow, the irony.

Me: See how that worked, right? Ironic as fuck. I laughed out loud at that shit. Got pictures and video too just in case he tried to pull anything.

St. Moe: Wow, man, that's a lot. Mice *and* roaches.

Me: And the maggots.

St. Moe: Huh?

Me: Yeah, bro. Went to use the broom in the kitchen I've used a few times before, and saw three maggots trying to run away from me.

Moe tightened his lips.

Me: Yeah. Landlord issues. Just recently he toned down blasting Christian sermons in Korean, but still wails gospel songs in every imaginary key found on not *one single instrument*. Up and down the hallway he does this shit. No thought of anyone else living there. But then his new thing is his "important work" keeping him home all day, everyday. Do you want to know what that work is, Moe?

St. Moe: Yes, I do.

Me: Korean Reality TV. A heatwave hit and all the tenets kept their doors opened, and all you heard and saw from the TV and speakers pointing right at his door from his room was Korean Reality TV. Then someone yelling a sermon —but from his room at least

—and then more Korean Reality TV. Important work. So important. The whole time I'm *desperately* trying to work on my research. Some people remind us that human evolution is still at work, which I guess is kind of promising.

St. Moe: Is this a joke?

I lowered my sunglasses and looked over the frames right at Moe's eyelashes.

St. Moe: Man, you're a prince.

Me: Thanks, Moe. Just trying to keep working and be patient.

Artist: Jimi Hendrix

Song: Hear My Train A Comin'

Album: Live At Woodstock (Live at the Woodstock Music & Art Fair, 8/18/69)

"Yeaahh/ I hear my train a comin'/ I hear my train a comin'/ Hear my train a comin?/ I hear my train a comin!"

St. Moe: Sounds like a good plan to me.

Me: Only one I got right now. But yeah, I don't live in a peaceful environment and peace is important to me.

St. Moe: To everyone, right?

Me: I don't know about that. Do you think peace looks different to each person?

St. Moe: I think that's a good question.

Me: Good questions and good answers have a hard time meeting.

St. Moe: And an even harder time staying together.

Something I hated happened. I hated remembering something I thought I remembered to forget.

What we didn't want remembered was the easiest not to.

What Moe said brought it back like a movie reboot.

Me: The staying together part is always the part I get *almost* right.

St. Moe: And you know what they say about almost…

I nodded slowly and bit the inside of my lip at the same speed. My chest felt heavy from the weight of swaying skeleton keys, each left by hearts who's locks were changed, chiming in low, long notes as they touched. Moe looked over his shoulder at the horizon where the sun setting made the sky blush with shy delight. He pushed his sunglasses up until the frames sat snugly on top of his head.

> Me: I never told you about my ex, did I?

> St. Moe: No, man. What happened?

> Me: Ugh, that's a lot to get into, but how we broke up was just very…

> St. Moe: Messy?

I considered the description's accuracy, but it wasn't close enough.

> Me: Exhaustive.

> St. Moe: Wow.

> Me: Yeah, "wow" would probably also work.

> St. Moe: Okay, so what exactly…

> Me: Yeah, so, we were already broken-up, right? I was at my place with the insane landlord living check-to-check, and she was…in hotels, and trap houses, or wherever—from what I came to understand.

> St. Moe: Yikes.

> Me: Very. So, some how she gets away from where she's staying and I pick her up.

Moe chuckled.

> St. Moe: She gets away?

> Me: Yeah, bro. She had a thing for living with men who wanted to control her —not entirely her fault. It gave her something to do, some kind of purpose, something to fight against, somewhere to put her energy—I don't know.

> St. Moe: Man.

I shook my head.

> Me: So she gets away and we hang out. I have to leave my house by around six to drop her back off and then go to work. I want to say we got together around noon.

> St. Moe: Got it. This is like the overture. Beautiful.

I laughed. I enjoyed the joke a little more because I loved live orchestras, and he was right about the overture.

> Me: Alright, Moe, let me focus. Okay, so, we get to my place and we have to be quiet because of the landlord and his mania. Bro, me and her end up trippin acid. I don't know how.

Moe laughed into a cough.

> St. Moe: Oh, now we're talking. What'd you have?

> Me: Uhh, hm—oh, the gel tabs, bro. I had the drops before that.

> St. Moe: Wait, acid? What color?

> Me: Oh, the tabs were dark blue-ish, but, with these gold flakes on it that—

> St. Moe: Is it a pyramid?

> Me: Get the fuck outta here, Moe.

He nodded his head and pushed his lips up, clearly impressed.

> St. Moe: Surprised they still make that stuff.

My jaw waved in the wind, shock running away with the bearings to hold it still. I refocused and recoiled it to the best of my ability.

> Me: We're definitely coming back to how you know about those. But yeah, I'm like ay, we usually really have good trips together. Joking, laughing, talking about ghosts, watching movies—it's usually chill. We do half a hit each but it's good acid, bro. Better than I understood at the time.

Moe was pretty much living with a constant rumbling giggle by that point.

> St. Moe: God, this is great.

I rolled my eyes.

> Me: So, the trip starts and she's being horrible. I'm trying to chill and watch a movie, and she just won't stop being loud. And I'm like listen, a mellow trip, remember? We set intentions and everything.

> St. Moe: Well that was good.

> Me: I thought so too. But yeah, she's just nagging

about everything. Mad at how I make her food, mad at this, mad at that. Then we sleep together. We both fall asleep—unplanned—and I wake up like fuck, I'm late for work.

St. Moe: Uh-oh.

Me: Precisely. So I have to rush and get my shit together and wake her up, and she's rolling hard still. She asks if she can stay over but I can't trust her.

St. Moe: That bad?

Me: A LOT went down, bro. It was half my fault for giving her chances she would spit at repeatedly. But get this. So I'm trying to get out the door and she's refusing to leave.

St. Moe: Huh?

Me: Yeah, bro. Says she's too high, and can't move, and she's nauseas. She's moaning, and groaning, and says she'll just have to stay and sleep it off. I'm trying to keep my cool because this is the type of shit she always pulls, so I'm mad at myself

for being the dumbest of fucking dumb-asses.

St. Moe: Been there.

Me: Not the best.

St. Moe: Not at all.

Me: So, I'm like "I will literally go get the car and pull it up front if it will get you the fuck up, without me having to drag you out and cause enough of a scene to get evicted." What does she say, Moe?

St. Moe: What?

Me: She says, "Oh, I thought we had to call a ride. I forgot you were driving." She's up like a light-switch, smiling like she wasn't just proclaiming to be dead forty-five seconds previously.

Moe's hand raced to cover his mouth, a levy against a flood of laughter surging within him.

Me: But that's when I was like okay, so this is, and will always be, a waste of time with this person.

Sometimes things lead nowhere, and if we're being honest, nowhere is where things lead most of the time.

We just hang out in Nowhere because we're bored with everywhere else.

St. Moe: We *should* be recording these.

I laughed.

Me: Told you, bro. But that isn't the end.

St. Moe: …how?

Me: I still have to get her home to god…blessed La Puente. I'm pissed the whole ride back to wherever she's living, and she's drinking the Yerba tea I gave her to wake her up. We get to the grocery store she wants me to park in because I'm not allowed to see where she lives, and I don't argue. She bitched about me not picking her up in the right spot when I got her, and bitched about where I parked when I dropped her off.

St. Moe: Was that just who she was as a person?

Me: I don't know who she was as a person, Moe. I saw a lot of sides of her. Maybe she thought the same about me too, but all my sides dress the same.

St. Moe: Good wardrobe.

Me: You know, just working with what I got. But yeah, she gets out of the car and asks me to text her when I get home. Granted she was the type to ask you to try and not give a fuck if you did. She just did shit for any kind of response.

St. Moe: Lonely. Unrecognized.

Me: Like many of us. So she asks me to text her—to please text her—and I can't hold back the laughter as I remind her how she wouldn't take the time to reply anyway. That gets her laughing and she turns, skipping as she walks away from the car. And she's tiny, like five-three or something, so it's adorable, right? Can't deny that.

I loved that girl. Anything she did I loved it.

St. Moe: What was her name?

Chills figure skated over my arms and neck in pairs. I didn't talk about my ex often. Her name made my face want to smile before I said it, although I was given little reason to and lost much of what I had.

Me: Lovella...Annette. Yup. She walks away and we're both laughing because we get the joke at the same time. This was the punchline. She found who she was and I did the same, we just...we weren't going in the same direction, and that was okay, it was just sad.

It was like going to a pizza place and ordering Chinese.

Moe smiled.

St. Moe: Okay...

Me: We all tried to be a pizza place. We can go to a pizza place and order Chinese, and they'll make the Chinese because they make anything, but it won't be the Chinese we wanted because we got it from a goddamn pizza place.

He laughed.

Me: Then we get mad at the pizza place for making shitty Chinese, when the blinking, neon sign of a fucking pizza slice hanging over the door says it all. The pizza place doesn't need to learn how to make Chinese, and we don't deserve our money back. We tried the pizza place Chinese, it wasn't what we thought it would be, and now we just needed to find a Chinese spot.

St. Moe: I feel smarter and hungrier.

I smiled.

Me: Makes sense though, right?

St. Moe: Oh, all the way, man.

Me: But, yeah. I was sure that neither me or her knew why we loved the other but we did, and we laughed at it all because we finally understood there was nothing to understand. We tried everything we could but none of it worked, and that was part of life we learned to accept. I laughed and then sobbed until the laughter faded, then I went to work and staggered my way through my shift. The tears were inspired by something she said earlier. She told me she wanted to pack a backpack and travel across the UK into Europe, which was terribly sad because I knew how slim the chances were of that happening for her. Her dreams were worlds away from where she slept. I cried hoping for her, even after everything she'd done. If another's happiness didn't endanger us, why not cheer them on while they find it? We didn't deserve each other, which meant a few different things I eventually forgot about. I never saw or heard from her again and I grew to be okay with that too. The story's ending wasn't anything less than I expected, who knows, maybe I should have expected more.

We parted ways like the Red Sea, in LA on LSD.

THE PHILOSOPHY

The Catalytic Principle [implores]
    - *Compais*: the Necessity of All. All possible was necessary. None happened without all. (pg. 16, 103)

Stabilization Assimilation Law
    - The recognition of our disconnect to traditionally conditioned perspectives, and when expressing such is wise. (pg. 225)

General Ownership Phenomenon
    - Possession is an illusion. We own nothing. We keep nothing. We lose nothing. We are free. (pg. 92, 182)

Authorist Futurism [implores]
    - *The Journey of Genesis*: the path we plan to take leads to the path we need. Creating the current. (pg. 156, 203)

Surrenderist Futurism
    - Allowing what needs to happen to happen. Following the current rather than creating it. (pg. 115, 165)

Displeasing Decision Consolation
    - Manipulating ourselves to enjoy what we don't.
    - Settling for the sake of ease. (pg. 154)

Base Barter Principle
    - All interactions include an energetic exchange.
    - Even generosity is traded for gratitude. (pg. 143, 182)

Emotional Truth Theory [implores]
    - The Frailty of Hate: hatred arises from unexamined experiences, increasing and perpetuating regressive behavior. (pg. 175)

Falsehood Theory
    - Lies and truths are both stories we choose to accept or reject. (pg. 34, 155)

ABOUT THE AUTHOR

ABOUT THE AUTHOR

Sean Aeon is a philosopher and author specializing in storytelling exploring our interconnected experience.

The examination of universal, inherent, and evident interconnectivity is central in his narratives.

Via the expression of this recognition, he is able to share applicable insight regarding the rhythmic nature of ourselves and our environment.

Sean's work reflects how the more we observe and understand of universal patterns, the more peaceful and harmonious lives we enjoy.

His literary influences include James Baldwin, Hans Christian Andersen, Joseph Campbell, James Frey, Alan Moore, Amy Cleveland, Frank Miller, Christopher Nolan, James Cameron, George Lucas, and Quintin Tarantino.

Made in the USA
Middletown, DE
08 December 2022

16417707R00158